# Star-Crossed LOVERS

By,

## CAROL EDWARD

Published by
Ace Lion Books
June 2017

*Ace Lyon*

*Published by*
*Ace Lyon Books*
*Acelyonbooks.com*
*First Edition*
*Cover Design by S. M. Savoy*
*Carol Edward*
*Star-Crossed Lovers*
*ISBN 978-1-947122-09-3*

# CONTENTS

# Star-Crossed LOVERS

# -1-

# CARA

Eighteen-year-old Cara NiClearin Martason gazed out her fourth-floor dormitory window. From there, Old Town University spread over the plains to the foothills of the Jennta mountains where thousand-year-old brick buildings nestled between Old Earth flora. Tourists came from all over Haven to visit the campus and admire the extensive gardens and old-world architecture.

In the distance, sleek tips of Copper City skyscrapers peeked over the forested, rolling hills. Their black glass and chrome glittered in the soft summer air. To the west, turquoise water shimmered. Framed by Old Earth mountain laurels and azaleas, the Gordon Sea beckoned, trying to lure her from her studies.

Below her in the quad, a group of girls played ball. Her gaze flitted to a boy sitting cross-legged in the grass. His tight, black leggings showcased his narrow hips. Long brown hair caught up in elaborate braids hung over his thin shoulders. Too far away to tell if his smooth skin was a result of youth or vanity, she assumed youth by his company.

Ten girls surrounded him, offering him drinks and snacks. Bright smiles lit their faces and even from this distance it was clear all laughed and joked comfortably. She observed them another ten minutes before returning her attention to her comp screen.

Thirty minutes later, her roommate, Fleur, entered the room. The wood-paneled door banged against the edge of Cara's dresser, another anachronism from Earth. Wood framed beds held thin mattresses and old world blankets instead of the usual heated gel-pads most Havenites slept on. The students kept their clothing in dressers and used actual water showers, which Cara enjoyed, much preferring them to sonic showers although she preferred sonic closets to washing laundry.

"Sorry." Muffled behind a stack of books topped with a heap of unfolded, clean clothing Fleur sounded distracted. "Tonison is in the quad, and it took me longer to cross than I'd planned."

Cara rubbed the small scar of her ten-year sterilization implant on her left arm and sighed hard. "I saw him. Him and his adoring fans."

Fleur giggled and dropped everything on the twin-size bed to the left of the door. "I also saw Professor Danson today."

"Really?" Cara peered up in surprise. "Is he teaching here?"

"Word on the street is his class will be invitation only. You're a shoo-in. Get me a pic."

Cara snorted and leaned back, rotating her shoulders to ease the soreness four hours of intense study produced. "He'll be dead before you're eligible to conceive."

"So?"

Cara snorted again and lifted the framed picture on the corner of her desk. A tap on the top-right-corner changed the display. She flicked through the pictures, lingering on the one of her father before setting it back down.

The frame automatically reverted to her preferred setting, a candid shot of her Uncle Michaelson on his last birthday. The women in the background were blurry and hard to make out. In the foreground, Michaelson smiled as if directly at her. Gray hair framed a kind, wrinkled face and laugh lines showed on the corners of his bright-blue eyes. Eyes Cara had inherited from his brother. At one-hundred and thirty-six, Michaelson still possessed all his teeth and walked without aid.

For a moment, a wave of sadness engulfed her. Her father had died tragically at eighty-seven in a senseless cab accident. Cara had been conceived thirteen years after his death, one of the last viable children Martason's sperm produced. Her older sister Bridget had been conceived with the same sperm.

In his lifetime, Martason had sired thousands of children both naturally and artificially. His line produced the occasional boy child so was much in demand. Add in his intelligence and good looks, and a breeding contract cost more than most women made in a lifetime. The cost had dropped dramatically after his death, although Cara's mother, Clearin, could've afforded to have Martason's children while he lived.

Reminded of her mother, Cara straightened and turned back to her books. Unhappy with the choice of her daughter's career, her mother had agreed to let her join Stellar Command when she graduated on the stipulation she remain in the top ten percent of her class.

Fleur tapped the picture lightly with a manicured nail. "Will you go again for his birthday celebration this year?"

"Yes. He's very kind and welcoming. I wish to see him as often as I may before we ship out."

Fleur grinned and thumped onto her bed, spreading out and knocking the books and clothing to the floor. "We're so lucky to get this opportunity to do something really worthwhile. I know your mom's worried, but the tech is sound. We haven't lost a ship in twenty years now."

"We haven't found more than one habitable planet either," Cara said.

"One is a lot. The first colony ships leave in two years. Maybe there they'll let us breed more men."

Cara's eyes widened, and she glanced toward the door. "Shh— they hear you speaking like that, and they'll kick you from the program."

Fleur shrugged but cast a nervous glance at the door. She rose to make sure it was shut, then stood with her back against it. "Everyone knows the birthrate is fixed. Well, everyone who ever took a biology class. Wouldn't it be nice to not have to share a man's attention with so many others?" Fleur rose an elegantly-shaped black brow. "I swear, before we finished yesterday, Franson had his eye on his next date."

A blush crawled across Cara's cheeks, and she spun away.

Fleur snickered and flopped to her bed with a dramatic sigh. One hand rose and passed over her breast. Her voice sounded wistful when she spoke. "It feels so much better when Franson touches me. It's exciting not knowing where he'll touch next or for how long. He's an amazing lover." She glanced from beneath thick, black lashes at Cara. "You don't know what you're missing, and it doesn't cost that much. Sell your copter, and you can visit him weekly. You'd really like him. He's tall with broad shoulders and a big—"

"Stop!" Cara laughed and waved her hands. "Is nothing personal?"

"I was going to say open smile. Get your mind out of the gutter." Fleur threw her pillow at Cara.

Cara batted it away and turned her back as Fleur continued to massage her breasts.

"It isn't the money; it's visiting the clinic afterward to ensure I'm not stealing sperm. Doesn't that embarrass you?" Just speaking of it embarrassed Cara, making her flush deepen.

"Meh, it takes two minutes. And it's dumb. I mean, I agreed to the ten-year sterilization so why would I steal it?"

"To sell?" Cara glanced over her shoulder, relieved to see Fleur picking up her scattered possessions.

While she didn't consider herself a prude, she hated to be present while Fleur masturbated. Somehow, she always felt as if she let her best friend down with her continued rejections of an intimate relationship. She found Fleur beautiful with her long, dark hair and bright smile, but she didn't want a relationship with any woman, at least until she had one with a man. Too many times she'd seen close friends break up over sex and Fleur meant too much to her to lose her.

Cara wanted a man of her own. A man like Professor Danson who lived with the same twelve women his entire life and sired all their children. Last year at a university-sponsored picnic, she'd met them and since then been consumed by envy for the close, easy relationship they displayed. The women seemed relaxed and friendly and had mostly ignored the other men present, content with each other and their professor.

As if reading her mind, Fleur said, "Stop obsessing over the professor. I only ever heard of three men like him. What are the chances you'll find an educated man happy in a monogamous relationship?"

"Twelve is hardly monogamous."

"Franson sees twelve a day..."

Cara giggled and tapped the stylus in her hand absently against her comp screen. "Think they get bored? Sex feels good and all, but doing the same thing day in and day out... I'd be bored silly."

"The boys at PH-One seem happy enough, and nothing's stopping them from pursuing any career they want or forcing them to date so many. Speaking of that, can I borrow a few hundred? I'll pay you back when I get my student stipend."

"Sure, but what for?"

"Franson is going to make a movie, and I want to visit him a few more times before he becomes famous."

"What kind of movie? A pleasure sensie or adventure story?"

"I'm not sure, but either would be a hit. He really is magnificent. He feels like a man, not all thin and soft like a girl. I swear to God; he can get me wet just by talking. His voice is all gravelly and low, and he lets his facial hair grow."

Cara grinned at Fleur. "You're a barbarian. You must have too many recessive genes."

"Pfft. I'm a healthy female with a normal sex drive. You're the odd one."

"That's true," Cara said thoughtfully. She glanced at the books lined neatly on the shelf over her bed. "But if I can find a habitable world, I'll be famous and get my pick of men."

"Be honest, it isn't the draw of fame, it's the thought of getting out from under your mother's thumb."

Cara winced. "True..."

"You're right though. If you lead a mission that locates a habitable planet, you'll be as famous as

Beatrice NiNancy Norason. She has nine girls and two boys now... can you believe it?"

"That might be a few too many children... I mean I eventually want a few, but eleven?"

Fleur heaved a deep sigh and scooped a science book from the floor. "Study is the only way to the top."

Cara glanced out the window, but the quad was empty now. Sunset lit the sky a pale orange tinged with rose and lights glittered from the tall buildings visible in the distance. Haven was a beautiful, peaceful planet. No pollution marred the sky. No dangerous animals roamed the thick forests or swam the salty seas. Terraformed to be idyllic in all respects, even the weather stayed mild and agreeable in all populated hemispheres.

But Haven had grown crowded. Most of the populous lived underground. Only the women who qualified in their exams were offered the opportunity of higher education and a chance to live on the surface. Men, of course, did what they wished. It wasn't unusual for a community to join forces to build housing or entertainment to entice a man's interest. The twenty-to-one discrepancies in male births saw to that.

Cara frowned. She'd seen a report in her mother's office that made her think those numbers were skewed, and the actual discrepancy was much higher. As a child, she'd believed when told more men lived in South Hampton preferring the warmer climate, but she'd visited and seen approximately the same amount of men there as here. In her entire life, she'd only seen a few hundred men in the flesh, yet millions of women. As of the last official census, Haven housed six billion souls, but the math didn't add up.

Not a problem as most women couldn't perform higher math. The average woman quit school by fifteen to begin work. Most jobs required only basic education. As long as you could type directions and read a comp screen, you could find work, as ninety-five percent of the actual work was automated.

Less than five percent of the population performed work that required higher education. Most didn't even need to leave their homes, as the programming to control a droid picking coffee beans in Athea could be done from halfway around the world.

The standard of living across the globe was high with plenty of free time to vacation or raise children. Travel could be expensive, but resorts flourished in every town, so you didn't need to travel far to enjoy a pampered vacation.

Women spent their time pursuing the arts or hobbies. Handmade jewelry and elaborate clothing were back in vogue, and the prices for such pieces could cost as much as a breeding contract.

A man's lifespan nearly doubled that of a woman. Cara could expect to live another hundred years or so, and not have children till she passed the half century mark. She'd begun to suspect the discrepancy in life span was artificial as well. A thought best not expressed aloud. She'd taken the basic medic courses and enough science to pass the advanced hibernation resuscitation classes, but found it hard to keep quiet at the obvious missing chunks from the medical journals.

The one time she'd questioned her mother, she'd been met by tight-lipped anger and veiled threats so desisted immediately.

Fleur stood and let her book fall to the bed. "I'm off to dinner. Want me to bring you something back?"

Cara handed Fleur her ID card. "Yeah, whatever's handy. Sorry I've been a pain, but if I don't pass this placement test in the top ten percent, I'm out."

"No worries. Take time to exercise and sleep though. Studies show that helps as much as intense study." She tapped Cara's forehead with one finger. "Let it percolate in here."

Cara nodded absently and returned to her book. Ballistics came hard to her, and if she wanted to pilot a shuttlecraft, she needed to understand it in all its intricacies.

When Fleur returned, Cara was busily writing out practice problems to predict fall speed at different velocities in varying gravities.

"Sorry, sweetie, but that answer is wrong," Fleur said as she placed the paper sack containing a soy burger and fries on Cara's desk. "At that velocity, in that ship, you'll burn up on entry. Don't forget to take hull strength into account."

Cara sighed and erased her work with a sweep of her hand. She snatched the bag and stuffed a handful of fries into her mouth. "Wanna go to the gym?"

"Sure, and when we come back, I'll teach you the mnemonic I use."

Cara placed her old-world books on her desk. Nobody used books anymore, but the university insisted on them. With a last wistful glance from her dorm window, she rose to follow Fleur. She wished they insisted on balancing the population as it had been then too.

# -2-

# GEIR

Geir jumped back from the honent's stamping feet. Hooves the size of dinner plates ringed with barbed claws kicked up clods of earth. Men shouting in the distance disturbed the animal. Normally placid, the bleating horn and yells had the entire pen of honents agitated.

"What the hells is going on?" Geir turned to be sure his three young brothers still cleaned the lep cages with the other boys and weren't causing mischief.

An older, grizzled man, grasping the halter of the honent, peered at him from narrowed eyes set beneath shaggy brows. Geoff had sired a son off Geir's mother and had taken him in when Geir's father died.

"Ne'r heard that before have you, son? Those be the horns warning one of the women is missing."

"Missing?"

"Aye, escaped or stolen. The double blow would mean we're under attack." Geoff yanked hard on the lead rope and dragged the honent to the fence surrounding the pen where he tied it to a metal ring bolted to a five-foot-tall hunk of rock. Snorting and twisting its head, the honent stamped the ground.

"Get the beasts tied tight, and then go check the lower pasture gate is closed."

Geir did as he was told. All around him, men quit their work and gathered in bunches. Most carried their swords or kept their hands close to their knives. Low mutters escalated to shouted questions as the jarl, and a group of arms-men cantered past on the backs of livered honents.

The jarl made no answer.

One of the arms-men halted. "We think she wandered off unattended. Triginta, a young girl of nine years, has a streak of curiosity, and a guard left a gate unlatched and unattended. Jarl Ludger is offering a reward for her safe return. One month of breeding rights in Autumn House."

The men around Geir stirred with excitement.

Geoff slapped his head lightly. "On your way, boy. Be sure the gate is closed. Gods help us if she wanders into the lower pasture."

Geir paled. The honents there were untamed and savage.

"I've sent men to make sure, but let's leave nothing to chance. Go!" Geoff cuffed his shoulder to hurry him away.

Geir went as fast as his legs could take him. The mile run to the lower pasture gate passed in minutes. Tall for his age, and limber, he excelled at all sports.

His mother, Septem, was from Summer House at his birth. His father had been killed in a raid acquiring two new women, ensuring his son a place on a raiding team. His father had sired a daughter before his death, which earned his son advanced training with a sword. Genes that fathered girls were dwindling so Geir received special treatment in the hopes when his turn came in a House he'd sire girl children too.

Unbroken honents wandered the lower field. The males snorted and pawed the ground, surrounding the females who stood placidly with their long tails swishing, cropping the thick grass with blunt, yellow teeth.

One of the males charged a keeper with shocking suddenness. At the last second, it reared to its hind legs and crow-hopped forward, striking out with its front feet. The man it charged held his ground and snapped the whip he carried. The sound echoed over the pasture. His partner grasped his spear, prepared to attack, but it wasn't needed. The honent dropped to four legs and whirled.

Spooked by the noise, the closest group of honents whinnied and pranced a moment before galloping away, heading to the lowlands and the river. Two man patrols guarded the honents from riptors and mega's around the clock.

A hand held to shade his eyes from the mid-day sun, Geir watched the honents run to the river that they knew better than to cross. The fish in the river could devour an adult honent in minutes. His gaze caught on the sparkling rocks lining the water's edge. As a child, he'd loved to play in the bright rocks. A fission of fear raced up his spine, and he vaulted the fence.

"Hey," the man with the whip called.

Geir ignored the hail and ran down the hill, cutting diagonally through the pasture. As a boy, he'd followed the bank of the river from the town to play with the rocks. Town law forbade drinking the water to the south of town or emptying waste to the north. Most boys preferred to play along the northern bank as the southern could be smelly with filth in it, but a girl wouldn't know that, and a wide border of colored rocks lined the southern stretch of river.

Rocks Geir had found fascinating as a child. He'd known of the dangers the forest represented and been careful of snakes. Living inside the sanctuary her entire life she wouldn't know. To her, it would be a pretty meadow dotted with flowers with sparkling water and glittering gem-like rocks.

He forced his feet faster.

The sight of the mounted patrol along the river relieved him, and he slowed his mad dash. With his hands on his hips, he leaned forward, breathing hard a moment before straightening and continuing at a jog. The mounted men ignored him. Beardless, he remained beneath their notice.

He peered over his shoulder at the high wall encircling the town. Likely, the girl had wandered from the food gate. If she'd crossed the wooden bridge directly on exiting the sanctuary, she'd be across the river now.

"Where would I go at nine?" he murmured to himself. Both hands rose to shade his eyes. "Assuming I didn't know that megas roam those woods, and packs of riptors lived in the fields, and I grew bored with the rocks— the lily trees..." he trailed off as he gazed at the flower-covered trees in the distance. A deep scowl on his brow, he jogged to the nearest guard. "Are we checking the lily trees?"

"I'm sure Ludger sent some men." The man turned his worried gaze to the distant white trees. "It's unlikely she would go so far... A child who never traveled farther than five hundred yards."

He said it as if to convince himself, Geir thought.

He began running again, ignoring the shouts as he swam the river. Most dangerous fish lived farther away, both human predation and the dirty water dissuaded them from staying so close to town, but there was always a chance a school of piranha or flat-back snapper lurked in the brown water.

He emerged wet, but unscathed, and ran through the waist-high grass toward the lily trees, keeping an eye out for riptors. Single riptors were easily dispatched with a knife or strangling; packs could kill, overwhelming you before you could fight them off. Riptors gray-green skin was hard to see in the thick grasses, but his honent leather boots and trousers would protect from their sharp teeth and claws if one leapt on him. A girl would have neither trousers or boots. He didn't even know if they knew of the small leathery carnivores except as food served to them.

Even from this distance, the lily tree's odor beguiled. Soft and delicate, it wafted to him on the breeze. The more scent breathed in, the more relaxed you became until you drifted to sleep without a care in the world.

As he grew closer, another odor, this one of decay and rotten meat, mixed with the flowery smell. He hoped it was corpses of those who came to die here and not the kills of a mega. He couldn't recall if anyone had come to die recently and cursed himself for not paying better attention to the doings of his seniors.

A glance over his shoulder showed the top of the town wall in the distance. Grasses and fluctuation in elevations obscured the men beside the river. Bluebells, honeysuckle, thorntips, and even precious roses grew fifty feet before the copse of lily trees. Tended by the loved ones of the deceased who choose to die here, the flowers bloomed in a riotous profusion.

And in their midst, a small girl knelt. Blond hair littered with bits of grass and picked flowers trailed across her back in a messy braid. She glanced up with bright, blue eyes and smiled, showing even white teeth. Her simple, pale-yellow shift was dirt smeared and damp.

"Hello," she said fearlessly.

Geir's heart pounded. Sweat trickled down his brow and dampened his palms. A coughing snort came from the trees, making the hair on his arms rise.

"Come away, sweetheart." Geir held out his hand.

She ignored him, content to pick and plait flowers.

Conflicting desires rooted him to the spot. He wanted to rush in and grab her but was afraid the movement would trigger the beast that lurked to leap. The knife at his waist was intended for eating, not fighting. Against a mega's claws, his knife would be useless.

The sheer differences of her mesmerized him. A corner of his mind wondered if that was the lily trees affecting his senses, but he felt as if he could stare at her for hours. Small, graceful hands and delicate bones, so different from any man he'd ever seen, revealed her defenselessness.

He vaguely remembered his mother as soft and smelling of flowers. He never tried to remember her as mostly he recalled tears and wailing. His father had told him the women cried when a child left the sanctuary and recovered quickly, but in his memory, the wails went on.

Like other boys, he'd snuck peeks through the inner fence, despite the penalties, and seen shrouded women cross the courtyard. As a young boy, he'd thought them happy. It wasn't until he was older he noted the downcast eyes and cringing behavior. But now here was this girl, and she smiled at him. He wanted to bask in it.

The befnir bush to his left quivered. He tensed and screamed for help as loud as he could.

Alarmed, the girl leapt to her feet.

Geir prayed help arrived before the mega finished eating him and chased the girl. He knew he would die fighting it, but it would be worth his life to save her.

"What?" Wide blue eyes peered around.

"A mega. Come with me now!" He drew his meager knife and offered his hand.

Tears filled the blue eyes, and she ran to him, grabbing his waist hard and burying her face against his chest. Automatically, he scooped her up, surprised by her slight weight. A tremble he couldn't contain shook him as the carnivore snorted again. He wondered what held it back and risked a quick glance behind him, praying someone had heard and was running to them.

"When it charges, get to the river."

"Triginta, my name is Triginta Olof Helgedr."

"I'm extremely pleased to meet you, but you must run as fast as you can." He glanced down at her. The dreamy disconnected way she'd said her name alarmed him. The wide pupils confirmed his suspicion. Triginta had inhaled a bit too much lily tree odor.

"Do you understand me?"

"What's your name?" Relaxed against him now, she appeared to have forgotten her fright completely.

"Geir Septemsz and I believe you're my sister. My father was called Helge." As Geir spoke he stepped backward, taking her with him. For a fleeting moment, he wondered if they shared the same mother as well. He had no idea what house his mother was in now or how many other children she had although he knew he was her first child and she had at least three other sons.

"I have three brothers and an older sister, Viginti Septem. My mother lives in Spring House, but it's so boring there."

Geir took another step back. Sweat beaded his brow and rolled down his back. The girl in his arms was priceless beyond being his sister. Her mother had produced two daughters while still in Summer House. Most women were lucky to produce one by the time they reached Winter House.

"Momma is expecting again. I hope it's another girl. I hate when my brothers leave us. Vigi is only a year older than I, but she's boring too. All she wants to do is play with dolls. I hate dolls and needlework. I like playing with my brothers."

"Someday you'll have sons of your own."

"I hope not. You should hear the women scream and moan. I never want to have boys or girls. I want to be a guard and be able to leave the sanctuary."

"You cannot. It's much too dangerous."

She shrugged and rested her head against his shoulder.

He turned and ran.

The mega's paw bowled him over. He tucked and rolled, trying to protect Triginta's delicate skin.

"Run," he bellowed over her scream and the mega's growl.

Sharp claws hooked in his gray leather leggings left shallow cuts behind as they shredded the thick leather. He released the girl with another command to run and stabbed at the snarling face with his knife. A young mega, not yet fully grown, faced him, but the animal was still bigger than he. Two hundred pounds of fur, muscle, and teeth, glared at him as it hacked its coughing roar again.

By luck, he connected with the black nose of the beast. The mega swiped at its bloodied nose and roared. He ducked and placed both hands over his face as the mega swatted at him with both paws, not connecting with either, feinting to judge his response.

Geir was ready when it lunged, and he rolled forward, stabbing at the throat, then abdomen as the mega bounded over him. The mega snarled and spun. His knife had barely scratched it through the thick, gray-spotted fur.

Wide golden eyes narrowed, and fur-tipped ears pricked back as the mega showed its teeth. Its glance flitted to the fleeing girl. Geir yelled and swiped with his knife, drawing its attention back.

White fire traveled down his arm and across his chest as the mega connected, ripping through his thin linen shirt and the skin beneath. Geir skittered sideways. The mega followed. In the distance, Triginta ran screaming, her head barely visible over the waving grass. The childish voice calling for help added power to his swing, and he made a solid hit on the mega's cheek as it snapped at him. Blood thundered in his ears. He grabbed the thick ruff in one hand, trying to get a choke hold and stab the mega's eye.

Teeth connected to his hip and the mega shook him hard, each movement a tearing agony. He managed to curl and stab again before the mega pushed him to the ground. Claws and teeth sank deep. A shrill scream escaped him as the world faded.

# -3-
# CARA

Sweat trickled down the side of Cara's face. For seventeen years, since she was five, she'd been practicing martial arts.

Fleur grinned, then stuck out her tongue before jumping to her feet and stretching. "Nice one, Cara."

The martial arts instructor snapped her fingers. "Attend. Note the correct placement of hands and feet when the attacker is bigger than oneself." The tiny woman placed her hands on Cara's wrist and elbow then planted her feet with deliberate firmness. "Just so. Then swing the hips. It isn't a matter of strength, but force. Use the body as a fulcrum and your opponent has no choice but to obey the laws of physics."

The students laughed as the teacher threw Cara to the ground.

"No. Stay down." She snapped her fingers again and beckoned the largest girl present to approach. "Once on the ground, and mobility is hampered, the fight becomes one of wits. What will my opponent do? To correctly access the available choices one must first decide on the opponent's goals. An opponent not bent on murder is unlikely to go for the neck, but instead the hands and legs."

The instructor stepped back and motioned the bigger woman forward. At six-feet, she was fifty pounds heavier and six inches taller than Cara. "Jena, show us how you would subdue Cara without killing her."

Jena knelt astride Cara, trying to pin her arms with her knees.

"And see? Jena has neglected half of Cara's body; the stronger half too. Cara, brace your left knee and twist your hips to the side. Keep in mind you owe an attacker no mercy. While they might wish to spare you, never leave yourself vulnerable by returning the favor. Attack hard and fast.

"Because we don't wish to kill Jena, we will instead film this and go over the options later. Pay special attention to the opportunities for harm Jena's position affords. See how close to Cara's face Jena's unprotected midriff is? Teeth and forehead are valid weapons.

"As Cara twists and pushes from the floor, Jena's left arm will come within striking range of Cara's teeth. A well-placed bite along the interior of the wrist will kill her. If Jena hunches to protect, she exposes her jugular. If she releases to hit back, now Cara is half free. Because of the laws of physics, a hit or slap will do little harm from this position, but clawed fingers to rip at delicate eyes or cause maximum pain to the delicate skin of nose or cheek can make the attacker back away completely, allowing you to leap to your feet."

She snapped her fingers again, and the two mock battled a minute. Cara easily overpowered Jena and ended on her feet with Jena lying panting on the floor.

"And so, we learn." Instructor Tiffin waved a hand toward the VR booths in the back of the class.

"Keep practicing on the virtual equipment, but don't neglect to practice against each other. Muscle memory is good, but feeling an opponent strain and hearing them gasp is indispensable training. Not all your opponents will be human, and no, I'm not speaking of alien life forms with intelligence, but animal."

Her steady gaze traveled the class. "You will be without back-up on strange worlds dealing with situations we can't imagine. New Haven taught us even the smallest animals can be deadly."

Cara winced. Two hundred colonists had been killed when animals they thought passive reacted aggressively during a mating season. No bigger than a common rabbit and built in a similar manner, when provoked their teeth and claws had proven deadly against the unprepared colonist. Now all who planned to travel off planet took mandatory self-defense courses.

Weapons training remained optional except for command positions. Cara took every class she had time for.

When *Odyssey,* the newest model galaxy class ship, was ready to launch in three years, she'd be ready. By then, she'd have the mandatory two years on interplanetary shuttles and completed all her classwork. Her goal was to command one of the twenty survey ships that would accompany *Odyssey.* Everyone said she was a natural pilot and she consistently tested in the top percentage of all her classes. The only thing that could hold her back would be her mother.

Unlike Fleur, who used parental influence to get into the academy in the first place after years of not applying herself, Cara tiptoed around, afraid her mother would use her influence to squash her dream.

★ ★ ★

To Cara's surprise, her sister Bridget waited in her dorm room when she returned. Immediately, a cold sick feeling filled her stomach.

"Relax, Mother doesn't know I'm here." Bridget hugged her hard a moment, then pushed her away to examine her. "You look good. Fit and happy. All this study agrees with you."

Cara bit her lip and ran a hand over her sister's dull blond hair. "You look exhausted and sick. Are you well?"

"Worried— and don't tell anyone I came." Bridget paced to the window and peered out. "You're going to be offered a chance to take the advanced history course. Don't take it unless you can keep what you learn to yourself."

Cara bit her lip. "If Stellar Command offers me a special class, I can't turn it down."

Bridget sliced the air with her palm in a frustrated gesture. "I came here to warn you, and believe me, if Mom finds out I spoke privately to you, I'm in big trouble. I can't make you refuse, but if you accept, your life will change."

"How can history hurt me?"

Bridget sighed hard and leaned her forehead on the glass, then jerked back and wiped the sweaty spot she left with her sleeve.

Cara realized her sister wore gloves and a shiver tickled her spine. "Bridge, you're scaring me."

"Good, you should be scared." Bridget gestured out the window. "All this is a lie, and while I can see why our founders did this, it's still a lie."

"The men?" Cara whispered.

Bridget jerked as if stung and peered over her shoulder. "Yeah, I should've realized you'd figure that out." She rubbed her temples and sat on Fleur's bed. "Not many people know our entire truth. Hell, I'm not even sure if what I know *is* the truth. I'm guessing only the elders really know and from what I learned..." She patted the bed beside her. "I'm not sure what I should tell you."

Cara sat and took her sister's gloved hand. "Tell me the truth as you know it."

Bridget nodded decisively and grinned wryly. "It's what I came here to do, but I put you in danger with this truth. As much as we need you to know, it hurts me to tell you. I love you. If this harms you..."

While Cara absorbed this shocking news, Bridget cleared her throat and began speaking. "Two thousand years ago, our ancestors came here aboard the hyper-ship *Haven* from a planet called Earth. *Haven* was a colony class ship carrying over two-hundred-thousand people in cryosleep."

Cara nodded. That was common knowledge although she'd believed the amount carried to be much less.

"We were taught only one colony ship left Earth and conditions on the planet prevented the building of another. The truth is eighteen ships left Earth for sure and maybe more afterward. Earth wasn't like Haven; it was cold and dangerous. Water covered most of the surface and contained dangerous fish, but worse, the people themselves were savage."

Tears filled Bridget's eyes, and she squeezed them closed. "I hope those books and videos were made up to convince us to follow this path we're on, but I'm afraid they weren't."

Cara released Bridget's hand and threw an arm around her. "We knew our ancestors had wars over land and resources."

"It's so much worse. They fought over everything. Men were in charge and treated women horribly. Women died in droves bearing unwanted children. The standard of living was so low we can't imagine it. And the planet was filthy. Packs of men roamed the streets and attacked weaker groups, stealing their clothing, not because they didn't have any, but because they wanted them. Buildings to house criminals equaled the buildings of the law abiding. Political corruption was so common that the populous accepted it without complaint, feeling grateful for any semblance of law.

"People locked themselves in their homes at night and hoped no packs of men or 'law officers' came to their door." Bridget rose her hands and pressed them against her face, muffling her words.

"What we did..." she took a deep breath and straightened. "By the time the colony ships left, they knew the planet was doomed. The women on the ship *Haven* killed their men. All colony ships carried sperm and ova banks. Five thousand diverse samples. They'd decide Earth men were too violent, that even on a fresh planet they'd revert to barbaric ways, and decided to keep the male population low. Just enough men are allowed to be born to ensure genetic diversity."

"They killed them?" Nausea roiled in Cara's gut and her palms sweat.

"One hundred thousand men killed in cold sleep and twenty-five thousand more in the fight for the ship. One hundred were allowed to live but kept in confinement as backup in case the sperm proved to be inviable. The mutiny aboard the *Haven* was fierce and deadly. Thousands of women died trying to take the ship back."

"That's horrid, but so long ago...."

"Our government lies about how many men are living now. Ninety percent of the footage on the comp showing healthy, happy men is faked. The women sent to New Haven have no men and will never have any."

"But why... and how can they reproduce?"

"Exactly. Our colonies will be dependent on the delivery of sperm from Haven. Haven will retain complete control."

Cara rose and strode to the window. The peaceful grounds of the university mocked her. "That's so dangerous and short-sighted. What if we have an illness or something?"

"The human race will die alone and childless."

Cara shivered.

"Cara, I don't know if Stellar Command will come right out and say this or not, but if you run across one of those other colony ships, I'm sure Haven will do its best to hide their existence, if not destroy them outright...and you. The underground needs you, Cara. I have no idea what 'truth' Steller Command will tell you. As her eldest daughter, Mother has been grooming me to take up a government position. Some of this I learned from my government classes."

A light blush covered Bridget's cheeks, and she withdrew her hand from Cara's to rub her temples. "Some of this I learned by sneaking into Mom's records. Jilla got me in touch with an underground movement, people like Jilla and I who have access to records because of who our mothers are. At first, we meant to stop the government corruption by going public, but then we realized how deep and widespread the corruption is and how ruthless they would be to protect their secrets.

"It's safer for you if you don't know details, just trust me when I saw they *will* be ruthless. Jilla and I have confirmed over twelve murders in the last five years alone." Bridget turned a pale, miserable face to her sister. "We believe, but can't prove yet, the destruction of the hyper-ship *Stalwart* was engineered by our government to cover up the murder of Stellar Command personnel who intended to tell the populous of New Haven the truth. Over two-thousand women murdered so they could keep their power...."

A tremor shook Cara. This was her mother they were speaking off. She'd always known her mother was a tough a woman, not easily crossed, but this... Jilla, Bridget's lover for the last eight years, was in a unique position to find information as her mother was the head of planetary security.

Cara turned bleak eyes on her sister.

"If you speak out..." Bridget slumped and cradled her head in her hands. "I don't know what will happen, but I'm afraid." She began to cry again and had to take a second to compose herself. "I'm afraid they'll kill our men again too. Michaelson is a good man, a kind, smart man. And Professor Danson, Wrenson, God, Cara, every man I've ever met has been kind and good company. How will we protect our men?"

"No, that's crazy. The women of Haven love their men. They'd never stand for it. In fact, I think they'd riot if they knew the truth about the male birth rate."

"How would they know? Who would tell them with what proof? Male births are already down. What's to prevent the government from allowing only the bare minimum needed for genetic diversity?"

"Dear God."

"You have to keep quiet, Cara. Accept it as if it didn't matter to you. Our only hope is to outlive the planners and take their place. Did you ever notice only those who eschew the pleasure houses rise in the ranks? It isn't because they're more focused, it's because the council considers they're less likely to protest the dearth of men."

Bridget rose and grasped her shoulders. "If you find another colony, you must never report it. To do so is to sign their death warrant."

"Bridge, there will be twenty teams searching."

"Yes. And we have three years to try to ensure only those who love men go."

Cara snorted.

Bridget winced. "Tell Fleur to lay off the pleasure houses, or she'll never get a command." Bridget searched her face and appeared satisfied with what she saw. "We aren't alone. There are others who feel as we do. I assured my friends you cared for men even though you'd never visited a pleasure house or sought male contact. Keep it up."

"How did you know I like them?"

"Michaelson." Bridget picked up the digital picture frame on Cara's desk and ran a finger over the aged face. "Keep his picture, but play another one first as if his importance has lessened.

"Who are your friends?"

"It's best if you don't know. This little I told you can't compare to the horror of the history classes. Please, when you view the recordings, remember Michaelson. Not all men are venal and corrupt. Some are kind, honorable people. We can raise men to love and respect women, and they can be equal, productive members of society."

Bridget grinned suddenly. "Imagine that? What if the ratio were balanced and we could all have our own man to love?"

Cara rubbed her eyes hard. " I thought we could if the colony on New Haven was successful. I'd hoped they would allow more men to be born as more space became available. Now I'm terrified it will be a success."

Bridget hugged her." Find us a good spot, Cara," she whispered. "A safe spot to raise children and we can steal sperm and start our own colony."

Cara trembled, the full import of her sister's treason sinking in. Bridget wasn't going to wait for the old regime to pass on, she was going to implement change despite the risks that entailed. The sheer magnitude of such an undertaking overwhelmed her. Even assuming the sperm could be stolen in the quantities needed without being caught, the weapons, books, and supplies needed was staggering.

"We'll have to let the world think we aren't in touch. If I'm caught...."

Cara hugged her sister harder.

"Don't tell Daisy or Aster."

"As if."

Despite her fear for her sister, Cara snickered. Her older sisters Daisy and Aster were sired by a poet, and both spent their days writing bad verse and socializing in the women's clubs. Their women lovers were countless. Both worked in their mother's office, enjoying the city social scene and hob-knobbing with children of other council members.

"Aster is certain she'll take mother's spot," Cara said.

"Aster is an idiot. Mother will live to three hundred easily." Bridget pulled away and peered into Cara's eyes. "You'll outlive me and everyone else you know. Our medics have the tech to keep everyone alive about three hundred and fifty years before the rapid onset of old age."

"What? That's crazy. Why wouldn't the council save themselves at least?"

"They do. Mom is on her second half. She lived a hundred and twenty years as Alifin Nikernin Friedason."

Cara's eyes widened. Alifin Nikernin Friedason had been the president of Haven for fifty years before her 'death' in a boat accident. Her mother now worked as the president's personal assistant and as an elder on the council of ruling governors. Even though cosmetic surgery was readily available and cheap, she'd never considered the government used it to continue to rule under new names. The thought terrified her. *If they broke the law so blithely for personal gain what were they really capable of?*

"Stellar Command isn't bothering to hide they're anti-aging anymore. Your training is too valuable. I helped write the paper explaining how living in space slows the aging process. Complete bullshit, but hardly anyone on Haven has the math or science to refute it. And those that do are generally in politics or work for Stellar Command."

"But Michaelson... they could all live twice as long?"

"We all could, but if we did this planet would be seriously overcrowded. The council is debating right now about giving the technique to New Haven. With low birth rates, longer life is fine."

Bridget straightened and glanced at her watch. "I have to go if I'm going to sneak out of here unseen. Keep contact with me to a minimum. If you need a private meeting, call and mention Michaelson's birthday. No matter what happens, I'm proud to have a sister like you."

"Please don't get caught." Cara tried to hide the tremble in her voice. Sperm thieves were hanged and their progeny sterilized. The thought of Bridget dangling in the city center horrified her.

"You too. It's going to be hard as hell to steal a planet."

Cara winced. Her gaze flicked to Michaelson's portrait, and her shoulders straightened. He was worth saving. A world without men didn't bear thinking of.

# -4-

# GEIR

Geir stretched and flexed his fingers before pulling the sword from the scabbard on his side. Keld's envious sigh misted in the frosty morning air. Fashioned of hammered steel, Geir's sword was an elder's weapon. Given to him by the hand of Jarl Ludger himself six years ago, he wore it with pride and a hint of bitterness. He'd rather have had the month in Autumn House, but he'd been judged too young and inexperienced so given the sword instead. He had six years to wait before he could battle for a position in any house.

Keld carried a bronze sword. Pale morning sun glittered along the length of the wavy blade. The soft bronze had been pounded and reformed so often the metal sported a permanent wave pattern and a dull edge.

Geir's blade was sharp enough to shave with. His envious gaze flicked to the bearded man lounging against the wooden rail. Custom dictate a man remained clean shaven until he sired a child. The gold hoop glinting from the man's ear informed the world he'd sired a daughter. As his reward, he now only patrolled the town.

Genes which sired daughters weren't to be wasted on raids anymore. As the father of a daughter, the man was assured of a spot in a House till his sixtieth year. If he managed to sire more daughters, he'd be let to stay in Winter House as long as his libido let him.

The women of Winter House terrified Geir. He couldn't imagine any man wanting to stay there voluntarily. He glanced behind him, but the twenty-foot wooden wall blocked the view of the squat, two-story wooden building of Winter House. Occasionally, crying or yells could be heard, but today all remained quiet. He'd stopped peeking through this section of fence ages ago, not wanting to confront the angry glares of old women.

"Going to day dream all day or spar?" Keld swung his sword and flexed. Two years younger than Geir, Keld was in a rush to prove himself. Hells, they all were. Without successful raids to boast of they wouldn't be eligible for anything except Autumn House.

Geir laughed and swung his sword, making Keld curse and jump back.

Keld threw his sword into his other hand and shook out his stinging palm. "Damn, you're going to break my blade. Let's wrestle instead."

Geir nodded agreeably, unbuckled his sheath, and pulled off his linen shirt.

Keld whistled as he always did at the sight of Geir's scars. "Man, I envy that blade, but you sure paid for it."

Four parallel lines scored Geir's back. Six crossed his chest. Multiple bites, small white scars, dotted his right hip and thigh. Three more long, runneled scars traveled the length of his left leg, leaving him with a slight limp and dull pain that grew sharp in bad weather.

"I only remember getting the first few."

"Lucky. Still, it must have a hurt like a bitch afterward."

"Yeah. She was worth it though. God, when I think of arriving just five minutes later..."

Keld nodded and ran a finger along the thin scar on the side of Geir's face.

Geir stepped back.

Keld sighed hard. "I wasn't going to kiss you or anything."

A blush heated Geir's cheeks. "Sorry, nothing personal."

"Whatever." Keld pulled his shirt over his head, revealing a broad muscled chest.

At six-three and two hundred fifty pounds, Keld was two inches shorter and twenty pounds lighter than Geir. Stolen from a nearby village the three years before Geir had received his sword, Keld's dark hair and eyes marked him as an outsider. Because of his youth and sunny disposition, the jarl had let him practice with the men. Now, he held a spot on a raiding team with a chance of winning acclaim enough to try for a House himself.

Keld flexed and winked at him, making his blush hotter.

Geir rolled his eyes. "Don't get cocky. I was just thinking you have no scars at all, but I could give you some."

"Aww, and here I thought my many charms were finally winning you over."

"As if." Geir threw a punch that Keld ducked.

Laughing now, the two young men fell to the ground, struggling for dominance.

"Mmm— you're doing it wrong, boys."

The fake falsetto grated on Geir's nerves.

"Come by later, and I'll show you how it's done."

High-pitched giggles and low whispers followed. Geir glanced to the fence. Sven and his cronies gathered and giggled, dressed in shifts like the women wore with hair curled and eye makeup, they looked nothing at all as Geir remembered the women being. Geir hoped the jarl put a stop to this new trend soon. He found it disturbing.

He didn't mind seeing lovers kiss or make love, but these boys pretending to be girls sickened him. They seemed a cruel parody of women. A man's body had undeniable needs. He craved a woman's touch with fiery desire. Sometimes, the desire overtook him, and he'd use his hand to give himself relief.

Once, he'd let Keld suck him. It had felt so good, better than he'd imagined possible, but he'd been unable to bring himself to reciprocate, and since then kept his distance, not willing to take pleasure while offering none.

Keld still flirted, and more and more lately Geir wondered if he'd enjoy it if he made himself, but nothing about Keld attracted him. None of the men attracted him.

His gaze flitted to the high wall again. In his opinion, the jarl didn't do enough to ensure the women's happiness. Too often lately they heard cries and screams from beyond the wall. More and more the sanctuary guards sported bruises and walked about town with sad, haunted eyes. In his youth, the women had seemed happier, or maybe he misremembered. It was a fact there were fewer women now. If the trend continued, his sons would have no chance for sons of their own.

Uneasy now, Geir gestured to the high walls. "What do you think the women do all day?"

Keld made an obscene gesture.

"No really? It must be boring as hell's stuck inside there."

"Believe me, I wouldn't be bored. Give me a scraggle-tooth, dried-up prune and I'd still be happy."

Geir laughed, the sound bitter in his own ears.

"Triginta will be in Summer House now. She was beautiful. Bright-blue eyes and hair like corn silk."

"Your sister though, so even if you win a position in that house in a few years, they'd make you choose another."

"No, my point was there are beautiful girls beyond this wall."

"Girls you'll never see if your lazy asses don't get to work," Geoff snapped.

Geir started in surprise; he hadn't seen the arms instructor approach.

Geoff snatched the sheathed sword from the dirt of the practice ring and handed it to Geir. "The jarl is sending a group out in two weeks if we have enough dried and prepared food..."

Both young men grinned and ran off.

Geoff turned and glared at the gigglers beside the fence. "Go make yourself useful before we put you out as useless mouths to feed." Hands on his hips, he glowered after the retreating boys.

# -5-
# CARA

Cara trailed a hand along the elegant fin of the scout ship *Intrepid,* her first command, walking the entire two city block length of her ship. Energy collectors gave the wing a shimmery appearance. Three-stories tall, the massive bulk of the *Intrepid* crouched on the deck with all loading bay doors open. Butterflies danced in her stomach in a mix of excitement and doubt. In one week, *Odyssey* would launch *Intrepid* to her assigned sector.

*Odyssey* had been traveling through hyperspace for six months, making stops along its route to launch the scout ships nestled against its hull. Cara and her five women crew would live aboard the *Intrepid* as they explored. Reports had shown a dense galactic cluster in which several viable solar systems contained numerous planets and gas giants. For two years— two, two-hundred, twenty-four-hour cycles— *Intrepid* would search their assigned sector for a habitable planet.

Currently, *Intrepid's* bulk filled most of maintenance bay one. Work crews busily loaded supplies and performed the last prelaunch checks.

Each scout ship would enter the bay, load supplies, and exit, carrying their five woman crews. *Odyssey* would return to retrieve and restock them in two years, depending on what they'd learned. A full circuit would take *Odyssey* four years before she returned to Haven to report and restock.

The thought of being in charge for two years both terrified and exhilarated her. Cara's glance flitted to Ilda who laughed with Teryl as they loaded medical supplies. Ilda and Teryl might be a problem. One she hadn't decided how to handle. Fahyim and Veta would cooperate and hide the existence of a viable planet from Haven to save the men. She'd known they were in the underground for three years now. Cara had hoped Fahyim would be assigned to *Gallant* or *Valliant* as neither scout ship had a member of the underground aboard as far as she knew. Her gaze returned to Ilda. With three of her crew firmly behind the idea of stealing a planet, it should be no problem to handle the two who might object.

Ilda and Teryl had no use for men, but maybe she could convince them with money. Both wanted the best sperm donors available. The cost was sure to be astronomical, but maybe Bridget could arrange to steal the sperm they wanted.

She shrugged irritably. She had years to decide and talk them into it and needn't do anything if they didn't find a planet worth stealing.

A grin crossed her face at that thought.

"Admiring your ship?" Fleur asked.

The clean lines of the dark-blue Stellar Command uniform showcased Fleur's lithe form to advantage. Similar in height, Cara had bigger breasts and rounder hips. Her gaze lingered a moment on Fleur's pert breasts, and she felt a pang of regret they'd never been lovers. *What if she never saw her again?* She firmly pushed the thought away.

"You caught me." Cara beamed at her best friend.

"Be careful. We're going to have some great stories to tell, but I'll miss you like crazy." Fleur hugged her hard, then wiped her eyes.

"You too."

Fleur turned to gaze at the launch bay doors. A live image of the exterior covered the massive expanse of metal, giving the illusion that the *Intrepid* could take flight at any moment. "Back home, staring up at the sky, you don't really get a feel for its vastness like you do out here. Don't get lost. Set the buoys."

"Yes, Mom."

Fleur glanced at Veta and leaned closer. "Take some chances on love, Cara. Veta is a good woman and not all relationships end when the partners move on to new lovers. Relationships can gain depth, not lose it with the addition of sex." Fleur straightened the collar on Cara's dark-blue jacket, resting her fingertips on the captain's insignia on Cara's left shoulder. "I know you're worried you won't be able to share your attention, but it can add spice when your partner desires another."

Fleur kissed her lips lightly. "It is possible to work through jealousy. Just because I desire others besides you doesn't make my love less real."

Cara flushed.

Fleur tweaked Cara's short, blond hair that had grown back since decontamination. For six months, the entire crew had lived in isolation, undergoing every treatment medical could devise to ensure they were as pathogen-free as possible. Inoculated, poked, prodded, measured, and weighed, they would repeat the procedure before being allowed to return to Haven.

"Fleur, be careful on your patrols, even near *Odyssey*. If you go off grid, and something happens, we'll never find you. Space is enormous. A million haystacks and one needle."

"Both good and bad news." Fleur winked and stepped away.

Cara nodded and straightened. Fleur would be looking for a safe place for the men too. Granted, her position attached to *Odyssey* wouldn't put her in a great spot to locate a planet, but every time the *Odyssey* exited hyperspace Fleur launched her landing ship, *Merris,* and began examining the local space while the *Odyssey* gathered energy for the next jump. Her real job would begin if the scouts found a viable planet.

She would bring her payload of fifty specialists to the surface and ferry women and equipment as needed while the scientist ran their tests.

*Odyssey* carried two fabrication plants that could land on the surface to begin preparation for a colony ship. Five landing ships nestled between the scout ships against the *Odyssey's* hull. Armed, armored, and containing the most advanced med-bays Haven could produce, the landing ships were also intended to be rescue ships if a scout crew required it or *Odyssey* herself suffered such a serious malfunction she needed to be abandoned. Landing ships could 'catch' escape pods and guide them to a safe landing or attach them to their hulls.

Because of the unknown and potentially hostile conditions of landing on a new planet, a group of five women specially trained in defense accompanied each group of scientists on every landing ship. As captain of a landing ship, Fleur held the rank of captain in the military division of Stellar Command and oversaw both the scientists and soldiers on her crew.

Much smaller than a scout ship, a landing ship was fast and maneuverable with only one small cafeteria aboard. Intended to be transport, fifty individual workstations, comprised of a single chair that reclined for sleeping surrounded by six screens, adjoined the bridge on the topmost level. The middle level contained the cafeteria and a state of the art med-bay.

The bottom level of the bulbous ships carried supplies for the landing parties and scientist. Designed to be offloaded fast in an emergency, the ship could dump its cargo and load five hundred crew within eight minutes

Cara turned her gaze to the captains gathering to see her off.

Rami and Fern, captains of scout ships, would also be searching for a home for the men. Marley, the captain of the landing ship, *South Hampton,* was in the underground as well. Cara wasn't sure of the others and made no effort to find out. What she didn't know, she couldn't reveal.

Admiral Tempo Sueson was Fleur's grandmother and in command of the *Odyssey.*

"You look better with eyebrows by the way."

Fleur's laughing comment brought Cara's attention back to her. Cara traced the regrown hair above her eyes with a medically enhanced nail. Steel fibers bonded to thin polymers replaced her fingernails. She was literally as tough as nails now and could use her fingernail as a screwdriver without fear of it chipping.

Tests had shown her nails could tear through thick animal hide with ease. As the captain of her ship, she would always carry a sidearm. The decision on when and what to arm her crew with was hers alone, but every woman of the two-thousand women crew of *Odyssey* had received the nail upgrade.

Cara had opted for permanent body hair removal, retaining only eyebrows, lashes, and the hair on her head.

Fleur had left a patch of pubic hair in the shape of a star. "Give them something to remember me by and set me apart," she'd joked.

Giving up the pleasure houses had been hard on Fleur. Seeing her suffering, Cara had been glad she'd never tried it. Too many nights she'd held her friend while she cried, yearning for something she'd never have.

But maybe if they could find a habitable world, the men could live there safely, and they could balance the population.

It was a worthy life goal. One worth dying for. Her gaze flicked to Ilda. And one worth killing for. She wasn't sure she could bring herself to murder though, no matter what the goal. The med-bay on board *Intrepid* had the capability to put her crew in cold sleep though.

Fleur followed her gaze, and her eyes narrowed. "A habitable planet by definition could support life. It would do some people a world of good to be alone with their thoughts awhile."

Cara brightened. It would be easy to strand Ilda and Teryl. With carefully chosen supplies they'd be safe and unable to stop the theft. "You always were smarter than me."

"Admiral on deck," a woman yelled, interrupting them.

The women in the maintenance hangar stopped what they were doing and straightened, falling into neat rows, and standing at attention.

"I just came to wish you well," Admiral Sueson said. "Haven's resources aren't infinite. Mineral rich astral bodies are also being sought, so don't focus solely on livable planets. You are our best and brightest children. Go make us proud." Admiral Sueson offered her hand.

Cara shook it, not fighting the grin on her face.

"Good luck, Captain." Admiral Sueson saluted her and spun on her heel. The room erupted into loud talk and laughing as the door sealed behind the admiral. Fleur's grandmother Tempo was in command of the *Odyssey,* and the family resemblance was clear. Both women were lithe although Tempo's short black hair was beginning to gray.

Cara wondered if Tempo would be willing to lie to Haven and Stellar Command to save the men. Or maybe she would jettison them like garbage like her mother would. A wave of shame over her mother's murders turned her cheeks red. She turned away and pretended great absorption in her reports till she regained her composure.

The rest of the scout ship crews entered, wearing their dress uniforms and bearing refreshments in what had become launch tradition. Cara accepted a glass of wine and exchanged well wishes with her fellow captains before overseeing the final checks.

Fleur found her at the maintenance bay bridge screens three hours later and escorted her to the *Intrepid's* hatch.

"Good luck, Captain," Fleur repeated and gave her a hug and a crooked grin.

Eye's sparkling and butterflies firmly tamed, Cara saluted and boarded her ship. For one week, she and her crew would live aboard, setting up the hydroponics and testing all systems before reaching their drop zone. Her com-screen showed the exterior of the ship. Blurred lights of hyperspace flickered past, each the promise of adventure. She couldn't wait.

# -6-

# GEIR

A rolling peal, one prolonged note, reverberated through the trees. Geir jerked his head around. Beside him, Geoff tensed. Both men gripped their spears tighter and began running. Loud crashing through the underbrush slowed as no further sound of alarm bells echoed through the thick firtin trees. By the time the other three men on the hunting team rejoined Geir and Geoff, Geir's heart had settled back to its normal rhythm.

The horn sounded again five minutes later. The men exchanged worried glances and spread further out, concentrating on hurrying through the dense forest at the edge of the broad plain. Thurji bushes abounded in the sparse edge of the forest making fast travel dangerous. The lead man continually cast small rocks about him to trigger any bushes before approaching. A single thorn flung from the dart-bushes would kill a man in less than five minutes. Five minutes of agonized writhing and screaming.

The town of Ludger, named after the reigning Jarl, laid on the edge of a prairie so vast no one had ever crossed and returned in Geir's lifetime.

The men told stories passed down from their fathers of the days when a dirt road connected Ludger to another town two months walk across the prairie. Rumor had it that a town nestled between hills so steep even beringei scorned them and brackish water rolled in continuous waves.

Geir wasn't sure he believed the stories of monstrous fish and water that formed waves higher than a man during storms. He also couldn't imagine living anywhere beringei weren't plentiful. The giant omnivores preferred rocky hillsides, but he'd run across them nesting in the plains too.

No paths remained to there or any other place. Steep hills ringed Ludger with narrow passes that men always guarded.

Once, when Geir was barely more than a child, a man had come with a woman and asked for sanctuary. He'd been allowed inside, and his woman offered a place inside the sanctuary, but every stranger since had been killed. The man had died soon after from a fleshy growth that bulged from his abdomen. As far as Geir knew, the women he'd brought still lived inside the sanctuary.

For a moment, Geir contemplated the man. He'd had a woman of his own, and knowing he was dying brought her to a town for her protection. It had never occurred to him before how dangerous it was for the man to keep her alone. Selfishly dangerous. Sure, having a woman you didn't need to share was a male fantasy, but the who stood guard while you slept or made love? To risk a woman for your own selfish pleasure was unthinkable.

Seventeen women had died in his lifetime. Each had been cremated with great ceremony in the town square. He'd attended hundreds of funerals for men. Most had been mass burnings at bonfires after attacks. Old men preferred to go to the lily trees. He forced his thoughts away from their deaths and back on the trail before him.

Narrow passes and steep hills helped protect Ludger. Twice, groups of men had attacked and both times been soundly defeated. When questioned, the few survivors had admitted to hearing of this place from stories told by their grandfathers. Supposedly, in the distant past, Ludger had been a trading town, dealing in weapons smithing.

While men remained who could shape metal, none remained who understood how the metal was retrieved from the earth. The caves in the hills led deep underground and now housed families of beringei that the men hunted for food and furs. Deer and mega abounded on the plains.

Geir couldn't imagine how dangerous a journey of months would be in the waist high grasses. Not only danger from mega, raptor, and snakes, but fire. Tales of the ancients who traveled in safety inside winged vehicles he dismissed as fairy-tales. In the summer months, lightning storms frequently lit the prairie grass ablaze. The prairie burned quickly, but usually the firtin trees on the edge of the plains kept it contained as it never built up much heat from the speed of its passage.

The men of Ludger maintained a wide swath of cleared ground between them and the plains to stop the fire from jumping to the wooden walls surrounding the town.

The thought of a woman alone on that dangerous plain chilled him. Traveling any distance from the town presented a danger for a lone man. Two together were much safer, able to fight off beringei and mega's and guard each other against snakes and riptors as they slept. The snakes without legs preferred to sleep beside the warmth of a human body over the cold ground and many a man had died from rolling onto an uninvited bed companion.

The town kept caged leps around the inner perimeter of both fences to attract the snakes and riptors that entered. Leps bred quickly, providing both fur and food and were easy to care for. As a younger boy, he'd liked the job of caring for leps. Now, he hunted with the men, a fact he was proud of. Much sought after because of his sword, most hunting parties asked him along.

Reminded, he dropped his hand to his sword and picked up his pace. He'd gotten the sword for rescuing Triginta. The guard who'd failed his duty to watch the gate had been hung in the square. Geir thought that too easy a death. Triginta had been seconds away from dying a horribly painful death when rescued. The horn sounded again for the third and final time. All those within hearing distance would be on their way back to town by now.

One of the women was missing, and gods help the man who took her. *Maybe she wandered out on her own*, Geir mused as he ran along the faint path that was all that remained of a once wide road. Younger than the other men, he quickly outdistanced them despite his limp.

The road hugged the edge of a rocky verge. Only a few scraggly befnir bushes grew between the jagged rocks, but snakes thrived there with the wild leps. The top of the palisade surrounding the town was visible, but the contour of the land hid the town itself.

He was shocked to see the woman running down the path toward him. She peered over her shoulder, staring back the way she'd come as she ran. The shift she wore reached her knees, leaving her feet and legs exposed. Sleeveless, with a deep V, every step bounced her full breasts. Geir was fifteen feet away when she turned back and stopped dead.

Her head swiveled, and she headed for the tall grass that lined the road.

"Wait, I won't hurt you," Geir called. "Please wait, there are dangerous animals in there."

Most of the fields surrounding the town contained nothing more dangerous than snakes and a lone riptor or two with the exception being the rolling hills to the south where the lily trees grew. Mega's loved lily trees. But she was to the north. Still, snakes were plentiful and plenty dangerous with bare feet. He cut diagonally through the grass and caught her easily.

To his shock, she fought him with desperate strength, scratching at his face and slapping his arms.

He held her as gently as he could, but knew he'd leave bruises on her arms; arms already covered with bruising. He shook her lightly to gain her attention.

"I won't hurt you. You're safe now." He spoke as if to a skittish honent, using a calm, soothing tone. She continued to flail and scratch at him. Despite his worry over her panicked response, her body pressed so closely against his aroused him.

"Please!" Her wild eyes scanned his face. Tears began trickling down her dirty cheek from a bruised eye.

His hand rose to cup her face, and his eyes narrowed. "Who has struck you?" Furious at the harm apparent on her skin, he pulled her closer, holding her tight to his side and drew his sword. Someone had hurt her; she ran from a cruel captor.

"Please— take me away from here. I'll be nice to you. We can be together, just us. Please."

She clutched his linen shirt and begged in increasingly panicked tones. Loud stomping feet and hollered questions announced the arrival of the rest of the hunting party. She wailed, the sound piercing his heart. Full of fear and desperation, the sound stilled the gathered men.

Geir loosened his hold on her. She slid to her knees, clutching his legs and begging him to help her.

"Come away now, Inkeri," Geoff said in a kind voice and offered her his hand.

"Please, you were kind to me. Wasn't I a generous lover? Have mercy. Don't make me go back there. He's terrible cruel. Please, Geoff!" On her hands and knees, she crawled to Geoff and grasped both his hands.

"It isn't my fault I don't conceive— I try. Never once did I turn you away. Tell them; make them stop." Her gaze traveled the men, and she hid her face in her hands. "The five of you could be my men. Please... I can't bare it anymore. It hurts so much."

Geir tensed. Her pain and fear were beyond refute. Surely Geoff would help her now that he saw her man abused her.

When they said nothing, she began laughing and scrambled to her feet. "Fine, you're all alike— rutting animals. Worse than animals! You care nothing for us except as vehicles to sate your lusts." She ripped the thin material of her shift open.

"Am I beautiful now, Geoff? Does the sight of my naked breasts inflame you?"

Geir stepped forward and pulled the shift closed while she slapped at his hands. Bruises and bite marks marred her body. Someone had left a ring of teeth marks around her left breast, leaving it black and blue and swollen. Long thin welts made from a lash crisscrossed her hip. The sight sickened him.

"You'll have to kill me then. I won't go back." She began to struggle wildly again in Geir's hold.

He wanted to take her away and treat her kindly, to ease her pain but knew he couldn't win a fight with the other men. He hoped Geoff would have a solution for this and be able to comfort her. Surely the jarl wouldn't allow such treatment if he knew of it.

"Come, sweetheart. Let us take you home and treat your wounds," Geir said.

She slapped his face. "Not my home! My men were kind. I hate you. You're vile, despicable!" Panting, she struck him again. He hugged her, letting her slap at him as she wished.

Geoff stepped forward and stroked her hair. "Let us help you."

"Yes, help me; take me away." She turned to Geoff eagerly.

"You know we can't do that, but tell us who hurt you, and we'll see the jarl punishes him."

She began laughing again. "Ludger himself did this." She touched her tender breast gingerly. "Rainer whips me as it pleases him and he and Sven fuck while I cry. They fuck, and laugh, and hurt me to excite themselves. The jarl knows and does nothing except watch occasionally. River House is a nightmare. The other houses are bad, but... How can it be our fault if we don't conceive? How can hurting us help? How will they know who the father is if so many use us?"

"River House?" Geir turned to Geoff for an answer and was surprised by his dismayed expression.

The other men stirred restively, but none spoke. Geir glanced at them, noting their surprised expressions. They hadn't heard of the new house either.

"How many live in River House now?" Geoff asked.

"Six. Two should be in Winter House, and three had children, but the children died after birth. There'll be more stillborn soon. The women are tired. We need sunlight and exercise. And not just on our backs. You make us weak, then blame us when we can't carry to term.

"Rainer beat Viginti Septem for miscarrying. Beat her till her back bled and left her laying on the floor beside her dead girl child and she barely more than a child herself. She has barely sixteen years. He gave her no time to recover either and mated while she still bled. You know it's wrong, yet do nothing."

Pounding hoof beats interrupted her. She turned terrified eyes on the approaching horses. Her gaze flitted back to the men, and she stared up into Geir's face. "My death is on your hands." Dry-eyed now, she turned to meet the approaching men and said nothing as they hauled her into the saddle and galloped away.

Geir stared after her, clutching his sword, tempted like never before in his life to steal a woman. "Was that true?"

Geoff glanced at the other men and straightened. "It sounded true. I'll speak to the jarl."

"What of her and her injuries?"

"I'll see to it."

They returned to town slowly. Geoff stopped at the gate leading to the jarl's residence. To reach the sanctuary where the women's houses lay you first passed through the jarl's house. A sandy floor covered the main room in the lower section. Two double doors opened to the town to allow spectators to view the fights held there.

Sometimes, men met on the floor to settle their differences, but generally, those who wished breeding rights, and qualified in all other respects, met to fight for a position. A red flag dangling from the balcony that faced the main road meant a fight would take place the following Saturday.

Occasionally, a few positions opened at the same time, but usually all those competing tried for one woman.

Every man who showed fought till one victor remained. Geir had seen five hundred men show and have to beat eight or more opponents to win the right of a month of a woman's company.

Now the doors were closed. The guard admitted Geoff and motioned the others on.

Keld grabbed his arm and dragged him to their barracks. "Did you hear? One of the women ran away. Ludger is furious and ordered her whipped. The women went crazy and began screaming and yelling. They were so loud you could hear them over the fence. Ludger sent for the honent trainers but backed down when more men gathered. He was going to beat them all with honent whips."

"No." Horrified, Geir turned back to the door.

"Wait, there's more. The women from Winter House demanded the destruction of River House. Ludger killed Sven for abusing women there and promised to see to their care. I heard Sven hurt Inkeri really bad, which is why she ran. Rumors are flying, and Ludger ordered all Sven's friends brought to the floor. The town is in an uproar that Sven even got inside the sanctuary."

"I spoke to her, was there when they caught her. She was injured and said Sven hurt her..." Geir trailed off not wanting to start rumors about the jarl with no proof. He found it almost impossible to believe the man responsible for the women would hurt one.

Geir glanced around their empty bunkhouse. "Why are we whispering in here instead of there?"

"It's best if I stay out of the way, being a newcomer and all."

"You're one of us now."

"True, but no reason to push my luck. Ludger's looking for leps, and I'm not tempting fate."

Geir leaned closer and lowered his voice, "You think Ludger hurts them too?"

"Yes, the woman shouted some really foul accusations. I saw his face; he was furious, so angry I think he'd have killed them to shut them up if there weren't so many witnesses. Those old women are brave. I'd be afraid of another plague were I them."

Geir grimaced, reminded of the odd plague which had wiped out Winter House and touched no one else when he was a boy. "What a mess. What are we doing about this?"

"Everyone is on edge and keeping their friends close. It'll be a nightmare if a free-for-all develops. Ludger better restore order quick before he has a rebellion to deal with."

"Rebellion?" Geir whispered.

Even saying the word could get you banished. That was one of the worst charges a man could levy against another, even worse than theft. Plotting against the jarl was a death sentence. A long, lonely death.

Both young men jumped when the bells began ringing. They ran out the door, grabbing the wooden buckets beside the door and heading to the well. Glendal, the man who ran the smithy, stood beside the well with his hands cupping his mouth.

"Not a fire," Glendal hollered. "An emergency meeting. Shake a leg or miss it."

Men milled in a thick pack before the open doors of the jarl's house. Ludger stood on the second-floor balcony. Greasy, graying, blond hair trailed along his back. Bits of food littered his unkempt beard, and his blue eyes appeared bloodshot in his sunken cheeks. He didn't look at all well. His arms-men blocked the entrance to the floor. All held steel blades and wooden shields. Geir dropped his hand to his hilt but left the blade sheathed.

"The women have a grievance," Jarl Ludger bellowed in a firm, deep voice. "I've been remiss in my duty as jarl to inspect them personally, and now they lack trust. To comfort them, choose from among you three trusted men who will enter monthly to hear any complaints they might have on their treatment.

"Anyone found abusing them will be banished. Rumors are flying about River House. It isn't a place of punishment but learning. The intent was to teach the boys of Sven's disposition to mimic women better to help ease the bodies needs we all feel. However, the men left in charge used their position to garner favors. And I'm sorry to say I believed their reports that the woman had been uncooperative and ordered punishments."

A loud unhappy stir met that. The grumbling escalated till Glendal stepped forward. "Punishment for what? not teaching the sissy boys to be sissier? They have no right being anywhere near the women. The rules are the rules. You want to be with the women, you fight your way there fair and square."

A loud cheer of assent followed.

Ludger let them yell a moment before raising his hands. "You're right. It was an ill-conceived experiment. One I'll rectify right now. Each man involved will get a chance, one chance, to prove his worth. Each woman has picked a champion who has agreed to a fight to the death."

A cold blanket of silence descended. Geir wondered if, like him, the men beside him thought Ludger was covering his tracks. None of the boys would stand a chance against the seasoned men. None of this should have been allowed to happen.

The boys were being blamed for Ludger's actions, but who knew that besides him and the four who'd accompanied him?

Uneasy now, Geir shifted nervously, feeling like a caged lep.

"Sadly, I can't take back the harm I did the women, but in my defense, I've been distracted planning a raid."

The men around Geir tensed.

"Rolf's raiding team returned with a report of a small village within two months' trek that we could easily take."

Ludger let the men exclaim a moment before grinning widely. "They have less than a thousand men, and Rolf confirms seeing thirteen women, three of who are under ten and none of whom were ready for Winter House."

A loud cheer sounded. Ludger laughed and waved his arms. "If we're to beat the snows, we must leave within the month."

The men beside Geir began making plans, trouble in River House forgotten. A flush climbed Geir's cheeks, a combination of anger and embarrassment over his cowardliness in failing to call out and demand justice for Inkeri.

"And what of Inkeri?" Glendal yelled.

Geir tensed, preparing to back Glendal up. He should have had the courage to speak. The women deserved to be treated with respect. Without them, the town was nothing.

"She'll be sent to Winter House to recover and allowed to stay three months."

"And River House?"

"Disbanded until safeguards are in place. It's too difficult to determine who harmed a woman when so many visit her and yet River House provides ease to many." Ludger spoke over the muttering. "See your team leaders before nightfall.

The quicker we go, the better. This ripe plum might fall to another if we aren't fast."

"Inkeri shouldn't have to suffer," Geir called out.

Ludger stared down at him with an impassive expression.

"Bring her lily flower to ease her pain."

Ludger nodded slightly, and a smile tipped his lips. "Good idea and fitting penance for the men who visited river house. They shall be sent alone to gather flowers."

Geir stood uncertainly. Gathering lily blossoms was dangerous. The odor could overcome you or just distract you and allow a mega to approach unnoticed. He hadn't meant for the men to be sent alone to gather it, which would increase the danger. He jumped when Geoff clapped him on the shoulder. "Go get ready to raid, boy, and watch your back." Geoff lowered his voice and leaned closer to whisper in Geir's ear. "Ludger is a wily one, but we're on to him now. He won't get away with abusing the women again. Causing a riot will hurt us all. River House can wait till your return. Most didn't know of its existence. Let the rumors fly and discontent rise."

"It's not right to use the women without their consent to slake your lust with no hope of a child."

"No, it isn't. But if you speak up now, Ludger will find a way to throw you to the riptors." As he spoke, Geoff pulled him away. "Go get ready," he said loudly and pushed Geir toward the barracks.

The only raid Geir had ever gone on had ended with a ransacked town. Someone had beat them to it. Haste was imperative if they wanted to be the ones to capture the women, but the timing was too convenient for Ludger. Scouts rarely found anything worth retrieving and seldom returned, killed by man or beast or maybe lost. Scouting was one of the most dangerous tasks a man could be assigned, but a successful scout was guaranteed a spot in a house and eligible to fight for any open spot afterward.

Geir glanced back at the boys huddled on the sandy floor waiting to die. He felt no sympathy for them. Inkeri's pain was too fresh. His gaze lifted to Ludger who spoke to Rainer. They should pay too.

Keld grabbed his arm. "Come away."

Geir shrugged him off and stalked toward the barracks. He'd let it percolate, but when he returned, he'd ensure it boiled over.

# -7-
# CARA

ntrepid fired its engines, acceleration pushing Cara firmly into her seat.

"Course correct to within point-zero-zero-zero-two." Teryl turned from her station and grinned at her.

Cara smiled back.

Teryl returned her attention to her screens and continued reporting, "Hull at one hundred percent, all systems green. Probes are at maximum power capacity. Ready to begin absorption, Captain."

"Proceed," Cara said.

On her screen, she watched the power meter fill, ready to slap her hand on the abort button, but all systems continued to read green. Her gaze flicked to the main screen, designed to resemble a window, and showing the exterior view from the forward sensor array.

Golden-yellow flames flicked across the hull of the *Intrepid,* which intentionally skirted the planet's atmosphere to cause friction and heat the hull, gathering the resulting energy for later use.

"Ninety percent, Captain."

Cara slid her finger over the direction controls along the bottom of the screen before her. *Intrepid* obediently turned and began climbing back into space. Her gaze firmly on her screen, Cara nudged her ship to the correct course and gave the engines full throttle, using fuel recklessly to gain speed. She cut throttle right as the ship broke from the atmosphere.

"Nice flying, Captain. We're on course within point-zero-zero-zero-three at ninety-six percent fuel. With a sustainable speed of two-point-one, we should arrive at our destination within four days."

Cara leaned back in satisfaction. She'd practiced countless hours on a simulator, but this was her first real course set up, and she'd done it textbook perfect. Sustainable speed meant the intake of energy on the ship was enough to keep this velocity constant, but with full fuel-cores, she could increase their speed and refuel on the other end.

If she screwed up and used all the energy, they'd have to coast to the nearest planetary body with atmosphere to refill, which could take a year or more depending on how far from the sun they were and the distance of the planet they aimed for.

This system was rife with planets and moons though and contained three gas giants so even a mistake would only strand them a few months.

"Maintain speed and position. Let's give the ship a day to settle in before we boost speed."

"Aye, Aye, Captain."

"Fahyim, launch the first probe."

Positioned behind Cara to the right, Fahyim sat in a semi-reclined seat surrounded by screens. Most remained blank as they had yet to dispatch any probes. Ilda sat before Cara to the left, positioned the same way. It was their job to oversee all the screens and correlate information. Veta sat before Cara to the right. Normally, only two or three women were on the command deck at any time, but everyone had wanted to be present for the first punch out.

Veta turned to her and grinned. "Captain, you make it look easy."

Cara laughed and stood to give Veta a high-five. As her backup pilot, Veta knew how hard calculating at speed was. The comp ran a countdown and estimates, but the pilot entered the course and pushed the icons on the comp screen that controlled the direction of thrust. The ship lurched as it fired the probe.

"Captain, the first probe is away and the first beacon set."

"Speed down by point zero-zero-zero-zero-one," Teryl said.

Cara nodded. Every probe launch would suck energy from the fuel reserves, but it was the force of the expulsion from the ship that affected their speed. Probes could land on planets, drop buoys for communication, and be redirected remotely. Equipped with imaging devices capable of sending pictures and video at a million-time magnification and an automated lab, a smaller version of their emergency medical bay capable of running complex tests on samples obtained from the scoops and waldos that extruded from beneath the protective covering, the probes were indispensable conduits of knowledge.

Each rocket-shaped probe weighed two thousand pounds and could refuel itself the same way the *Intrepid* did under the careful guidance of the remote handlers. With their large batteries, which formed the bulk of the weight, the probes traveled twice as fast as *Intrepid*. *Intrepid* carried one hundred and twelve probes, and their machine shop aboard could reproduce them if supplied with the materials.

"Second probe prepared for launch."

Cara glanced at her readouts to be sure the coordinates had been entered correctly. "Launch."

Fahyim triggered the probe, and the ship lurched again.

Cara peered over her shoulder and met Fahyim's gray eyes. The women grinned at each other. Fahyim had barely made the height requirements. Her chair engulfed her petite form, but her small size hid a large personality. Fahyim's quick wit and humor made her an excellent traveling companion. Fahyim and Teryl were both older than she with more real space experience.

Cara turned to Ilda and frowned. She was going to be a problem. Surly and unhelpful, she took orders in an increasingly sulky manner, and they'd been aboard less than three weeks.

Ilda wore her Stellar Command uniform on and off duty and gave everyone aboard a hard time over the most minor of infractions, complaining of talking too loud or laughing at station. Cara would have to talk to her soon and dreaded it. The tight, pinched expression on Ilda's face and clipped way she spoke grated on her nerves.

As if sensing her regard, Ilda turned to Cara. "Veta, Teryl, and Fahyim shouldn't be on deck. This borders incompetence. They should be in quarters resting for their shifts."

"Ilda, see me after shift in my quarters. Return to your duty."

Ilda's thin lips tightened even more, but she turned around to face her screens.

Veta rose from her chair.

Cara gestured Veta to return to her seat and stood to face her crew. "I'm captain here and say who may be on deck at any given time. This is a momentous occasion we all wished to be part of. No regulations have been broken on my part. If you wish to spend your free hours here, you may."

Cara returned to her seat and changed the view screen to show the aft view.

Veta turned a bark of laughter into a cough. Familiar with Veta's sharp sense of humor from university, Cara had to bite back her answering laugh. The other three women remained quiet, but the happy excitement had vanished from the bridge.

The off-duty crew left within the hour, and Ilda turned to watch them leave, a smirk dancing across her thin lips.

Information continued to come in from all stations, reporting the condition of the ship and the probes. *Intrepid* was performing flawlessly.

Eight hours later, Cara rose and stretched as Veta entered. "Veta, you have the con. Teryl, take second chair and notify me at once when probe one reaches its destination."

The women took their new seats and continued speaking in low voices.

Twenty-six probes had been launched with only one malfunction. Already they'd spotted a mineral rich asteroid field surrounding a lifeless moon, and probe one had been repositioned to take samples.

Cara headed directly to the cafeteria to fix herself a cup of soup, which she took to her room. She was filling out the daily log when Ilda knocked and pushed open the door uninvited.

"You wish to see me, Captain?"

"Yes, come in. In future, don't enter until invited. Your attitude has become a liability; one I'm afraid I'll have to report."

"My attitude?" Ilda lifted a brow and placed her hands on her hips.

"You are addressing your captain." Cara glanced pointedly at Ilda's hands.

Ilda flushed and assumed the correct at rest position. "Sorry, ma'am," she said as if the words choked her.

"Ilda... we're all friends here. Discipline is important, but keep in mind we have to live together for the next two years. If you have a problem with someone aboard, I expect you to handle it in a professional manner."

Cara held up her hand as Ilda opened her mouth. "I want a pleasant, professional tone from you. In the future, you will inform me privately on issues with any crew member or myself. File written reports of any complaints you may have to Stellar Command. I expect professional, polite behavior from you. Dismissed."

Ilda spun on her heel and stalked from the room.

Cara sighed and finished her soup before stripping and stepping into the sonic shower. Technically, a sonic shower cleaned better than water, but psychologically she missed soaking in a tub and long hot showers. The three minutes of vibration and lights felt odd and not at all relaxing.

When she emerged, she dropped her uniform on the floor of the shower and changed the setting to clothing. Naked, she padded to the bed and curled on the heated gel pad under the soft blanket. From her nightstand, she picked up the picture frame and flipped through the pictures until Michaelson's smiling face greeted her.

Before *Odyssey's* launch, he'd sent her a voice mail wishing her a safe journey that she'd attached to the picture. His kind voice brought tears to her eyes and firmed her intentions.

Six hours later, Cara halted before the cafeteria door, shocked by the vicious tone of Ilda's voice as she ranted to Teryl.

"— Everyone knows she got this command because of who her mother is."

"Don't be stupid; Cara was in the top of her class." Teryl laughed uneasily.

"Because of her mother. All the professors treated her as if she were their only sons. I was there, you weren't! I'm telling you, she isn't competent for this command. She had the nerve to tell me she was putting me on report when she's the one who broke regs."

"You did break regs, not her, and you're doing it again right now." Teryl rose and gathered her plate, her expression stern. "I want no part of this mutiny. Never come to me again with these baseless, childish complaints."

"Sycophant," Ilda spat.

"How the hell did you pass a psych examine?"

"I'm a loyal member of Stellar Command. They see how Cara used her connections to get this posting."

Cara cleared her throat noisily and entered the room.

Both women flushed and turned to stare at her.

"Good morning, Captain," Teryl said and inclined her head.

Ilda said nothing. Her lips were pressed so tight together they disappeared as if the effort to bite back what she wanted to say required her to bite her lips. She glared at both Cara and Teryl.

"Shouldn't you be in hydroponics?" Cara rose an eyebrow at Ilda and tapped the comp on her wrist.

"Heading there now." Ilda omitted the honorific and stalked from the room.

Cara sighed.

Shoulders slumped, Teryl stared at the floor, then straightened to meet her eyes.

Before she spoke, Cara said, "Everyone is entitled to an opinion. I'll speak to her about appropriate methods of displaying one's concerns again and send her to medical. Negative gossip amongst the crew can severely damage our performance. I'd appreciate discretion over this incident."

"Yes, Captain." Teryl offered a formal salute that Cara returned. "Kinder than I would've been to that little bitch," Teryl muttered under her breath as she left the room.

Cara bit back her laugh, then grimaced as she turned to head below deck to hydroponics. This confrontation was going to suck. Teryl being upset with Ilda was bound to escalate Ilda's discontent. The two had been chummy until this point, sometimes sharing their quarters for off hours.

Ilda stood before the softly glowing tubes with a comp screen and stylus, making notations. At her feet, a small bucket and clippers rested. An assortment of clippings littered the bottom of the bucket.

The air smelled green and clean, the scent of growing plants overpowering the smell of metal that permeated most of the ship. Broad green leaves sprouted from the tube before Ilda. Cara was happy to note the small white flowers that heralded the arrival of fresh beans.

Beside the beans, bright yellow flowers of impending tomatoes nestled in the dark green foliage. With any luck, they'd have fresh salad before their supplies from *Odyssey* ran out and they were forced to use the dried stock.

They had enough dried stock to last a year, but it was intended for emergencies, not everyday use. Hydroponics were an integral part of the *Intrepid*, supplying both food and fresh air. Studies had shown a monotonous diet had a depressing effect, while fresh food prepared in imaginative ways promoted mental health.

"Have you checked tubes twenty-nine through thirty-two yet?"

"No. I go in order as directed by Stellar Command."

"Yes. That's fine. What isn't fine is your continued hostility. Report to medical for a full scan after this shift. While you're free to harbor any doubts or opinions you wish, you will in future keep them to yourself. That is an order. I won't tolerate insubordination on my ship. I hope I'm making myself clear."

"Yes, Ma'am."

Cara examined Ilda a moment then nodded once and turned away. Ilda hadn't sounded enthused, but she hadn't sounded hostile either. Maybe she finally realized Cara could ruin her career with reports. Cara didn't care what kept her in line as long as she stopped being a source of conflict.

A guilty twinge made her shrug irritably. She was being tough on a woman she planned to strand on a viable planet if they found one. A small smile tilted her lips. "At least then she'll really have something to complain about," she whispered, then laughed.

Still laughing, she headed to the gym.

# -8-

# GEIR

Autumn's chill deepened as eight-hundred men marched along a winding river in a valley nestled between steep mountains. Dark circles ringed Geir's eyes. Keld hiked sluggishly beside him, exhausted from the nightly patrols. Neither young man complained.

Geir hadn't needed Geoff's warning to see the writing on the wall. Rainer ran his squads with an iron fist, not being shy about whipping men he deemed not fast enough following orders.

Geir preferred being sent on bivouac details, jogging ahead to hunt and make camp. Not only did he like the freedom to hunt and rest as he pleased, but being out from under Rainer's watchful gaze was peaceful.

In camp, he and Keld took turns guarding each other while they slept. Glendal had woken twice now with a snake beneath his cloak. The three other men who'd been present when Geoff questioned Inkeri had succumbed to a thurji bush on a night patrol a bare week after they left home. Geir kept his head down and his eyes open, doing what he was told instantly without complaint.

Rainer had taken to smirking at him, which made him extremely uncomfortable. He hoped the smirk was because Rainer thought he wouldn't make trouble and not because he desired him. The thought of Rainer lusting after him made Geir sick to his stomach.

When the raiders returned to Ludger, he'd do his best to wipe the smirk from Rainer's face, but to return required he keep a low profile. Turning down a sexual advance would be sure to cause a stink and draw more unwanted attention. And if Rainer had his friends hold him...

The majority of the men would side with Rainer while on a raid, their hope for a future rested on the women. A successful raid meant sixteen more chances for a child. The older a man grew, the more he seemed to feel the lack of children and doted on the young boys.

Of the men who'd raised Geir, only Geoff and Einar still lived. Geir was glad neither had come on this raid. Both would be outraged over Geir being assigned to night patrol every night. The thought of Rainer revenging himself on them disgusted him. The smart thing to do was stay out of Rainer's way and give him no chance to try use either force or seduction.

Rolf, a man Geir had hunted with in the past and considered a friend, approached. "Rainer wants you and Keld to run ahead and tell Chal we'll be stopping to hunt and smoke the meat. There'll be no fires after next week, so we need a large supply." He stepped closer and lowered his voice. "Watch your back. Better to take a whipping then get killed trying to fill an impossible quota. He means you ill. Stay alive, and we'll handle this back in town, but now isn't the time."

Geir nodded and ran to gather his pack.

Keld squatted on his heels, gutting a lep beside the cooking fire. Both their packs sat behind him.

"Leave it. We've been ordered to meet Chal."

Keld handed the half-skinned lep to the man beside him and shoulder his pack. He waited to speak until they left camp. "What's up?"

"Rolf warned me we'll be set impossible meat quotas and it'll be better to take the whipping."

Keld's lips tightened. "He'll beat us to death."

"He has to follow some semblance of law. Not every man is his crony.

Keld snorted, breath pluming in the frosty air.

"Get a move on. We'll tell Chal and get a head start. In this cold, meat will keep."

✦ ✦ ✦

"Fucking, great," Keld hissed.

Geir unhappily eyed the deer the megas swatted at. He and Keld had stashed it yesterday when they were lucky enough to catch two. "Two mega are more meat than one deer."

Keld rolled his eyes but nodded slowly and tightened his grip on his spear.

"The male will drag the carcass off and eat while the female grooms. He'll fall asleep while she eats. We attack then. If we're fast, we can kill the male before he wakes."

"Yeah sure. If the wind doesn't change or a cub wanders by..."

Geir slapped Keld's shoulder, being careful to do so quietly. Eight-hundred-pounds of fur and muscle made short work of dragging the deer from the tree where they'd left it. The female brushed against the male, stopping to lick the yellowed tusks jutting a foot from the male's mouth before settling to her six-hundred-pound haunches to begin cleaning the fur between her ten-inch claws.

Attacking two mega was nuts, but going back without the required meat meant another whipping and his back still stung from the last one.

The coppery odor of blood filled the air as the male mega ripped the deer open and began feeding. Within minutes, he'd reduced the fifty-pound deer to scraps. The female nudged him aside and began worrying at a thigh bone.

The male swatted her with claws retracted. Snuffling and snorting, he sauntered to a sunny rock where he stretched out on his side.

Geir held a finger to his lips and crept forward. Mega were fast. All it would take was two seconds for the animal's enormous paws to swat him like a bug. The memory of pain from much smaller clawed paws tightened his shoulders, making the fading bruises from the last whipping twinge.

He glanced at the female less than fifty feet away and rushed forward, swinging at the males exposed neck with all his might.

The mega jerked and grunted, falling limp before it could gather itself. Blood gushed from the severed jugular. Keld screamed a warning. Geir ducked and rolled as the female pounced, landing where he stood a second before. Bloody breath warmed his cheek from her outraged roar. Instead of swatting at him, she turned and snapped at Keld who stuck her right shoulder with his spear.

Geir swung at her neck and caught her cheek as she turned back to him. Instead of running back, he ran forward, between her swatting claws, too close for her to reach with her paws. She ducked her head to snap at him.

Keld struck again and swore as the mega leapt away, taking his spear with her. Geir ran to the nearest tree, putting it between him and the enraged mega. The mega roared again, the coughing snort that proceeded a leap.

"Run," Geir screamed, and dove from his hiding spot as the mega sprang forward.

Instead of running away, Keld ran forward and slid on his ass beneath the mega, stabbing upwards with his sword.

The mega roared again and landed gracelessly, kicking up leaves and firtin needles as she scrambled to turn. Geir struck, stabbing his sword deep into her exposed flank and tearing a jagged cut, which gushed blood. Slower now, the mega backed away. Bloody spittle drooled from her lips.

Keld scrambled to his feet. "It's hurt bad, but not out."

"Go left." Geir ran to the right and connected solidly with the paw that swatted at him. The weight of the paw knocked him to his ass. The mega snuffled and swatted again with the bleeding paw before staggering forward and landing on her chest.

Geir darted in as she struggled to rise and swung again, scoring a line across her left eye. A shaky howl ended in a grunting huff as her head flopped to the ground. Geir slammed his sword against her neck, blood fountained and the paws stilled.

"Keld, you okay?"

"Good," Keld said breathlessly. "Holy gods, how the hells are we getting this back to camp?"

Geir began laughing and collapsed in the dirt. White flakes of snow began to fall, the first flurry of the year. *No more whippings,* he thought in satisfaction as he leaned against the mega's still warm side to catch his breath. He and Keld were unstoppable.

* * *

For two months, Geir and Keld had been assigned every dangerous job Rainer could devise. Sleep had become a fond memory. The next time he and Keld were assigned hunting duty, he planned to find a hidden spot and sleep instead.

If he survived the attack on the town.

Torvald continued to go over the attack plan and hand out assignments. Less than a mile away the town slept. They'd already dispatched the far sentries. For four days, Torvald had men spying to learn the patterns of the town. For a town of over a thousand men, they set out few patrols, and their walls were weak and low and studded with unguarded gates.

Rainer trotted up to his squad as the meeting broke up. As an arms-men, Rainer oversaw four squads of twenty-five men each. Geir cursed the luck that put him under Rainer's command.

Leather jerkin gaping, revealing matted chest hair, Rainer scratched absently as he spoke. "We're going in the front gate. Our job is to take the women's house. Chal's squad will be in charge of bringing them back here. Ours is to hold off their men. Glory enough for everyone."

The men around Geir stirred excitedly. Being in the front was the most dangerous, but also offered a chance to impress and move up in the ranks.

Rainer grinned and gestured the four squads forward. He slipped from his honent and handed Geir the reins. "You and Keld guard the beasts."

A furious wave of anger flushed Geir's cheeks. The hard leather reins cut into his palm as he yanked the honent to a standstill. "Yes, sir," he bit out.

Rainer smirked and ran his hand along Geir's stubbled cheek. "That's my boy."

Geir stood, clenching the reins in impotent fury. He'd been certain he and Keld would be sent into the most dangerous spot Rainer could devise but this... this was reserved for those either ill or injured or under punishment; none of which applied to him. Cold air nipped his nose and turned his cheeks red, camouflaging the flush of anger as he dragged the honent back to camp. Keld trailed, not saying a word. When he reached the picket line, Keld had disappeared, and he hadn't noticed his leaving.

He debated tying the honent and following. He could always claim he'd misunderstood his orders. His gaze flitted to Rolf astride a honent twenty feet away. He'd get a whipping but could be in the fight. But if the charges stuck they wouldn't take him again. Rolf had heard his orders and given him a commiserating shrug. Rolf was unhappy with his assignment too, but with a sprained ankle he couldn't move without being astride a honent.

Resigned, Geir paced before the tied beasts with his hand on his sword. Two hours later, smoke drifted into the dawn sky. Hands held to shade his eyes from the rising sun, Geir peered toward the town. Distance and forest blocked the view, revealing nothing except the thickening plume of smoke. Too far to hear the fight, he tensed and pulled his sword when pounding hoofbeats approached.

Men's raucous laughter vied with the crying, screaming women. The men passed him, carrying their prizes and headed to the wagons six-hundred-yards behind the picket line. Laughing like a loon, Rainer handed Geir a shrieking toddler before spinning his stolen honent and racing back to town.

Tiny bare feet kicked at him ineffectually. Horrified by her deep sobbing, Geir murmured endearments in a soft tone, trying to calm the baby. She couldn't be more than three and screamed for her Da-Da. Tears streaked her dirty, red face. Little fists hit at him as her cries changed to Ma. Over and over again, the baby called for her parents. It was breaking his heart.

Disobeying orders, he headed back to the wagons. Rolf galloped up on his honent and grabbed his arm, almost falling from his mount in the process.

"No, stay here. It'll be worse for her to see..."

"See what?" Geir narrowed his eyes, inadvertently tightening his grip on the toddler, making her scream louder.

"Don't be so naive. What do you think the officers are doing right now?" Rolf yanked him to a hard stop. "They have to do it. Any child born afterward might be theirs, and the women will accept them quicker."

"That's... " Geir trailed off and hid his face in the child's hair.

He was a fool. An angry snort of laughter gusted the girl's hair.

"At least I won't spawn more fools on the world," he said bitterly to the child in his arms.

In his imagination, he'd thought the battle would be like the one he fought at home to protect his town. But this time they were the cowardly attackers who struck at dawn— and he hated it.

The child in his arms stopped screaming and began taking deep, shuddering breaths.

"Give her to me and get the fur from my pack. She'll sleep. When she wakes, I'll ensure she sees her mother."

"And what of her father?"

Rolf shrugged and held his hands out for the girl.

Geir handed her over and tucked the fur over her.

"Likely dead, but if not, Torvald will decide if we bring him home or not. Get to your squad."

"Yes, sir," Geir said through clenched teeth and jogged back to the town.

Smoke wafted from the town in billowing black clouds, and Geir put some extra oomph in his step. Metal clashed on metal and men yelled, trailing off as he ran through the main gate. He arrived in time to help throw the dead on the funeral pile. The smell of burning hair gagged him, but the weeping of those who'd lost loved ones made his eyes tear. Unarmed men glared at him as they threw their dead on the pile under the supervision of Chal and his squad. Stone walls of a two-story home muted the screams of the injured. There would be more for the fire soon.

Chal led his captives to the stone house and mounted a honent tied to the front door.

Geir scanned anxiously for Keld, his apprehension mounting when no one he asked knew where Keld was. Mud churned from blood lay six inches deep before what had been the women's house here. Dreading he would uncover Keld's corpse from the mangled remains still there, he began sorting the dead with the rest of his squad.

Chal galloped up. His honent pawed and danced beneath him. Darker in color than theirs, it stamped and snorted, clearly unused to being ridden. "Lou, take six men to the east wall. Stay alert. We're still finding loose men. The rest of you, come with me."

He wheeled away and galloped to the south gate. Geir ran after him. Torvald stood on a barrel speaking when they arrived.

"—Two-hundred or so. The smaller group that exited from this gate is the more likely one. Rainer, send a small group of men after the two-hundred and our best riders after the small group."

Keld grabbed his arm, distracting him from Torvald. Blood trickled from a shallow gash on Keld's forehead, and he glanced behind him with a worried expression.

"What?" Geir whispered, following the glance. Without thinking, he hugged Keld tight, relieved to see him alive and well.

Keld returned the hug, a surprised expression on his face. "I locked a storeroom. Hopefully, our men won't find it," Keld whispered. "Rainer is burning their supplies."

"Gods, what about the little boys?"

Keld shrugged. Geir eyed him warily. Keld wore an unreadable expression and seemed on edge as if he was about to do something drastic.

Geir returned his attention to Torvald just as he said, "Pack up. We move out tonight. Chal, round up the children under six, but don't bother with the ones who won't come willingly."

"What about the older boys?" Chal called.

"If any volunteer to come, but none over twelve and make sure they're unarmed."

Geir sagged in relief. Loud shouts to the right drew everyone's attention. Geir drew his sword and ran to the sound along with everyone else.

The fighting stopped as Torvald pulled his honent to a snorting halt before the low wooden building.

"Drop your weapons," Torvald ordered.

The six men eyed the group of fifty and slowly lowered their swords. A dark-haired man with a blood matted beard stepped forward. A long gash in his leather trousers leaked fresh blood with every step. "Our young sons are inside...please... they can do you no harm. If you kill us all and burn the winter storage, they'll die. Have mercy."

Torvald slipped from his horse. "Let my men inspect. If, as you say, only boys remain within, we'll leave them in peace."

"Our food?"

"You may keep it."

The man glanced to a thick plume of smoke rising from the left. "This is the last storage we have."

Torvald held out his hands. "I swear it."

The man's hard gaze traveled them again before he stepped forward and touched his palm to Torvald's. Torvald gestured, and a group of men pushed past to search the building.

The man stood silently but shifted his weight. Twice he made as if to speak before blurting, "I have another child, a daughter. The only girl we have so young. Is she well?"

"She is," Geir said, and stepped forward. "We'll treat her kindly and care for her well."

"Her name is Lily. Please... her mother and I..."

Geir's throat constricted and tears clouded his vision. The desperate pain in this man's voice hurt.

"She's ours now," Rainer said in a hard voice and leaned from his honent to slap the side of Geir's head.

Geir hadn't heard him arrive.

"Before you go falling in love, you and Keld can chase down the group that snuck out through the northwest gate." Rainer turned and spat at the man beside Torvald. "You're a weak fool and not worthy of breeding. This town was pathetically easy to take. Your defenses are laughable—"

"Enough!" Torvald barked. "Don't get cocky and no more fires— that's an order! Get back to the wagons and head out."

"And leave them alive to follow?"

"Follow how? Don't be stupid. They have their boys to care for. Following us is a death sentence. The snow will arrive and cover our trail. They're injured and weak."

"Kinder to put them out of their misery."

"I'm in charge, and I say we got what we came for, and there's no reason for murder." Torvald dropped a hand to his hilt.

"You're the boss." Rainer chuckled as if delighted and swung his honent away. Still laughing, he galloped from sight.

The men around Geir relaxed.

"Get to your assignments!" Torvald bellowed. Then he leaned forward and lowered his voice to speak to the townsman. "Don't make me regret this."

Geir grabbed Keld's hand and tugged him from the crowd. "Let's get our packs before Rainer has a chance to mess with them."

"I'm glad we got guard duty," Keld muttered as he ran back to camp.

"Me too," Geir whispered, ashamed of both his weakness and presence there. Lily's sobs and Inkeri's begging were sounds he never wanted to hear again. He could give up raiding, stay safe at work in Ludger, but never have a chance for a child of his own, never feel a woman's embrace. His future seemed cold and bleak no matter what he chose.

*Cold wind made his eyes water,* he told himself as he dashed the tears from his cheek.

# -9-
# CARA

Ilda turned in her chair and stared at Cara, her eyes bright. "Shall I send a beacon, Captain?"

"Not till we have concrete information to report."

A look of triumph lit Ilda's eyes, but she turned away before Cara could be certain she saw it or pin the source. Cara herself felt both triumphant and worried. The very first planet they'd approached had what appeared to be man-made artifacts orbiting it. Still too far for the ship's sensors to take clear, concise readings, she ordered a probe launched.

"Send a probe, but keep it at maximum range."

"Aye, aye, Captain."

The ship jerked with the probe's launch. Fahyim peered over Cara's shoulder and pointed to the data flowing across the screen. "Two distinct devices. I'm betting one is a sensor of some kind and one a weapon. I recommend we slow our approach and give the probe plenty of time to investigate."

"Run the calculations to put a probe in an elliptical orbit." Cara tapped the screen before her to bring up a magnified view of the planet. "Send another to scan the moon, but keep both as far back as we can and still get clear readings. We don't want to start an interstellar incident. We'll treat them with the respect we'd want from visitors."

Fahyim tapped the screen, changing the view. "This asteroid field will pass that planet every thirteen years. If they're space capable, they'll likely be mining it. We should approach it with caution. "

Cara nodded, paying careful attention to Fahyim's advice as she pointed out likely spots for space traffic or weapons.

Fahyim had over fifty years of experience in Stellar Command, most in the science labs on the orbiting platforms. Haven had two small settlements on both their moons. A space habitat orbited the bigger moon from which technicians controlled mining droids.

Fabrication of all space vessels took place on the smaller moon. Remotes handled most of the work. The jobs that required a personal touch paid very well and were much sought after. Stellar Command headquarters appeared in Haven's sky as a glittering wheel with seven spokes. The interior was opulent, the finest Haven had to offer. Stellar Command top personnel lived aboard in lavish apartments.

Sixteen small wheels spun in space placed strategically for Havens defense; shuttles traveled between them daily. Stellar Command Academy orbited their closest planetary neighbor. A mockup of a galaxy ship, aspirants to Stellar Command lived aboard for four years. To attend required four years of college and passing a plethora of tests including psych evaluations and peer recommendations.

The best and brightest Haven produced attended Stellar Academy. Fahyim had taught weapon systems there for five years. Cara was happy to have a woman of her experience along and even happier to know she was part of the underground.

Everyone aboard had taken the advanced history course and realized they'd likely found one of the missing colony ships. Repressed excitement practically hummed through the air as the women continued to examine the probes reports.

Teryl arrived for her shift.

Cara stood and tapped Fahyim's shoulder. "Join me for dinner. Teryl, you have the con. Notify me at once if we have any major changes or discoveries."

Fahyim followed Cara out.

"I never thought we'd find a colony. I find myself wondering if the inhabitants will be violent and warlike like our ancestors were," Cara said as they entered the galley.

Fahyim held out a pizza she'd removed from cold storage. Cara nodded her approval and poured two glasses of wine.

"No decisions need to be made in haste," Fahyim said as she slid the pizza into the microwave and set the dial. "Take our time and explore. For all we know, they're much more advanced than we and can swat us like flies."

"I can stall sending a beacon for a week tops. On your next maintenance shift, you'll have to put in the decoy beacon."

"Two days till my next shift in that department; it shouldn't be a problem." Fahyim removed the pizza from the microwave and slid it onto the countertop. Both women pulled out stools and sat.

Cara handed her a glass of wine and paused to inhale the garlicy fragrance emanating from the pizza. "I'm excited and terrified."

Fahyim smiled. " Me too. Whatever happens, our lives will change forever."

★ ★ ★

Everyone gathered on the bridge the next day to view the probe's first in-depth reports.

"A clear pattern, but missing sections." Teryl tapped a button on her console, putting a picture on the main screen. A metallic, oblong object rotated before them. Broken metal poles jutted from one edge. The unbroken pole led to a smaller rounder object twenty feet in diameter. Much smaller, baseball-size, metallic balls made a clear pattern between the bigger devices, surrounding the entire planet.

"See the pitted edge of the metal extrusions?" Fayhim traced the edge in question without touching the main screen. "That's thousands of years of space dust damage. This is an old, unmaintained installation. Can we send the probe closer? Maybe even scoop one up?"

Cara used her stylus to do a few quick computations. "Send the probe closer and match orbit with this one." She pointed to the last device before the empty space where the pattern discontinued. "If they're still monitoring, maybe they'll think whatever happened to this missing chunk is happening again when one disappears. Let the probe send us two days of pictures before we scope it up. Take all noninvasive measurements we can before touching it."

"Shall I send the beacon now?" Ilda asked.

Cara glanced at her and frowned. The repressed excitement and odd tone weren't like Ilda.

"It's killing her to be polite," Veta whispered.

Cara bit back her laugh. "Negative. We're nowhere close to the planet and in no danger whatsoever. As soon as we have concrete information, we'll send a comprehensive report. We don't have unlimited beacons. I wonder if any of the original settlers are alive down there." Cara turned to Teryl. "Have any other probes reported anything that could be remotely considered man-made?"

"No, but only probes one, three, and six, have reached their assigned sectors."

"We're making history here, folks," Cara said excitedly. "Let's do our best work. Fahyim, any idea yet if this is a sensor or weapon?"

Fahyim sent her findings to Cara's screen. Cara took a sip of coffee. "Anyone on free time is welcome to stay, but if it's your sleep shift, get some shut eye. Let's stay sharp."

Ilda and Veta left the room.

Fifteen minutes later, the comp notified her Ilda had visited sickbay and requested a sleep aid. Cara made a mental note to speak to her and order a psych-eval. She'd been requesting sleep aides and mild tranquilizers daily since Cara put her on report. She did her job and disappeared, not socializing with anyone, even taking meals alone in her room.

Or maybe it wasn't contacting a lost colony, but the break-up with Teryl had hit harder than she thought. *Either way, I need to handle this. Cold sleep was always an option if she becomes dangerously unstable.* Cara considered putting Ilda in cold sleep and claiming she was unstable, but she had a few days to decide. She turned back to the reports.

Fahyim cornered her before she left the bridge the next day.

"Captain, we had a malfunction in sickbay, and I didn't get a chance to finish that project we spoke of, but I'll for sure get to it tomorrow."

"What happened in sickbay? I received no reports."

"A minor jammed door from improperly replaced pharmaceuticals. I've repaired it, but needed to fabricate a part."

"Send me a report."

"Yes, ma'am."

"You have the con." Cara rose, stretched, and headed to the gym.

✷ ✷ ✷

The probe sent back grainy long range scans of the surface of the planet, which Cara poured over on her next duty.

"Take us closer, Veta. There's no sign of advanced civilization. Approach from their moon and maintain position behind it. One more day of pictures and we'll let the probe examine the device."

Veta flashed her a grin and began planning a trajectory. Cara waited for Ilda to suggest they send a probe, but she said nothing. *Maybe she's given up*, Cara thought hopefully. After her shift, Cara headed to her cabin, slowing when she heard angry voices. Teryl and Ilda argued outside Teryl's room. Ilda stormed to her room before Cara arrived. She decided to let her cool off before speaking to her and went to bed.

✷ ✷ ✷

She was about to pour herself a coffee the next morning in the cafeteria when Veta paged her, sounding excited. Coffee forgotten, she raced to the bridge.

"Captain, we've received pictures of people," Veta said unnecessarily. The picture on the main display showed a rough collection of wooden houses surrounded by a wooden wall. Cultivated land surrounded the main town.

"Fahyim will want to see this," Veta said, her voice quivering with excitement.

Ilda entered and handed Cara a coffee, then offered one to Veta and Teryl before taking her seat without comment.

"She's resting; we can tell her when she wakes." Cara took a sip of the coffee. It tasted bitter so she spat it back in the cup, hoping Ilda wouldn't notice and get insulted. The small gesture of bringing them coffee was a big step for her and Cara hoped it proceeded a real change of heart. "Thanks for the coffee, Ilda."

Ilda nodded without turning and flicked through her screens.

"We've gotten a few good close-ups." Veta enlarged four still shots and placed them on the screen. "Men, and all are carrying knives; some big enough to qualify as swords. And see how they stand beside the doorway? Obviously, they're guards, which means something dangerous is in the vicinity."

Veta rose from her seat and strode forward to peer at the images from close-up. She absently sipped her coffee, making a face at the bitter taste, but drinking it anyway. "Teryl, can you show the close up of the field behind the town again?"

The screen flickered, and Veta pointed. "See those skins? The animal it belonged to must be enormous and the weather cold to have such thick fur. The o—"

Without warning, Veta collapsed.

Ilda rose. "I'm relieving you of command and taking over this ship by the authority of Stellar Command section one, forty-two. The captain is incompetent and dangerously unfit for duty, blatantly disregarding Stellar Command policy." An edge of manic glee in her voice, Idla grinned at Teryl as if expecting her to be pleased.

Cara made no reply, all her efforts remained on trying to move her finger the inch it needed to travel to hit the medical alarm button. Teryl jumped to her feet.

"Are you crazy? This is mutiny."

"I'm under orders from command itself to make sure a beacon is sent if the captain of the ship refuses to." Ilda turned to her screen and tapped a moment. The ship jerked as it fired off a beacon. "I told you she was a figurehead because of who her mother is. Command knew it, and sent me as backup."

Teryl knelt beside Veta and felt for a pulse in her neck. "What did you do? Captain?" She seemed to realize Cara had made no response and stood.

Cara remained motionless unable to even blink. Whatever was in the coffee was strong, and she hoped it wasn't fatal.

"Calm down, Ilda. Veta needs medical care, her pulse is thready and weak. The beacon is away. Your job is done." Teryl spoke soothingly. Sweat trickled down her cheek as she stepped toward Ilda with her hand outstretched.

Cara wished she could turn enough to see Ilda, but she couldn't even make her eyes move.

"Cara?"

Teryl glanced at her, paled, then grabbed Cara's wrist.

"Teryl, you see, right? She wasn't going to send the beacon. One excuse after another. I had orders to send one."

"But not orders to murder them. Let me get them help. Intrepid, sickbay alert on the bridge. Veta is incapacitated—" She dropped Cara's hand and jumped back as Ilda strode forward.

Cara's pulse accelerated. The comp had automatically switched Veta's controls to her when Teryl called sickbay and reported her incapacitated. Her hand landed on the acceleration slider, and neither woman noticed, too intent on each other.

"It isn't murder or mutiny; it's my command, and I'm taking it back."

Teryl licked her lips and nodded, her gaze darting to the door. "Fine, you're captain now. Let me get her help.

Veta's lips had turned blue, and foam had collected on the corner of her lips. Cara tried to force her fingers to lift, but couldn't manage it. The planet's moon approached, growing on her screen with frightful speed. Ilda was going to kill them all.

Teryl turned away and slapped the intercom. "Fahyim, grab a med kit and report to the bridge."

Cara could've told her it wouldn't work. If she were able, she'd have been her by now at the first alarm.

Teryl reached the same conclusion and reached down to drag Veta up. Ilda let her leave. She stared after her with an expression that changed from triumph to fear and back. A shiver skittered up Cara's spine. Ilda was crazy, there was no telling what she would do. Cara's finger jerked, sliding on the throttle and she wanted to sob with relief. The moon slowed its crazy approach. She had about five minutes to impact now.

*Please*, she prayed and strained to make her hand touch the all stop button.

Teryl returned three minutes later. Tears tracked her cheeks. Without her saying a word, Cara knew Veta had died. Ilda knew it too.

"It isn't murder or mutiny!" she screamed.

"I know, sweetie, I'm sorry I doubted you. Can we go talk about this? Help me bring Cara to medical. I can't access Fahyim's room without medical override from the captain.

"I'm the captain," Ilda shrieked.

"Medical needs to confirm Cara is incapacitated first."

Eyes glittering with malice, Ilda yanked a kitchen knife from her beneath her shirt. Teryl jumped forward and grabbed the hand holding the knife with both of hers as Ilda swung it at Cara.

"Stop!"

Ilda ignored Teryl's pleas. The two women struggled for the knife. Ilda bumped Cara's arm, sending her hand over the controls. The ship spun too fast for the speed at which they traveled for the interior gravitation to keep up, and the two women slid across the floor and into the main screen on the wall. In the pilot chair, webbing encased Cara, holding her in place.

No longer aiming toward the moon, *Intrepid* aimed toward the planet. If no one corrected course, they'd skim along the edge of the atmosphere missing the planet by less than two miles but going so fast the hull would take catastrophic damage.

Ilda and Teryl continued to fight. Unable to turn her head to see, Cara had to rely on pants and grunts to predict who was winning. To her dismay, it sounded like Ilda.

Apparently, Teryl thought so too as she spoke. "Intrepid, record to permanents." Ilda TiHelena Dawnson has murdered crewwoman Veta NiJantra Quinson, poisoned the captain, and is attempting to kill me to get control of this ship. She claims to be acting under secret orders from Stellar Command, but from personal talks, I believe her jealousy has caused a psychotic break. She did have a code to launch a beacon but has no code to override the captain and used homemade poison to subdue the crew.

"The condition of crewwoman Fahyim NiDentra Clarason is unknown, but I assume she has been murdered as all attempts to reach her have failed. Captain Cara NiClearin Martason has acted in all ways appropriately, and any reports to the contrary are lies."

Ilda screamed for her to shut up. "I'm the captain. I didn't murder anyone. They're just sleeping."

"Intrepid, place message inside beacon and launch it." Teryl gave the emergency code, and her ID number as Ilda thrashed and shouted both threats and promises.

Teryl made a sharp sound of pain and staggered into view, swiping at a gash on her cheek. A large bloodstain above her left hip grew bigger by the moment.

Ilda shrieked and jabbed with the knife. Their uniforms were made of a special blend of plastic and metal which made them impervious to punctures or slashing. The knife connected but left no damage behind. Teryl kicked out, sending Ilda crashing into Cara's seat.

Cara groaned as her head suddenly fell forward. The muscles in her neck felt weak and strained, but she could control her head now. She turned in time to see Ilda yank up Teryl's shirt and stab her again.

Teryl screamed shrilly.

Cara groaned again, trying to speak. "Shhiipp," she managed to gasp.

Neither women paid her the slightest bit of attention. Ilda screamed as Teryl ripped her nails across her face. Teryl wrestled the knife from her grasp and stabbed Ilda in the neck.

"Crash," Cara bit out.

Teryl turned to her and tried to rise, then fell back, unable to stand. Blood seeped from her hands clenched over the wounds on her stomach. "Intrepid, report position."

"Approaching – " A soundless explosion rocked the ship, flipping it on its side, then rolling it twice. *So the devices ringing the planet were mines*, Cara thought as sirens blared. The lights flickered and darkened. Emergency power kicked on. Cara watched helplessly as *Intrepid* headed for the planet's surface.

"Intrepid, correct heading to one-point-four-two-seven," Cara managed to bite out.

Cara's screen remained dark. Before she could panic, it flickered, and the rebooting logo appeared. The comp came back online and proceeded to answer the last question asked of it.

"Disregard last question. Adjust heading to one point-four-two-seven," Cara said through dry lips. She wished she could lick her lips or wipe the drool, but the effort to speak took all her strength. She was grateful speech came easier and hoped movement returned soon.

Teryl's dead glassy eyes stared at her accusingly. Ilda amazingly hadn't died from either the knife in her neck or the ship rolling. She'd landed beside her chair and pulled herself into it.

The *Intrepid* began changing course. Wavy lines crossed the comp screen. Ilda was trying to scan the surface. Cara noted the reports but didn't have time to take them in, too busy doing the math in her head to enter a safe trajectory. Damage reports lit her screen as alarms began ringing. Atmosphere was leaking faster than the ship could regenerate it. No longer space capable, the ship was going down. Fleurs laughing lectures to never forget to take hull capacity into account spun through her mind.

"Intrepid, set speed to negative five-point-two. Adjust heading to two-point-zero-two-seven. Lock out all users except myself."

Ilda shrieked a bestial grunt.

"Ilda TiHelena Dawnson is under arrest for the murders of Veta NiJantra Quinson, Teryl DerFrancis Amilson, Fahyim NiDentra Clarason, and the destruction of the *Intrepid*. Log that, attach complete recordings of command deck for the last week, and send a beacon."

The screen before her brightened as the comp stopped trying to send or receive information through the fire that surrounded the hull of the ship.

*I'll be terrifying the natives*, Cara thought absently as she continued to give voice commands to adjust the path of her ship. Half her systems weren't responding at all, knocked out by the blast. The comp responded sluggishly, she suspected because of the work overload Ilda had given it while it was trying to reboot its systems.

*Intrepid* continued to fall to the surface at speed. Braking at the limits of hull endurance, she tried to shed enough velocity so that she wouldn't leave a crater the size of the Gordon Sea. She blazed through the atmosphere, leaving a glowing trail behind her.

*Intrepid* began to shake so hard Cara feared it would fly apart. Every system on her board showed red as they careened toward the surface. They were going to hit hard and do serious damage, and there wasn't a damn thing she could do about it.

Except one.

"Intrepid, disengage all seatbelts except mine."

Ilda made another bestial groan and crawled from her seat, heading to the door. One hand held the knife in her throat as if she debated removing it and trying to finish the job she had started before she bled to death.

"You won't make it," Cara said with vicious satisfaction as the ground rushed up to meet them. "Intrepid, prepare for imminent impact, encase me in safety foam.

White mist billowed from her seat and reached her face right as the *Intrepid* impacted the ground.

# -10-

# GEIR

"What a colossal waste of time." Geir kicked a rock into a thurji bush.

Keld jumped back with a cry of dismay. "Idiot, you trying to kill us?"

"No. Did any thorns shoot out? Of course not. Look at these tracks. A hundred people passed by here within the last day. Assuming Torvald isn't a moron, and the fugitives who escaped from the raid have women with them, they'd have sent a patrol along the expected route to ensure all such bushes were disarmed."

"What if Torvald was wrong?"

Geir shrugged. "I didn't see any thorns."

"Still... don't do it again while we're so close. I have nightmares about getting stuck with a thorn and choking on my own tongue."

"Fine."

Keld followed as Geir stamped through the light snow. "Why is this a waste?" Keld finally asked. "The bush proves they went this way and women are with them."

Geir ripped a dead branch from a firtin tree and broke it into smaller pieces, which he cast at another thurji bush. "No, it doesn't. It proves somebody went this way and set off the shrubs, but it could just as easily have been done to throw us off." Geir squatted and laid his hand alongside a clear print in the snow. "Big shoe and small stride; what's that tell you?"

"A man?"

"And?"

"He carried something heavy?"

"Nope, the print would be blurred and deeper, but all these prints are the same depth. Granted, most you can't make out, but all clear ones so far have been similar. So, men, and either sick or old, not men sent to escort the women."

"Unless that's what they want us to think."

Geir brightened. "True... keep alert. Old or not, they might have left traps."

Keld swept his spear over the snow-covered ground before him. Geir let him take the lead. The two men followed the trail for three days. It ended in a patch of lily trees where they came across their quarry.

Geir grabbed Keld by the arm and yanked him away from the rotting corpses.

"A beringei has been here," Geir whispered through the hand clapped over his nose. He scanned the still bodies searching for movement or black fur.

The men they'd chased had pulled lily leaves into piles and burned them. Huddled together in a tight circle around the fire, the dead men had embraced and held hands to meet their fate. Smoke drifted in eddies from the still-smoldering piles. Burned lily blossom was especially potent and could make you hallucinate. Beringei had torn into a few of the bodies, eating the softer flesh of the stomachs and scattering uneaten limbs. Blood saturated the ground, turning the snow red.

"Keep your eyes open and face covered. We'll have to circle and make sure all are here," Geir said, keeping his voice low in case the beringei remained close by, sleeping off its feast.

Keld's horrified, blue eyes stared at Geir over the hands clasped against his nose and mouth. He followed without speaking as Geir circled, searching the ground for prints. Both men slunk as quietly as they could passed the tracks of a herd of beringei.

When he was satisfied no one had continued on, he led Keld back to the open plain.

"The beringei should be satisfied with that feast awhile, but we'll take turns resting just to be sure."

Keld stabbed a suspicious mound of snow with more force than necessary. "Why would the men do that? We couldn't have harmed them; there were too many."

"What else remained for them? You saw them, old and weak. What they did was heroic."

"No, it was tragic."

Geir jerked his chin in acknowledgment and turned away to give Keld a minute to wipe his eyes. "Yeah, the deaths were, but trying to make us chase them to save their women... that's heroic. They could've stayed near town. Even if we spotted them, we wouldn't have bothered to attack them. They have nothing we want. Instead, they tried to lure us away."

"But you and Torvald knew it was a ruse."

"But you didn't. The ruse might have worked, and it took two good warriors from the fight. It was clever sending the old and useless away in small packs. It splits our forces, making us chase them all down to be sure no women got away."

Keld nodded thoughtfully. "They probably hoped it would take more than two warriors. If we hadn't scouted first and gotten a good estimate of how many women were there and where they kept them, it might have worked." Keld peered over his shoulder toward the lily trees. "Such a waste."

"I agree. Only the beringei profits."

Geir wished now he'd taken Inkeri and run despite the danger. Not to keep her for himself, but to save her. He wasn't an idiot and realized he'd been sent on this patrol in the hopes these men killed him. If he and Keld returned without information, they might even be killed at the pass as if they were strangers, but what else was there except to return? *What was the point of anything with no hope for a child?*

Depressed by his musings, he followed Keld into the woods where they made camp beneath the drooping limbs of a firtin tree. Not bothering to make a fire, Keld swept the ground with his spear, checking for snakes before laying his leather cloak atop the snow.

A clap of thunder made Geir start in surprise. Overhead, a brilliant, white light lit the sky. The thunder continued, one long rolling peal. A ball of flame streaked over them, seeming almost close enough to touch, accompanied by a distant rumbling. White hot, the ball shaded to dark orange with blue edges. The trailing flame left a smoking path in the sky.

Both men leaped to their feet.

Hands held to screen his eyes, Keld peered upwards. "What the hells is that?"

"Meteorite. Come on." Geir grabbed Keld's arm and began running.

"Why are we chasing it?" Keld asked.

"Two reasons. One, meteors contain metal. But more important, others will come, and we can follow them back to find their hideouts."

"Brilliant." Keld snatched his cloak and cape and picked up his pace. The two men ran after the glow.

"We'll never find it," Keld complained two hours later through short panting breaths.

"Sure we will. It'll be straight in front of us, and sure as shit, it'll start a fire when it lands."

"It could land miles away. Days away!"

"So what? You got something better to do?"

Keld chuckled and rubbed his bare hands over his arms. The day chilled rapidly as night deepened. "You got me there."

Geir halted them before a tree-lined ridge. "Sleep four hours. We'll wait for full light to cross the ridge. That's a prime beringei hunting ground, and I don't fancy stepping on a snake."

Reminded, Keld scoured the ground before settling down to sleep. His pack carried a thin hide he used for both cloak and bedding. Neither man had bothered wearing the cloak despite the light snow covering the ground. Exercise kept them warm enough.

Now, with the sun's retreat, and sitting still, a chill covered Geir's arms in goosebumps. He removed his cloak from his pack and put it on. Cross-legged, he sat in the snow beside Keld to guard his sleep.

Keld woke him at sunrise. Both men scooped up handfuls of snow to quench their thirst as they climbed the ridge. Shale and loose rock made for treacherous footing. The dusting of snow made the snakes visible as either squiggly trails or short pyramids. Most snakes preferred to sleep in holes in the ground, but some of the bigger ones with short stubby legs remained active even in deep snow and would bite if stepped on. Neither man approached them.

"I hate snake. The taste makes me gag." Geir shuddered dramatically, making Keld laugh.

✦ ✦ ✦

By mid afternoon of the second day, the wind brought the scent of smoke.

"Hope we aren't heading into a forest fire," Keld said.

"If the smell grows too strong we'll wait for it to dissipate."

"Won't we be in trouble for not returning?"

Geir debated mentioning his worries over that and decided to wait. No point in freaking Keld out till he had too. "Nah, I bet they saw that fire in the sky too. And besides, I'm hoping we come back with valuable information."

"Me too, but... I hate this," Keld blurted.

"We can go back if you really want to."

An uncomfortable expression on his face, Keld observed Geir from the corner of his eye. "No, not this. This is fun, tracking a meteor. I never saw one before. But I hate being the guy leading the others to attack a town."

"Ahh." Geir hiked silently, not knowing what to say. He didn't like it either, but he liked the idea of earning the right to a house more.

"Them or us," Keld muttered.

"Ain't that the truth."

Geir considered his options, liking none of them. To be banished was the worst punishment he could conceive of, worse even than death. No town containing women would take a man in for any reason and would kill a lone stranger to prevent him reporting the towns whereabouts. Usually, even young, beardless boys were left to live a barren life in a sacked town with only the hope of a successful raid to sustain them. *Keld had been lucky a sickness had just wiped out a good portion of the younger children in Ludger when his town was taken.*

The memory of those days made Geir flinch. Boys under four lived in Winter House during the winter as it was the only heated house in the village. Small wooden caskets had burned with the old women on the funeral pyres. More women died that day than in his entire lifetime. The men had cried and sat vigil the entire night till only cold ash remained.

Geir had expected the sickness to spread and waited with dread for the bells to ring on Summer House but the illness had been completely contained in Winter House. Even the men who'd rushed in to help had emerged unscathed.

Keld must have been considering his luck in being allowed to join a town with women and remembering the cause; his spoken thoughts matched Geir's closely. "Do you think the death in Winter House was poison?"

"At the time no, but now... I hate to consider it, but it never spread and only affected the one house. And Ludger had their food burned... I don't know. Maybe an accident. I can't believe anyone would kill so many women, even old women, on purpose."

The memory of Inkeri's injured breast, caused by the man who was supposed to protect her, haunted him. If Ludger could do that, what else was he capable of?

✦ ✦ ✦

Geir knelt beside Keld on the edge of the tree line and peered through the thick foliage of a firtin tree. Before them, spread a deep valley boarded on three sides by forest and a wide lake. Bigger than any body of water Geir had ever seen, the water met the horizon in a thin gray line. Normally, such a sight would've awed him, but his gaze remained riveted to the girl crouched on the shore.

Small boulders and dull gray rocks studded the waterfront. The girl had formed a crude pile of rock and made a fire. She huddled with the rocks behind her, the firelight dancing on her short blond hair. Her thin, delicate build made him think she was barely more than a girl, but her shirt revealed the curves of generous breasts so in her teens at least and technically a woman. She stood and shaded her eyes to peer around the valley, then squatted again to hold her hands to the flame.

Keld grabbed his arm hard. "Look." He pointed to the grass of the valley, which waved as an animal passed through it.

From where they stood, they could see the valley dipped and rose with high and low spots. Geir tried to convince himself the movement was an innocent deer hidden from sight by the contour of the land. The hair on Geir's arms rose. He knew better.

"Mega," he whispered and yanked Keld down when he stood. "Don't be stupid. You rush down there, and she runs, she'll run right into it. Stay here. It'll take me an hour or so to follow the tree line to get behind her. I'll approach nice and slow. If she runs, she'll run right to you."

"That beach must be littered with snakes." Knuckles whitened on the spear Keld carried.

Geir nodded. "I'm more worried about beringei in the forest to the south of her. Those hills are their ideal habitat."

"How'd she get here? I didn't see a weapon, no knife, or even a long stick, just the small bag. How the hells did she make it through that forest alive?"

Geir's shoulders tightened. He and Keld had fought off beringei twice getting here, dealt with a pack of riptors, and killed a mega, not to mention the countless snakes they'd passed. His boots were constructed to withstand a snake bite. Knee high and formed of thick leather, numerous punctures marked where he'd taken an unwary step.

The woman wore dark-blue leggings and a long-sleeve shirt of a type of shiny material he'd never seen before, but it appeared thin. Too far to see her footgear, he didn't think it adequate and hoped she wore shoes at all.

His gaze raked the waist-high brown grasses for signs of movement but the mega, if that's what it'd been, had stilled.

Keld grasped his arm hard a moment. "Be careful."

"You too. Keep your back to a tree and your eyes peeled on the woman. Be ready to help her..." Geir slapped Keld's shoulder and stepped into the trees.

Keld was too far to help if a mega attacked. By the time he crossed the eight-hundred-yards, the mega would carry her off to snack on. But this was the best plan. Chasing her would likely result in panicked flight, leading to her death.

Geir pushed through the trees recklessly. Firtins had soft needle-like-leaves but grew close together with entwined branches. Pushing through them could be time consuming and noisy. It also left a trail a two-year-old could follow. If the noise attracted and inquisitive male beringei so be it. While much larger than a human, a male beringei could be bluffed with an aggressive stance and might retreat.

Considering his options, Geir purposefully made more noise, hoping it wouldn't travel far but be enough to alert a foraging female beringei he was near to give her time to wander off. Female beringei never retreated, but they also never approached and would leave if not startled. Gods help you if you accidently ran into one while forging though. They fought viciously with teeth and claw. Averaging three hundred pounds and up, only quick sword work would save your life.

Spears where better to hold them off and he and Keld working together could defeat them without injury. Keld would distract and antagonize with his spear while Geir rushed in for the fatal stab.

But they tried to avoid beringei when possible. A lucky swing of a clawed, hand-like paw would kill. He'd seen a beringei rip the head from a mega's body and pull rooted trees from the ground. Strong, smarter than a mega, and faster than a human, the mated pairs where the most dangerous as they would assist each other.

Geir held an arm before his face and pushed through the branches. The scent of pine filled his nostrils, growing stronger with each step he took. Sticky sap dribbled onto his leather clothing and hair. He was halfway when he heard the choking cough of a mega. Sweat sprang up on his brow as he pushed his way through the trees at the edge of the grassy valley.

His forlorn hope the earlier movement had been a harmless deer was dashed. A ripping snarl ended in the sounds of the struggle. From where he stood, he couldn't see the woman, but had a clear view of a small mega, under two hundred pounds, with a dead fawn dangling from its mouth as it dragged its prey into the tree line.

Adrenaline made Geir pant. A mega that small would have a mother nearby and maybe siblings. As if in answer to his thought, another, louder snarl ripped the air to his right.

Geir stood frozen with indecision. He was only about twenty feet past the woman. If she saw him approach, she could run down the shoreline and reach the forest before he could catch her. And panic would make her careless on the sure to be snake strewn shoreline.

But if he waited, the mega could reach her before him. There was a good chance the mega would attack the fawn's mother. If he ran through the grass, it might attack him instead, and without Keld and his spear, it might kill him.

While he debated, the woman screamed. Without conscious decision, he rushed forward. In moments, he'd gained enough elevation to see Keld running down the steep mountainside with the spear grasped in both hands. Keld leapt over bushes and boulders in his path with a blithe disregard for snakes and thurji bushes and ran full speed down the hill.

Geir couldn't see the woman. The rocks she'd stacked blocked his view. The crouched mega between them he saw clearly. Back haunches hunched tight to the ground and the tip of the mega's tail twitched. It would spring in seconds.

His pulse pounded so hard blackness edged his vision. He yelled, hoping to draw the mega to him. It leaped. The mega seemed to hang in the air, front legs outstretched, back ones pushing from the ground. Six-inch claws glinted in the afternoon light. A curved white tusk, extending from a snarling mouth lined with razor sharp teeth, engraved themselves on his mind.

A brilliant white light enveloped the mega. It crashed to the ground.

Geir continued running. He and Keld had approximately the same distance to cross. He lost sight of Keld again as the ground dipped. A shiver traveled his back as he ran past the mega's nest. Bones were scattered before a circular patch of matted grasses, and a musky odor permeated the air.

She'd made camp fifty feet from a den.

He bolted up the shallow rise through the already crushed grass. His legs strained, and breath came in shallow pants. There would be another mega. Whatever miracle had stopped the first, he hoped reoccurred. Somewhere close, the dead mega's mate would be lurking. From the size of the second mega, and proximity to the nest, he assumed it was the male that had sprung at her. Usually, the females hunted and brought back their prey although sometimes they hunted in pairs.

As he gained the top of the shallow rise, he saw Keld now standing still and peering over the waving grasses. He yelled and gestured with his spear. Geir turned to follow the gesture in time to see the grasses to his right ripple. He continued running forward.

The woman stood now, leaning over her rough, rock wall. Both hands gripped a small metal box. Tears streaked her dirty face, and wide blue eyes stared at him from beneath the blond strands.

Her gaze flicked from the dead mega to Keld, before returning to him. Geir stopped running when he reached the mega corpse and spun. The woman stood less than fifteen feet away. With his back to her, he inched to the right to put himself between her and the approaching mega.

The mega's head peeked from the tall grass. Golden eyes narrowed on him, and the head sank from sight. The ripple revealed it still approached, slinking through the grass. Ten feet from him, the grass stopped moving. He braced himself, holding his sword in both hands with his left foot back. The mega would leap any second.

Geir flinched when the woman touched his arm.

She babbled something incomprehensible, but her meaning was clear by her tugging.

"Run," he said, knowing it was useless. "Keld!"

"Coming," Keld shouted back.

Before he could holler for Keld to grab her, the woman yanked his arm hard and knocked him with her hip. Surprised by her strength, he staggered back as she stepped forward and rose the metal object in her hand. A beam of light traveled in a straight line from the box to the leaping Mega. The mega crashed to the ground.

The mega corpse beside him twitched. *Not dead then*, he thought as he spun to pull the woman to his side. Keld crouched beside her now with his spear extended and his gaze searching the waving grass.

"Keld, I saw a young one. There could be more, and I think this big guy is still alive."

As he spoke, Geir ran a hand over the woman's face and down her arm. His worried gaze traveled her, checking for injuries. She held still, but her posture revealed her tense state.

He sheathed his sword and felt her face and hands again. Ice-cold skin flinched from his touch. From this close, the freckles crossing her nose became apparent. Thick black lashes framed her blue eyes. *Wide, terrified eyes,* he noted. Smooth, wrinkle-free skin and even white teeth made him think she was young, but her demeanor contradicted that. She didn't look ready to flee but to fight as if she fought often.

Moving slow, he removed his pack and shook out his cloak, which he placed around her shoulders. Her wary gaze followed his every move.

"She's freezing, Keld. And likely hungry."

"The mega is waking. Get her away from its paws," Keld replied in a soft voice as if speaking to a child.

Geir turned to grin at him. The woman smiled. The smile made her look years younger, and again he was conflicted on her age. *Not as young as sixteen but no older than thirty*, he decided. He didn't care how old she was.

One hand clutched her metal box although from this close he could see it wasn't a box at all, but a short round pipe with a square end lined with buttons and, amazingly, small lights. Her other hand clutched his cloak closed. Made for him, the material dragged on the ground.

"The box thing in her hand is a weapon, so go slow," Geir said.

"Did you see it knock that mega right down?"

"Yep." As he spoke, Geir fumbled in his pack and offered her a piece of jerky.

She took the proffered treat and sniffed it before hesitantly tasting it. She made a face, but swallowed and handed it back to him. He smiled and offered her his last oat cake. Pressed oats bound with honey and dried berries, the cakes could be stored for months if kept dry.

Her eyes lit, but she shook her head, said something incompressible, and shook the jerky at him.

Geir tapped his chest with two fingers. "Geir." He pointed to Keld who stood behind him now. "Keld."

The woman smiled and tapped her chest. "Cara."

Light and musical with an odd lilt, he wanted to hear her voice again.

Geir beckoned and backed away. "Come."

She peered over her shoulder and bit her lip, then followed.

At her fire, he paused. Keld drew his knife and slit the mega's throat. The woman screamed, the sound cutting off abruptly as she covered her face with her hands.

Keld had jerked upright and spun to face the grass.

"Cara." Geir offered his hand. Horrified blue eyes met his. Fresh tears tracked her cheeks. He sighed in relief when she took his hand.

"You're scaring her, Keld. Kill the other when she isn't looking." The hand he held trembled. "It's okay," he said in a soft voice and drew her close. Suddenly, she was sobbing and clutching him. "Easy," he murmured as he stroked her hair. For a minute, she cried and clutched him before pushing away to wipe her face.

In that minute, he fell in love. He wasn't going back and leaving her at Luger's nonexistent mercy. His gaze flitted to Keld who he loved like a brother, and his hand dropped to his sword.

Bloody knife in hand, Keld stared at him. "She's ours."

Geir's shoulder relaxed. "We need to find a safe spot for her."

"Far away."

"Yes."

"Since we have a fire already, let's butcher the mega and make jerky," Keld said,

"No time. Get us three days' worth of steaks. She'll be being tracked. Whoever she belonged to first will want her back."

"What if she won't come with us?"

Geir froze. He couldn't force her or hurt her. "Then we go with her— and fight."

"She needs boots."

Geir knelt and ran a hand down Cara's leg. Her shoes came to her ankle. Black with cloth laces, they felt thin and insubstantial to him. Of course, living inside a sanctuary there would be no need for boots. The women in his village didn't even wear shoes.

He drew the knife from his belt, and she leapt away in a surprisingly fast and graceful move.

"Sorry, come back, Cara." He tapped his boots with his knife and pointed at her feet.

She peered down and held up a foot. She said something he didn't understand, but let him approach. He knelt before her and began cutting the bottom of his cloak.

"We might need your cloak too. This leather is thin. Even wrapped a few times it might not be strong enough."

Cara removed the cloak and spread it between them to make it easier to cut. Keld draped his cloak over her, and she smiled.

Geir paused, surprised by the twinge of jealousy he felt over her smile. He wanted her to smile at him.

Keld squatted in front of her and took her hand. "She's freezing. Damn it, I wish we had time to skin the mega."

"Not with her here. Imagine how bad she'd freak?"

Keld nodded and continued to rub Cara's hands with his.

Geir had to fight the urge to push him away. A scrap of leather fell away to lay on the rocks beside his feet. He stood and shook out his cloak before removing Keld's and draping his over her shoulders. He wanted her to wear his cloak, to belong to him and him alone. Each glance and smile at Keld felt like a knife in his heart.

Keld cut the scrap into two equal lengths and attempted to wrap it around her ankle. For a moment, she watched before backing away. Two, deep lines furrowed her brow.

"You're scaring her again." Geir knelt on one knee and pointed to his boots, then her leg. She shook her head and took another step back while saying something incomprehensible. She leaned down and tugged at her pants, stabbing the taut fabric with a finger.

She peered through the blond hair, which had swung forward over her cheek, and smiled. The smile went right to his groin. Instantly, he was as aroused as he'd ever been. Painfully hard, his cock pushed against the lacings of his leather pants.

"She doesn't understand," he said in a rough voice.

Keld knelt beside him and made a slithering motion with his hand, then stabbed Geir's boot with two fingers.

She nodded and did the same to her pants.

The men exchanged exasperated glances.

"Maybe we should kill a snake and show her?" So saying, Keld stepped away, his eyes scanning the rocky verge of shore.

She stepped forward and held out her hand. When Geir took it, she smiled but dropped it. She clipped the metal object on her belt and pointed to his knife, then held out her hand again.

He handed her the knife. On one knee, she knelt and pulled the end of her pants taut, then stabbed the fabric. Her nearness distracted him, and it took a moment to realize the knife hadn't marred the material. She handed him the knife and offered her leg for his inspection.

The small movement shattered his composure again. Crouched uncomfortably, he ran a hand down her leg and tentatively tried to cut the fabric. Her low laugh sounded like music and intoxicated like wine. He grinned at her, his smile widening when she took his hand and slid it under the cuff of her pants.

When she stabbed with the knife, he felt the pressure but no sharpness. She pulled the pant leg up, exposing her ankle. The sight of her skin made his cock throb. He trailed his fingertips over the exposed flesh, making her inhale sharply. From inches away, she stared into his eyes. A tense moment passed as they gauged each other.

"Geir?"

His name on her lips filled him with lust like never before in his life. He wanted to kiss her, to rip her clothing off and press her naked body against his, to use her body to quench the fire in his soul. Unconsciously, he leaned toward her.

"Cara," he whispered in a voice that cracked.

Her eyes darkened, and she licked her lips, raising one hand to his face before dropping it and jerking back. A blush flushed her cheeks as she scrambled away, laughing and kicking her leg to straightened her pants. He remained crouched before her. His expression must have been intense because she laughed again nervously and peered over her shoulder while wiping her hands on her pants.

"Cara." He beckoned her forward and lifted her foot, catching his breath when she balanced with both hands on his shoulder.

He examined her shoes and socks, testing both with his knife, and couldn't resist running a hand along her calf. Her skin shivered under his hand. He was so entranced with her Keld speaking startled him.

"Will she let you bind her legs?"

"No need. Cut me two thin strips to tie the pant legs closed, but the fabric is tough. My knife can't pierce it."

"A bite will hurt with no padding."

"True, but we can ease her into it. Let's get away from here and then we'll hunt and make her better clothes."

While Geir spoke, Keld cut two thin strips of leather from the scrap piece and handed them over. Cara stared with wide, inquisitive eyes as Geir tied the pieces around her leg. She nodded and grinned. His answering smile made her grin wider.

Keld used the rest of the leather scraps to wrap around his hastily butchered steaks. Geir offered his hand. She glanced from him to Keld and the bloody meat and took his hand. The tight expression on her face stiffened more as she paled and jerked away, doubling over and grabbing her stomach.

"Cara," Geir said in alarm as she vomited.

She pushed him away and leaned against her rough rock wall, panting. A grimace crossed her face, and she vomited again. Geir placed himself between her and Keld.

"Hide the meat, Keld. She's really squeamish."

"We better get out of here before this kill draws more predators."

Speaking in a soft voice, Geir approached and held his hand out again. He stopped immediately when she spoke sharply and waved him back. She pointed to the ground at his feet and barked a word he knew meant stay. Her hands dropped to her belt as she put the wall between them.

"Not squeamish—sick," Keld said unnecessarily as Cara relieved herself behind the rock.

Keld opened his pack and removed the stack of leaves he carried for just such occasions. Saying her name in a soft voice, he held the leaves over the rock wall. A snort of bitter laughter met his offering, but she accepted it.

The two men waited for her to reappear. Retching and foul odors accompanied their wait. Five minutes later, she stood and staggered to the water's edge where she rinsed her mouth and washed her face. Geir squatted beside her and held out a linen shirt from his pack as a towel. With his thumb, he traced the lines of strain that had appeared on her face.

She offered him a weak smile and stood. Clutching her borrowed cloak closed, she bent to retrieve her bag. Keld snatched it and put his arm around her.

"She's shaking. I think she's really sick. We need to get her somewhere warm."

Geir straightened and gestured south to the rugged hills. "That way. Maybe we can find a cave or something."

Cara followed his gesture, then squatted to clear the rocks from the dirt. With her fingernail, she drew stick figures of men holding knives and pointed to the east. She tapped the picture then opened and closed her hands five times while shaking her head.

"Fifty men with knives back the way she came from," Keld said and exchanged a worried glance with Geir. "See if you can find out how far away."

Geir tapped her drawing, then pointed back the way they'd come. With his fingers, he made a walking gesture then pointed to the sky. He drew a rough sun in the dirt and pointed to the sky again.

When he held up five fingers, she nodded and smiled. She pointed back to the trees, made the walking gesture, and held up two fingers.

"Armed men are two days behind us, likely chasing her. Our best bet is to still head south." Unable to explain complex reasoning, Geir pointed toward the hills and shrugged.

She sighed and glanced toward her pack hanging over the crook of Keld's arm, then rose and dusted off her pants. After squinting back, the way she'd come, she waved him forward and began walking.

Keld strode forward to take the lead. This time he put five feet between them and stabbed snakes with his spear. Along the half-mile stretch of shore leading to the rocky hillside, he killed four snakes. She stopped to examine each.

Geir mimed vomiting and convulsions making her laugh, but she used care in her examinations, using a stick she'd picked up to pry open the mouths. Color returned to her cheeks as they hiked, and her stride loosened as if the cramps had passed.

"Thurji bush," Keld warned and motioned them back.

She stared in apparent fascination as Keld threw a rock at the bush.

"Dangerous," Keld said.

"Dangerous," she repeated.

Keld grinned. She returned it.

Geir pointed at a thorn on the ground. "Poisonous."

She smiled and repeated the word. Geir took exaggeratedly careful steps around the thorn spattered ground. A smile on her face, she mimicked him. As they hiked, he named the trees and bushes they passed. Once they reached the tree line, Geir stopped and opened his pack, offering her the jerky.

She grimaced and waved her hands, then made gagging noises.

His eyes widened as he brought the meat to his nose to sniff. "The meat is bad. It got her sick."

Keld groaned and peered at the half-eaten piece he held with dismay.

"Maybe yours is still good," Geir said.

Keld brightened but didn't finish eating. He stuffed the remainder back in is pack. Geir offered her the oat cake. She sniffed it and sighed, then took a small bite and handed it back. She took her pack from Keld and removed a metal bottle from which she drank, then handed it to Geir.

He sipped tentatively. Water with an odd metallic taste. She pulled up the sleeve of her shirt, revealing glass jewelry on her wrist. Arm out held, she showed it to Keld, then pointed at the sky and tapped the glass.

Geir peered over her shoulder. Small lights blinked inside the glass. The pattern changed as he watched. She pointed to the sky and tapped her finger in a steady pattern. The display changed again. She grabbed his hand and tapped his finger, stopping right before the display changed.

"It's keeping time," he said in awe.

Geir pointed excitedly to the sky, pretending to tap as he motioned to the west. She grinned and tapped the glass with her fingertip. A new picture appeared. A red arrow inside a black circle intersected with black lines and four dark blue symbols. She stood and turned, then pointed.

"West," she said clearly.

Her accent was odd and the word inflected differently, but he understood it. She stared with exaggerated emphasis at her wrist.

She turned again. "East."

The red arrow spun, continuing to point in the same direction no matter which way she turned.

Before she could say anything, Keld said, "North."

Geir laughed and pointed ahead of them up the steep hill. "South."

Keld stood and shouldered her pack. She grabbed his arm and rubbed her stomach with her free hand, then pointed to the sky and flicked her fingers.

"She wants to wait to make sure the food doesn't make her ill," Geir said.

"Maybe the food is fine, but she's sick? Or it makes it her sick like when you eat snake."

"Offer her yours."

Keld withdrew the jerky from his pack and offered it to her. She grimaced and made gagging noises then smiled and ran her finger over Keld's bottom lip. Keld's eyes darkened, and he stepped closer. He grabbed her hand and pressed it to his lips. Cara stepped closer, then jerked away, busying herself with retying the leather strips holding her pants closed around her shoes.

Geir cleared his throat. Both hands clenched, and he had to force himself to remain still.

Keld glared at him, then smiled ruefully. "I don't want to share her either."

"She'll be safer with two of us."

"What if she wants neither of us?" Keld hesitated. He brought her hand to his lips again and kissed it, making her giggle. "Or one of us?" he finished softly.

White hot jealousy scorched Geir. A blush burned across his cheeks.

She drew away from Keld and turned to him. Her laugh faded and an uneasy expression flitted across her face. The smile she gave felt forced and unnatural. He was scaring her with his angry glower.

He sighed hard and gave Keld a quick one-armed hug. "We're partners and can work things out. Making her safe is our top priority. If she's cold now, by nightfall she'll be freezing. We need to find a more permanent shelter for her before the heavy snows come."

"What will we feed her if deer makes her sick? We have no more oats and berries."

"We'll try the mega steak tonight. Maybe she can eat that."

Her smile lightened to a more natural one as they spoke. She stood and linked her arm in Geir's and began walking up the hill again. The three hiked for six hours, continuing their language lessons.

Sunset surprised him. He hadn't meant to walk so long, but she kept up easily without slowing or complaining, and he lost track of time. Despite Geir's worry over the men following, he enjoyed every minute with her and sought her smile eagerly, doing his best to answer her questioning glances and gestures, repeating the same words endlessly. Her grin of triumph when she understood his mime brought an answering smile to his lips.

He and Keld did their best to ease her way through the thick firtin trees, but branches slapped her face and sap stuck to her hair and hands. The trees thinned as they reached the peak where sunset lit the sky a deep red. She paused to admire the view before tapping the glass on her wrist.

"Comp."

Geir dutifully repeated the word, earning another smile.

She took the metal box thing from her waist. "Gun."

He nodded his understanding, and she tapped the glass and frowned, then rubbed her arms. She tapped as if counting out time and flicked her fingers "Cold. Dangerous."

"The night cold will be dangerous for her, and she knows it." Geir turned to examine the hill top, but nothing in sight offered shelter. Steep and rocky, the tip of the hill exposed them to brisk winds. While safer from predators, the danger of freezing was greater.

"Let's cross the peak and get her out of the wind. We'll clear a spot and make a nest with the branches. It'll be impossible to light a fire with that green wood. Grab a few flat rocks. We can burn the needles. And maybe our body heat will be enough. We can take turns guarding her. With her gun—" Geir's tongue tripped on the unfamiliar word. "We should be safe enough."

Keld nodded agreement and began up the hill, talking over his shoulder. "I never even heard of a weapon like hers before. Her village must be amazing and teeming with ancient artifacts."

"She isn't from this planet."

Keld stopped dead and turned to stare. "What?"

"Think about it. We saw her arrive. That flaming ball in the sky. She can't eat our food and has clothes and weapons we could neither make nor imagine."

"But she's a woman..."

"Yep, I can't explain it, but I know I'm right."

Keld laughed. In moments, he laughed so hard tears streamed from his eyes, and he held his stomach. Cara patted his arm and looked worried.

"Women are falling from the sky. I think I've died and gone to glory," Keld gasped between peels of laughter.

"Just one."

"How do you know? That flaming rock was enormous. Maybe it was full of women."

Geir turned back, his expression bleak. "Too late now. We'll ask her tomorrow, but I doubt she had friends and left them behind."

Keld continued to chuckle as he resumed walking. "Women falling from the sky," he mumbled and laughed again.

# -11-
# CARA

Eddies of warmth teased Cara's chilled fingertips. Tiny flames flickered and died away as the fire consumed the dried firtin needles. Huddled against the thick base of a firtin, tree limbs enclosed she and Geir in a cocoon, giving the illusion of warmth and comfort.

Cold air still nipped her exposed face and fingers, causing progressively worse shivers. Taller and wider than any tree she'd ever seen on Haven, the firtins towered over them. Everything on this planet seemed bigger to her and slightly wild. Grass waved at chest height and leaves on familiar maple trees were twice the size here. And the animals... the animals were enormous with teeth, claws, and poison fangs. Haven possessed nothing of the kind.

She'd seen footage of big, dangerous animals from New Haven but seeing them up close and personal was entirely different.

The cold didn't seem to bother Geir at all. The roughspun tunic and leather vest he wore appeared adequate to keep him warm. Her uniform wasn't up to the task of keeping her warm once night fell. She'd spent the last two nights huddled miserably beside the biggest fire she could safely make and still shivered from cold.

A sharp crack startled her. Geir dropped the firtin limb he held, placed his hand on her shoulder, and gently pressed down, indicating she should stay seated by the fire. She rubbed the grip of her gun nervously.

"Keld," he said and carefully placed a small broken limb across the fire.

An aromatic mixture of pine and smoke rose into the dark. Geir squatted beside her, his bulk warming her more than the fire.

"Safe?" she asked and gestured with her chin toward the sharp cracking noises.

This world contained a myriad of dangerous animals and plants. She shuddered, remembering her wild flight from her crashed ship two days ago. Luck had saved her from her carelessness. She'd run through the forest with no thought that the plants themselves could be deadly.

"Keld good. Back soon. Safe." Geir's warm hands caressed her cheek for a moment, and a frown grew on his face. "Cara cold."

She nodded agreement. Firelight flickered across his face, lighting the hollows of his chiseled cheekbones and sparkling in his blue eyes. A bolt of lust warmed her, and she smiled. His return smile warmed her even more. He resumed clearing the ground of stones and sticks, laying a thin mat of firtin branches along the ground in preparation for sleep.

For the first time in days, her shoulders relaxed. The competence he and Keld had shown getting them this far, and making camp, reassured her they were used too, and prepared for, the dangers their world presented.

Dangers she couldn't imagine and hadn't prepared for when leaving the safety of her ship.

When the foam encasing her had dissolved, and she'd recovered enough for movement, she'd dragged herself to the med-scanner. It took the machine thirty-three hours to repair the damage Ilda's homemade poison had done. Twelve of those hours she'd been conscious and in pain trying to stop the spread of fire in and around the ship while being treated.

The heat of *Intrepid's* reentry through the atmosphere had destroyed sections twelve, thirty-seven, and forty-three through fifty-two of the power receptors. Numerous other sections were partially destroyed. The landing had torn the bottom of her ship wide open. Buried in the ground at an angle up to the second deck, her ship wasn't going anywhere for a while, if ever.

As soon as she got the fires out, she'd retrieved her crew for burial. Tucked into nenobags their bodies would remain intact for autopsies when *Odyssey* arrived and retrieved them. She couldn't bear the thought of Veta in a storage hold waiting. Somehow it seemed more respectful to bury her.

She realized now she hadn't been thinking clearly, whether from the poison, or stress and lack of sleep, she didn't know, but at the time burying them felt like the right thing to do. But right or wrong it comforted her to think of Veta resting on the sunny hillside beneath the wide-leafed maples instead of a cold, dark hold. Looking back, she couldn't clearly remember carrying them the half mile to the hill. She'd been in a daze of fear and loss.

A strong shiver gripped her. The memory of that day scared her to her toes. She'd just finished burying the last of her crew when a pack of velociraptors attacked. Smaller than the ones in her history books, she'd been astonished when the first one leaped and landed on her chest, knocking her to the ground. Bolder then the other eight, which surrounded her growling low, chittering howls, the first one went for her throat. Luckily, her uniform foiled its ripping claws. Two more had jumped on her and ripped ineffectually at her arm by the time she knocked the first away and drew her gun.

Frustrated by the material of her uniform, the small animals had screamed their odd clacking call as they used their inch-long hooked claws to rip at the fabric of her pants. Made of the same material as her shirt her pants held up to the swiping claws without marring. Her gun made short work of them, leaving them unconscious on the ground. A gun she almost hadn't bothered to take. But Ilda's constant harping on correct procedure had made her grab the pack and gun before leaving the ship.

An ironic laugh escaped her. She stifled it quickly when Geir looked alarmed. Ilda had saved her life. The velociraptors had turned on their unconscious brethren, tearing them to shreds while she ran back to her ship. When she drew close enough to see her ship, armed men surrounded it, holding swords and yelling angrily at each other. Astride shaggy gray animals and waving unsheathed swords, they were the very picture of ancient barbarians shown in the history texts. She'd run again, meaning to hide in the trees till they left but a family of gorillas had chased her further, and before she knew it she was miles away.

She snorted, annoyed with herself for overreacting. On the *Intrepid* she'd under-reacted, letting Ilda get out of hand and causing the death of her crewmates because she was unwilling to act and here she acted too quickly, without thought. A groan escaped her as she rubbed her eyes hard.

Geir felt her face and hands again, then pulled her into his lap, wrapping both arms around her. The kindness of the gesture warmed her more than the closeness. The sun had set and the night chilled rapidly. Her every breath plumed in the frosty air.

"I'm good." She made as if to rise.

He pulled her back down. "No. Stay. Warmer."

She had to agree it was warmer so close to him and she relaxed against his broad chest. His presence comforted her with more than physical warmth. Nothing was as she expected it here.

This planet contained species of animals that hadn't lived at the same times back on Earth. She'd been attacked by gorillas, seen white-tailed deer, and a bigger version with long pointy antlers and dark shaggy fur.

The sabertooths had confirmed her earlier observation of multiple types of old Earth animals from different eras of Earth's history. Dark gray instead of traditional orange and black, the enormous cats were clearly of Earth descent. Not so the many varieties of reptile. Her quick examines had shown startling differences from Earth reptiles. She thought the smaller ones with legs might be indigenous to Jord.

Scientists from Odyssey would have a field day here. It would take a lifetime to sort out the varying plants and animals to determine which were native Earth animals and which from here, and which a manmade combination. Or maybe there was alien intelligent life here. The thought made her shiver again.

Geir tightened his grip, running his hands over her arms and chafing her hands between his.

"Keld," he called.

Keld answered immediately. They spoke too fast for her to catch most of what they said but she got the gist. He was returning. Loud crashing and quivering tree limbs accompanied Keld's return. He'd brought a log as thick around as her waist.

Comprised of dead, rotting wood, it should burn nicely.

The two men spoke again. Geir stood in a surprisingly graceful move, taking her with him. With his boot, he nudged the limbs he'd placed farther from the fire.

"Stay," Geir said firmly when he placed Cara on the small pile of firtin limbs.

Geir ripped a length of rotted bark from the stump and brought it to her. Hunkered beside her, he traced a line of one-inch gouges that lined the wood with his fingertip.

"Riptor, dangerous." He pointed to the trees, then scuffed a small hole in the dirt with his booted foot.

Fingers spread like claws, he mimed climbing and burrowing, teaching her the words and warning of danger. He handed her the piece of wood.

"Toamalm, dangerous. Firtins safe, no riptor. Rotte firtins." Geir mimed a small furry animal.

By his descriptions, she thought he meant rats or mice lived in the firtin trees. The animal he called a riptor she thought was a velociraptor-like the ones that had attacked her. From what she understood of his warnings, riptors preferred to live in deciduous trees and open fields at the edges of forests, which matched what she'd observed.

Keld offered her a piece of meat warmed on the fire, pulling her from her musings on native wildlife.

She gingerly bit into the offered roasted haunch of Sabertooth, the animal Geir called a mega and listened to the two men converse.

Geir spoke a mixture of completely unidentifiable words and mangled Latin with the occasional clear word thrown in. His deep voice and accent made discerning his meaning difficult. She tended to forget to listen for meaning, enjoying the sound.

He distracted her utterly. She'd never spent this much time in the company of a man. Keld's laugh made her grin, his smile made her feel warmer. The simple touch of Geir's hand heated her from head to toe.

These two had been kind and helpful. Perhaps the other men by her ship would have been as well. Weapons were a necessity to deal with dangerous wildlife and didn't mean the men were hostile or dangerous to her. The history books she'd read had disgusted her. At the time, she'd assumed the stories wildly exaggerated, but seeing the men carrying weapons mounted on the shaggy, horse-like animals, had unnerved her, and she'd run, convinced they meant her harm. And yet, here she was, being cared for by two strangers.

Keld offered her another piece of meat, which she declined.

The first bite settled into her stomach and she waited uneasily for her body to react. On the wrecked hulk of her ship enough supplies remained she could live off for years, maybe even the rest of her life if she could get the hydroponics working again, but she only needed to live two years, three tops before *Odyssey* arrived and retrieved the beacon Ilda had sent.

The sensors aboard *Odyssey* would scan this planet and locate her ship. If she were within a mile of her ship, she could use her comp to contact them. Her panicked flight had taken her a good ten miles from the crash, and they'd come another ten since. But she had years to kill.

A blush heated her cheeks at the erotic nature of her thoughts for killing that time, and she laughed at her imaginings. These two had been heading somewhere and were still heading there. They'd stopped to help her, but she was sure they would drop her at the first safe settlement they came across.

The mine which had blown her ship from orbit had partially destroyed her sensor array, but she's seen enough scans on her way down to know this planet was sparsely settled, and a good portion was too cold to be habitable without technology. Technology she'd seen no signs of at all except for one densely metal area on the other side of the globe impossibly far to reach on foot.

Her quick readings made her think she'd located the colony ship which brought people here in the first place. The reading was almost identical to the ship which remained as a museum in orbit above Haven.

The fauna she'd run into so far convinced her this planet was barely habitable. Large dangerous predators roamed freely.

She glanced at Geir admiringly. He'd leapt between her and the giant cat with only a sword to fight it off.

The bravery of that act sent a tingle down her spine. Unlike the history book's warning, neither man had tried to force her anywhere or to do anything. Instead, both had done their best, at great risk to themselves, to help her.

Geir's kind smile reminded her of Michaelson's. Michaelson had the same blond hair and sparkling blue eyes, but Geir's build... her blush darkened.

Much bigger and bulkier than Haven men both Geir and Keld towered over her. Bulging muscles rippled under their leather vests. Geir smelled fresh and clean, like pine trees and woodlands. Keld smelt of sweat and leather. She found both scents wildly erotic.

When Keld had kissed her hand, she'd wanted to pull him closer and kiss his soft lips. The light stubble on his cheeks drew her. She wanted to feel it against her skin.

The attention had angered Geir. She didn't know if in Geir's eyes she'd behaved inappropriately, or Keld had, but something had annoyed him. Her mind flashed back to warnings from the histories about how barbaric men behaved over women, being possessive to the point of murder. Uneasy, she rubbed her hands over her arms and hugged her knees to her chest.

Geir touched her hands then moved closer, pressing his chest against her back. His warmth infused her, and she leaned against him gratefully. She'd never been cold before. A temperate planet, snow only formed on Haven's uninhabited poles. She found the chill in the air distinctly unpleasant.

She made a mental note to form a cloak like Veta had made for fun. Veta had loved fashion and designed clothes in her spare time, spending her free hours sewing intricate patterns. Reminded of her dead friend, tears filled her eyes.

Her mission had been a failure. She was a failure. Her incompetence had gotten her entire crew killed. She rested her head on her drawn-up knees and cried.

Geir stroked her back, murmuring words she didn't understand but knew were offered as comfort.

His kindness made her cry harder. When *Odyssey* returned, she would be saved, and he killed.

Ilda had gotten the beacon off.

Keld hugged her now too. The two men tried their best to comfort her, their every kindness making her feel worse.

How could anyone just kill them?

In sudden hope, she grabbed Keld's hand. Maybe she could convince the landing ship pilot who arrived they were worth saving. If the pilot would lie for them... the problems felt huge and beyond solving. The *Odyssey's* sensors would have to be blinded, the logs replaced. Technically, she could do it, but access... How could she do it undetected? How could she silence those who already saw?

If only she'd been faster and not trusted that Ilda would obey orders.

"What's done is done," she said aloud and straightened. She'd just have to think of something.

Geir handed her his shirt again. She laughed when she took it. "You must think I'm crazy. I'm not. I'm a bit shocked and overwhelmed, and really worried."

He smiled his kind smile not understanding a word she said. She needed to change that. Without help, she wouldn't be able to convince anyone of anything. Her panicked flight had already taken her too far from her ship, and she had to go back.

She turned in Geir's arms to face him. A delicious tremor rippled her skin at the light in his eyes. "Business," she muttered and held up one finger. "One."

Geir leaned forward and kissed her fingertip.

"One," he repeated in his deep, husky voice.

# -12-

# GEIR

Eyes closed, Geir feigned sleep. Cara cuddled against him beneath his spread cloak, her face tucked against his neck. Warm breath caressed his skin, and he'd never been happier in his life. Soft and warm, her body fitted against him as if made for him. For her slight size, she was surprisingly heavy. She weighed a good fifty pounds more than she appeared to. Weak morning light glowed on his closed eyelids. Keld would know he was awake, pretending was futile, but he had no plans to move until she woke.

Last night he'd resented when she curled up with Keld and fell asleep, but now he was glad he'd taken the first watch. The sheer joy of waking with her in his arms thrilled him.

She'd spent the evening learning to speak with them and seemed to have quickly grasped their method of counting. Exhaustion had slowed her attempts to understand his efforts to question her on where she came from. Wide yawns covered by her fisted hand made him give up and let her sleep.

When he opened his eyes, Keld smiled. He sat with a hand resting against Cara's shoulder, holding his spear across his knees.

Geir tightened his grasp on her, making her mumble and squirm. Her hand trailed across his arm, and he knew when she woke by the sudden tenseness of her body.

For a minute, she lay against him. When she sat, she did it slowly as if worried to wake him.

"I'm awake," he said.

She wouldn't understand the words, but maybe his intent to be reassuring. Balanced on one hand above him, she laid her other hand lightly along his cheek, her bright-blue eyes smiling into his.

"Good morning." He repeated her greeting, making her laugh.

She jumped to her feet and spun to face Keld, greeting him the same way. Keld offered her a hunk of broiled meat, which she devoured with gusto. Geir found the meat gamey and tough but ate his share without complaint. When she finished, she sipped from her metal bottle then stood and pointed to the ground.

"Stay," she said in his language and ducked behind the tree.

He and Keld separated to relieve themselves and returned before her. Before he could become concerned, she reappeared, straightening her belt.

She rubbed her arms and frowned, then rubbed his. "Cold?"

"No, I'm fine."

Head cocked to the side, she regarded him with her lips pursed before smiling and saying something he didn't understand, but assumed was a thank you.

He offered her his hand and frowned when she said no and sat.

"Dangerous," he said and gestured around them.

"Yes. Gun. Sit." She patted the ground beside her.

Reluctantly, he sat. She laughed softly and patted his knee. For a few minutes, she reviewed numbers with him. With a booted foot, she scraped the limbs and needles from the ground and spent a moment arranging dirt and rocks. She spent a few minutes gathering pine needles, then pointed to the biggest rock in her picture and carefully placed three needles atop it.

"Cara, Geir, Keld." As she named them, she touched their hands and then the rock. He nodded. She pointed at the wavy line she'd drawn. "Water." She tapped the picture of the sun and traced her hand in an arc above them. "One day."

Geir nodded he understood she was showing them where they were and where they'd met.

She handed him the handful of counted pine needles. "Two hundred and fifty men." She tapped a pebble she'd placed carefully on the ground. "Cara." Another tap on the sun. "Three days."

Geir scratched outlines of houses in the dirt. "Geir's home. Fifty days."

Cara drew stars around the sun then pointed into the sky. "Cara's home." She flashed her hands, wiggling her fingers at him till he grabbed them and laughed.

"Far, far, away; I get it."

She shrugged and smiled, then pointed at Keld and Geir and tapped the drawing of his home. Then she tapped her chest, pointed to the sky, and then the small rock. "Three hundred and eighty days."

A thoughtful frown on his face, Geir tapped his chest. "Geir man. Keld man, Cara woman."

She nodded and repeated it, then indicated the handful of needles he still held and said, "Man."

She tapped the pebble. "Ship. Women. Three hundred and eighty days."

After another two hours of mime and confusion on both sides, Geir sat back on his heels and eyed the food before him on the ground unhappily. He now knew the name of her planet and she his.

"She can't eat our food, Keld, or not much of it anyway. Nothing that eats grass. The grains give her a stomachache. She can keep them down, but they might be harming her. Her ship contains supplies though, and women will arrive in three hundred and eighty days to get her if she's near her ship."

"She'll leave?"

"Yes."

"Maybe we can go with her?"

"Look at her, Keld. To her, we must be primitive. She can travel through the heavens. I can't even imagine how amazing her world must be. She's never been cold or hungry before..."

Keld nodded unhappily. "Hundreds of women ... if we could capture them..."

"Don't be stupid. They'll all have guns, and besides, I want her to want to stay, not force her to stay where she'll be unhappy, and they can't live here. Even assuming we could capture them, it would kill them."

"What are we going to do?"

"Take her to her ship, but not for a while. Let's give the men there time to return to their home."

While they spoke, she peered between them with wide eyes and a worried expression.

Another few minutes of mime and writing in the dirt and he'd convinced her to go with them a few days away to give the dangerous men by her ship time to leave. They headed down the hill together. She repeated the words he'd taught her and pointed and asked about everything she passed.

"She's exhausting," Keld said four hours later.

Geir laughed and took her hand. "I don't mind." He continued his lesson, naming parts of her hand.

When they stopped to eat, she shook her water bottle.

"More soon, Cara."

She ate the meat Keld handed her, and sipped from her bottle, then sat quietly till they were ready to go. The few birds that flew overhead riveted her interest. She said nothing as they continued their trek. By late afternoon they reached a grassy plain. In the distance, a line of high mountains with snowcapped peaks blocked the horizon.

To their left, water glittered, seen in small glimpses through firtin trees and waist-high brown grass. The hill they'd climbed down curved to their right. A wide swath of burned forest sported new growth through the charred remains of firtin trees. Between the burned section and where they stood a copse of lily trees grew onto the plain. Not yet cold enough to completely kill the white blossoms, the browning white flowers hung in long folds.

"Dangerous." Geir pointed, then mimed sleep. "Poisonous."

"Eat?"

He tapped her nose.

"Smell?" she wrinkled her nose and sniffed.

"Yes."

"Where to now?" Keld asked.

Cara opened her pack and rummaged a moment, emerging with a long, metal tube that she held to her eye. For a few minutes, she fussed with it, hitting buttons on the side and glancing at her comp. Then she handed it to Geir.

"Ten days walk." She pointed at the mountains, then her comp.

Geir made no answer. Her device fascinated him. The lily trees appeared to be directly before him, close enough to touch. She took it from him, touched the side, and then handed it back as she gestured at the distant mountains.

To his shock, the mountains appeared to be within touching distance too, the firtin trees so close he could see individual needles and count branches. When he swung the device to the lily trees, a blur of color filled the end.

She took it back and showed him the slider on the side pointing to the lily trees then a row of symbols along the side of the tube. She drew a circle in the dirt at her feet and made markings he realized represented the small symbols in white writing below each picture inside the tube. Excited, he aimed the device at the glitter of water, then matched the symbols on the picture to the ones on the side of the device.

The picture jumped into focus. Each wave became clearly defined as if he stood over it.

"What are you doing?" Keld asked.

"This is amazing— look." Geir handed Keld the device and showed him how to use it.

"It's cool and all, but where should we go?"

"This plain is bound to have mega's. It seems silly to cross it and then return. The burnt section is unlikely to have beringei."

"And we could have a fire; the char will hide the scent of smoke."

Geir glanced at the sky. "We have about two hours of daylight left. We can skirt the lily trees and make the edge of the burned area."

"Cut through the plain?" Keld asked doubtfully.

"Yes. Her gun can kill a mega."

"Before it pounces?"

"Stay alert for waving grass."

"I don't have eyes behind my head."

"If we go through the firtin trees, we'll leave a trail. If we head straight toward the distant mountains, then cut to the burn, we might be able to shake a pursuer. They'd have to be really persistent to risk chasing across this plain."

Keld gripped his spear so tight his knuckles whitened and strode forward. His head scanned from side-to-side as he strode through the waist-high grasses.

"Come, Cara." Geir took her hand and nudged her before him.

Ten minutes later the comp on her wrist beeped. "Dangerous." She pulled the gun from her belt and turned to the right. A deer bounded away from them.

"Gun, Cara," Geir said excitedly and lifted her arm.

She glanced at him, then frowned and lifted her hand. A yellow light leaped from her gun and brushed the rear legs of the deer. It flipped head-over-heels. Cara's hand trembled as she lowered the gun.

"Stay with Keld." He took her hand and placed it in Keld's, then ran through the grass.

The deer struggled, trying to lift itself with its front feet. His sword slipped easily into the exposed neck. He removed his shirt and gutted it with the knife on his belt, working as fast as he could. With his sword, he hacked off the legs and head. While the blood drained, he used handfuls of grass to wipe his hands and clean his sword before throwing the carcass over his shoulder and heading back to Keld and Cara.

Cara hid her face in Keld's shoulder a moment before straightening. Her lips in a thin line, she followed Keld.

Keld picked up the pace, trusting her comp to beep if an animal got close. He cut diagonally across the field, and they reached the edge right as the sun set.

"Stay." He motioned Cara back and headed up the low, brush-covered hill, casting handfuls of rocks every few feet. Geir nudged her forward as Keld reached the charred trees.

# -13-
# CARA

Geir followed five steps behind her, carrying the deer carcass. The iron tang of fresh blood drifted to her on each breeze, noticeable over the charred stench of the trees burned in the past.

Limbs brittle from burning snapped easily, making travel quick. Keld ducked and wove before her, trying to break as few limbs as possible.

The frown on her face deepened as she realized Keld was worried about leaving a trail a man could follow.

Someone followed them or her, but why? Were they criminals on the run from justice or were strangers treated cruelly by locals? Or were men following her; maybe thinking she was an alien bent on harming them or something. She flinched as she realized she was. Her presence on this planet endangered the inhabitants.

Her gaze flicked to Geir. He'd easily accepted her being from a different planet with no sign of distress. She doubted they were thieves; they had nothing. It seemed unlikely they were killers or violent men. They'd been kind to each other and her. What other crime would get you followed for days? It seemed much more likely she was being followed.

The care Geir was taking to scuff her tracks confirmed her suspicions. She spent the next thirty minutes pondering why they were going out of the way to help her, but couldn't come up with an answer.

Night descended with a spectacular sunset. Shades of red and orange darkened to purple and faded too black. Cara tapped her comp and shone the beam of light on the ground before her, causing both men to exclaim in wonder.

They spoke a moment, too fast for her to catch more than a few words. Geir wedged the deer in a tree and gathered limbs to make a fire. She amazed them again with her lighter. She ate the mega meat despite the charred taste and tough texture. The men let her leave without comment to relieve herself. Tomorrow, she'd ask them to return to the water so she could wash and refill her canteen.

She handed Geir her scope again and showed him how to change the settings for night vision and infra-red. Too tired to talk, she lay on the ground as close as she safely could to the fire and fell asleep in moments. She woke briefly when Geir settled beside her and snuggled gratefully against his warmth.

When she woke in the morning, she lay across Keld's chest and hadn't woken at the change of position. A blush heated her cheeks. Pressed against him it was clear he had a morning erection. Well versed in male anatomy, she realized this was common in young men, but it still made her feel like a tease.

He grinned at her, brown eyes sparkling, and ran a hand over her hair. She was tempted to kiss him, but it felt like taking advantage, and she wasn't sure an overture would be welcome or wise.

He released her with no hesitation but looked disappointed. His hand dropped to his groin, and her blush deepened. Eyes locked on hers, he rubbed a hand along the laces of his trousers. She stared for a moment before jerking away and hurrying behind a tree trunk.

Hands pressed to her cheeks, she took a deep breath then slapped her hands over her mouth to stifle the giggles. She'd been tempted to watch or help, but both would be foolish. For all she knew, they practiced the ancient rite of marriage and had wives or each other. If she chose one, perhaps the other would leave, or attack, or both.

She did her business and lurked behind the tree till Geir called her. While she'd slept, he'd skinned the deer and placed thin strips of meat over the low, smoky fire. Smeared with a paste of ash and blood, the hide hung from tree limbs.

"Cara, no eat. Poisonous." Gear gestured to the strips hanging above the fire.

She nodded she understood. She shook her almost empty water bottle. "Water?"

He pointed to the gray clouds dimming the morning light. "Snow soon." He turned to Keld, and the two spoke a moment ending in Keld shrugging and him looking worried. Hands on his hips, he surveyed the surrounding trees then began breaking branches.

She watched for a moment before joining him. Soon they had a stack of branches that he arranged in a rough teepee.

She stepped back to examine it then drew her gun and adjusted a setting.

"Stay."

Twenty feet away she used the thin beam to topple a tree and slice it into rough planks. When she had a waist high stack, she cut the tops from a close grouping of trees, dodging the falling limbs, then slicing them into manageable sections. By noon, after two battery changes, they had an irregular shelter built with the rough-cut boards stacked and tacked with limbs in holes she drilled with her gun. More leafy limbs chinked the cracks. The eight-by-eight room had a low, flat, ceiling barely high enough for Geir to walk inside without ducking. Leather strips held an ill-fitting, narrow door in place.

When she finished cutting the limbs, she removed the battery pack and attached it to her solar collector and inserted her last spare. Geir and Keld collected limbs and rocks to form a crude fireplace inside.

The smell of roasting meat made her mouth water and stomach rumble. Keld handed her a hunk of meat from his pack that she ate without enjoyment while Keld and Geir ate strips of the fresh, roasted meat. She was tempted to eat one of her ration bars, but the meat would spoil, and her bars would last years.

Geir cut the bloody scraps of leather, which had wrapped the mega meat, into strips and left after telling her to stay with Keld. Keld stared after him worriedly, then smiled at Cara. They spent the afternoon talking.

Geir returned, lugging bundles of dead grass. White flakes covered his head and shoulders. She stepped from their shack and stared with amazement at the white, swirling flakes drifting from the sky. Hands outstretched, she twirled and laughed, lifting her face to try to catch the flakes in her mouth.

While she admired the falling snow, Geir brought in the leftover planks. When she entered, she found he'd built a crude bed frame and spread the dead grass in it. Barely wide enough for one, their feet would dangle on the ground, but their torsos would be cushioned from the cold ground. She grinned with delight. Without thinking, she kissed Geir's cheek. His sharp intake of breath made her realize her faux pas.

He pulled her closer when she stepped back and whispered her name, his voice so full of yearning tears filled her eyes. She kissed him. The kiss deepened till her pulse thudded and limbs trembled. She'd never felt such desire. A deep moan escaped him as his hands slid down her back to press her tight against his erection.

# -14-

# GEIR

The heat of her kiss seared his soul. Her gasping breaths enflamed him. When he drew back, she kissed his cheek, then neck. Keld stalked from the room, his shoulders tight. He couldn't make himself worry about it. Her hands, fumbling with the laces of his vest, stole his breath. He felt lightheaded from desire. A deep moan escaped him when she pushed his vest off and ran her hands under his shirt.

He kissed her again as she pressed hard against him, making a low moaning noise. Her response thrilled him. She seemed to want him just as much as he wanted her. He hadn't been sure. The men in town gave conflicting advice and told different stories. Some claimed women liked sex, others said they hated it. He'd asked Geoff once and believed his answer that some enjoyed it and some didn't. He'd advised speaking in a kind voice and going slow till the woman relaxed and kissed him back.

Cara kissed him passionately and touched him eagerly. When he dropped his hands to her belt, she stiffened and peered over her shoulder, then giggled and kissed him again, letting him remove her clothing as she struggled with the laces on his pants.

He knelt before her to remove her shoes then his own. Her fingers ran through his hair, and her eyes sparkled. She dropped to her knees before him and kissed him again. The kiss got him so hot he came. She didn't appear to notice. A hot blush scalded his cheeks, it faded as she continued to kiss him, seemingly perfectly content in his arms. Goosebumps covered her as he lifted off her shirt. Beneath she wore a covering over her breasts.

Laughing, she removed it. "Bra." She stood and shimmied out of her pants. "Panties." The thin scraps of material got tossed on their piled clothes, and she stood before him naked and shivering.

He'd never seen anything as beautiful. Her shiver escalated as he traced his fingertips over her full breasts. In a breathless voice, she continued her language lesson. He happily complied when she asked him to kiss her breast.

The sound she made went right to his cock. He wished the room were warmer for her or they had furs to lay on. The grass would scratch her delicate skin, and the ground was cold. He pulled her into his lap and caressed her body. Kissing her nipples made her moan and writhe. He kissed them till he was fully erect again then stood to remove his pants.

Her eyes widened, and she touched him delicately with her fingertips, making his cock throb.

"Geir and Cara," she said in a soft throaty voice. "Yes."

She giggled when he picked her up and laid her on their discarded clothes. Her body against his made every inch of his skin feel alive. Delicate fingertips traced his scars before gliding over his cock. Legs outspread and hips tilted to welcome him, she hissed as he slid inside her. He moaned and thrust hard, making her cry out.

Tear filled eyes met his.

"Wait."

Sweat sprang up on his brow as he tried to comply. Her every small movement made him surge.

"Kiss Cara."

He complied, and she began rotating her hips. In moments, they surged together. Her panting breath competed with his. He came again in hard spurts and rested his forehead against hers as she continued to jerk against him. Both hands on his ass, she pressed him tight against her body.

"Stay."

"Yes. Geir and Cara."

Tears trickled from the corner of her eyes, and suddenly she was crying and clutching him, mumbling words he couldn't make out. He smiled against her hair as he kissed her. He felt like crying too, but men didn't cry. Emotion overwhelmed him. He petted her hair and kissed her till the crying stopped.

Her skin cooled, and she shivered. He realized the fire had burned to embers and sat back on his heels. The blood on his cock alarmed him. He'd hurt her. She hadn't cried from passion but hurt.

Filled with remorse, he splayed his hand across her pelvis. "Hurt?"

A deep blush bloomed on her cheeks. "No. Good. Geir first." Smiling, she drew him down for another kiss.

He kissed her for minutes before he realized what she meant. Shocked, he drew back to examine her, running his fingertips over her breast and down to the V between her legs. Unlike him, she had no hair on her body. Her breasts had convinced him she was mature, but the lack of hair confused him. She might be younger than he thought.

While he stared, her teeth began to chatter. He was going to kill her with his lust.

"Keld?" she asked softly and almost fearfully.

Shaking, he gathered her close and buried his face in her hair. He didn't want to share her, but that was completely unfair to Keld. It would kill him to be banished while they made love with no hope of touching her skin. And she needed Keld's warmth. A hot flare of jealousy scorched him. Maybe she wanted him too. Logically, it made sense. They both wanted her, why shouldn't she want them back. But if she had sex with Keld, how would they know whose child she carried? Normally, a man kept a woman for a complete cycle.

*It didn't matter whose child she had*, he realized. All her children would be theirs until she left in three hundred and seventy-nine days. The thought of losing her hurt. He squeezed her so hard she squeaked.

"Keld," he called before he lost his nerve.

She stiffened in his arms.

# -15-
# CARA

Keld entered right away, carrying the deerskin, which he placed on the grass. Cara ducked her head, hiding her face in Geir's neck, fighting the urge to laugh. Keld's eager expression left her in no doubt he hoped to make love to her too. Slightly sore from Geir, and happy with his attention, she had no real desire for Keld, but it was clear they expected her too.

If she and Keld were alone, and he showed interest, she would accept his advances, but it felt odd in front of Geir. She didn't want to hurt either of their feelings.

"Cara's cold," Geir said.

Keld draped his cloak around her shoulders then hugged her, being careful to keep his hands above the leather. His erection pressed into her back. She turned in Geir's arms and kissed him.

"Oh gods," he moaned and kissed her back, sliding his hands over her naked breasts. Geir's arms around her waist and her back pressed to Geir's chest she kissed Keld till he panted and struggled with the laces of his pants.

"Geir, yes?" she peered over her shoulder to meet Geir's eyes as Keld undressed.

"Geir and Cara," Geir said in a deep voice then sighed and said softer," Cara and Keld, yes."

"Geir and Keld?"

"No."

"Geir, Cara, and Keld?"

"Yes."

She turned and kissed him. Naked now, Keld leaned against her back. The two men spoke too fast for her to follow but the end result was Geir laid back and drew her down beside him as Keld knelt between her legs. Geir kissed her as Keld fumbled and slid inside her. Thicker than Geir, Keld stretched her painfully.

"Wait."

Geir placed a hand on Keld's shoulder and spoke again. She caught the words 'first time' and 'slow,' and a blush flushed her cheeks again. Legs wrapped around Keld's waist, she rocked slowly. He came in five thrusts. She wished they had wash water, but the men didn't seem to care. Both caressed her.

Snuggled between them with Keld's cloak over her, she was almost warm. Drafts, as they knocked the cloak, made her shiver. Geir rose and pulled her up. He spread his cloak, and their clothes on the deer hide then laid and pulled her down beside him.

Keld built up the fire and was turning the roasting meat when she fell asleep. She woke a few hours later in a smoky room wedged between the two men. Her small movement woke Geir.

"Bathroom," she murmured.

He followed her outside naked. She wore Keld's cloak and her boots and shivered as she peed in the two inches of snow. Back inside, she leaned over the fire still shivering. Geir pressed against her back and cupped her breast, teasing the nipples between two fingers.

She turned in his arms to kiss him and fondle his growing erection. Her glance flitted to Keld who watched from the bed. Geir's hands and kiss made her forget her audience. He laughed when she dropped the cloak and pushed him to the ground to kneel astride him. His laugh changed to a deep moan as she swayed atop him.

Eyes closed and head thrown back, she rotated her hips, finding just the right rhythm. The power of the orgasm surprised her. She'd masturbated in the past, but had never felt this before. Collapsed against Geir's chest, her hips bucked uncontrollably against him.

"Cara!" his shout seemed to echo in the room as he came in deep hot spurts, each one triggering a small orgasmic aftershock, leaving her panting and weak atop him.

She'd forgotten all about Keld and started in surprise when he said her name.

Completely sated, she had no desire at all. She wanted to snuggle with Geir and feel him breathe. His hands roamed her body in slow, gentle strokes. Perfectly content, she didn't want to move.

He seemed to sense it or felt the same.

"Later, Keld. Cara needs rest."

She understood all his words and his tone was kind. Keld glared, then sighed hard and smiled at her.

She debated making love to him anyway. It likely wouldn't take long, but she didn't want to set a precedent that if she made love with one she owed the other. She fell asleep in Geir's arms and woke when he picked her up to return to the bed. She didn't wake again till late morning.

Keld gazed at her so eagerly she laughed. Half-dressed, Geir feed the fire.

"Good morning. Cara good?"

"Cara and Geir," she said, and grinned at him, making his eyes light.

"Keld and Cara," Keld whispered as he kissed her neck, making her giggle.

He continued to kiss down her body making her squirm and moan as he licked her nipples. This time he lasted longer. She was almost there when he came. She groaned with frustration.

"Geir and Cara now." Geir's deep husky voice and intent gaze made her hot.

She reached for him eagerly, knowing he would make her come in moments, she wasn't wrong. She came hard and screamed his name. He continued to thrust, panting and groaning. She pulled her legs as far back as she could and encouraged him with her hands on his ass groaning, "Yes, Geir," till she screamed, "Yes," and came again.

"Geir and Cara," she whispered in his ear and pressed him tight to her chest. He tightened his grip on her.

Her legs trembled, and her body felt weak. The wet spot on the deer hide embarrassed her, but Geir didn't seem to notice it. The pulse in his neck thudded, slowing as his breath steadied.

She didn't want to let him go. What she felt when they made love she didn't feel for Keld. Keld didn't touch her soul like Geir did. With dismay, she realized she was falling in love. The thought of never seeing Geir again hurt. Warned since birth of the folly of falling in love with a particular man, the realization that she had scared her. Men were to be enjoyed or ignored, shared among friends and treated well, but not to be loved.

For hours, she lay awake contemplating the position she'd found herself in. She'd be the envy of almost everyone she knew with the undivided attention of two handsome, kind men. She ran her fingers through Geir's hair without waking him. Relaxed against her side with an arm around her waist, his warm weight was a comfort. One she never wanted to lose.

Her gaze traveled the dimly lit cabin and settled on Keld who fed branches to the dying fire. Each breath she took plumed in the chilly air but beneath Geir's cloak, pressed to his side, she remained warm. Keld glanced over and seeing her awake smiled his sweet smile.

She couldn't help but smile back.

Never had she imagined living so rough, and she surprised herself by not minding it. Geir and Keld's company made up for the lack of running water and bad food, but as much as she didn't mind it, she wouldn't survive long without nutritious food.

She needed to get to her ship for supplies and the lab. There must be some food she could eat here to live on. She would return and beg whoever came to leave them in peace. The planet Jord was her home now, and she would stay even if it killed her.

# –16–

# GEIR

Geir glanced at Cara who slept curled in a tight ball beneath both their cloaks. The cold sapped her. She never complained, but she tired easily and fell asleep as soon as she sat down. He'd begun making her wear her uniform to sleep in and missed the feel of her skin against his, but each breeze on her bare skin woke her and caused shivering that could take an hour or more to stop. For forty-two days they'd lived in this rough building, spending their days talking and making love and he'd never been happier.

The bed was now deeply piled with dried grass and covered with two roughly cured mega skins. A small building, she called an outhouse, attached to this one now by a narrow hallway so she could relieve herself without going into the snow. A two-foot-deep coating of snow covered the landscape. They'd rigged a crude wooden box that they kept filled with snow, which melted and trickled into their canteens.

He smiled at himself for using her word for a water holder. Her canteen purified the water.

They'd found if she drank the unpurified water she got the runs, which embarrassed her horribly.

She hated to be dirty and cleaned herself daily despite the wild shivering that followed.

Thinner than she had been, the bones in her wrists appeared fragile now. Rib bones jutted from her back. Yesterday, when he'd run his fingers through her hair while making love, the golden strands had stuck to his calloused hands. She was starving to death. Whether he liked it or not they had to go to her ship soon. Mega meat couldn't sustain her, and she'd finished her supplies a week ago.

"Come to bed," she murmured and sat to wipe sleep mussed hair from her cheeks. Her freckles had faded, leaving skin so fine and clear he could see veins through it.

"Eat something first."

She grimaced, but crawled to the edge of the bed and joined him beside the fire. Lips pressed tight, she swallowed and chewed the mega jerky as quick as she could.

"I'm so sick of Sabertooth." She flashed him a grin. "Haven has no dangerous animals at all. We have museums though with reproductions of Earth animals. Your mega's are amazingly like ancient sabertooths."

She had to explain the word museum to him, but her other words he understood. She spoke his language much better than he spoke hers.

"Your honent look like a cross between a horse and an elephant. Leps are original Earth rabbits. I might be able to eat them. Maybe not though as they eat grass. I need to bring one to my ship to see. And your columba birds are doves. The fish might be good for me too. We have them at home too, and I can eat them. With samples, I could check. My scanners will tell me what's safe to eat and my comps can optimize a diet for me."

He nodded he understood, which he did. What he didn't say was he had no way to get those things for her.

"I can manufacture you clothing and get you weapons like mine aboard my ship if I can get the power back on. There will be medicine and vitamins there for all of us."

"Will the men have been able to break in?"

"I'm not sure. I locked the door behind me but all systems were down and I had no time to try to fix anything or search for holes in the hull. When I woke, I put out the fires, set out sensors, and buried my crew." A pensive frown flitted across her face.

"I don't think I was thinking straight." Red spots appeared on her cheeks, and she ducked her head. "One of my crew mutinied."

Again, she had to explain the word.

"I should've seen it coming, but I never imagined..." She slashed the air with one hand. "It isn't important. Ilda drugged me, and I'd just regained movement when we hit the mine."

"The mine?"

Cara explained the word to him before continuing her story. "When your colony ship landed, they encircled Jord with sensors and mines. We spotted them way out. We'd just begun scanning the surface when Ilda tried to take the ship." Both hands rose to rub her eyes. "We hadn't even been on our own a month. I knew she would be trouble..."

Keld entered with an armful of wood. "Who's trouble?"

"My shipmate, Ilda. I killed her."

Keld dropped the wood. Geir pulled Cara close. The distress in her voice was evident. "Did she try to kill you?"

Cara peered up at him with a rueful smile on her lips. "I didn't give her a chance. You have to understand; it wasn't about her attacking me, but..." Cara shivered and hugged him tightly. "This is going to sound horrid, and I don't want you to think we're all bad people. Haven has very few men. So few, I've only seen a handful in person." The blush on her cheeks darkened. "Mostly because I never sought them out. Anyone could visit a pleasure house whenever they wished and ask to spend time with a man. If the man was agreeable, you could visit. Most charged money, but some would spend time with women they liked for free. To entice men, towns built them fancy housing and gave them gifts. The young men lived in these houses till they made enough money for fancy homes of their own.

"If you wanted a child, you visited a clinic to buy sperm or dealt directly with your choice of donor. Some men charge astronomical amounts, and some practically give it away."

Geir laughed. "We have the opposite problem."

Lost in her musings, Cara sighed hard, not commenting on his disclosure. "Our government is purposefully keeping the male population low."

"How come?" Keld took her hand and kissed it.

She smiled and relaxed against Geir. He kissed her cheek, then her neck, and she relaxed even more. The small aroused sound she made excited him. He hid his rueful smile in her hair. Everything she did excited him.

"Because men are dangerous. Or they used to be. Back on Earth, they brutalized women."

Geir exchanged an uneasy glance with Keld over her head.

"Because men are bigger and stronger they could force women to do what they wished. For a long time, thousands of years of Earth's history, women had no rights and barely any worth. The women aboard the colony ship *Haven* decided they would make that impossible on their new planet.

"It worked. We're happy and peaceful. Science has advanced dramatically since we arrived Most of the women don't seem to mind the shortage of men. But we do respect them. Most of the citizens would be horrified to learn Haven won't allow men in the new colony." Her voice lowered, and tears filled her eyes. "Some of the scout ship captains had decided if we found a viable planet, we would steal it. And underground formed on Haven dedicated to saving the men."

Keld laughed. "How could you steal a planet?"

"It would be super easy. Space is huge. If we lied and reprogramed our sensor readings, how would Haven know? Stealing it would be easy. Defending harder, but not impossible. We planned to steal a sperm bank and the tools we'd need. With an outer perimeter warning system and laser platforms, we could destroy a Haven ship if it entered our air space.

"It was crazy risky, but we didn't have a choice if we wanted to save our men."

"Save them from what?"

"Haven. The government has been letting the number of male births decline. Entire towns have never seen a live man. Our media is being censored, limiting mention of men, and worse, they began showing men as being violent and unreasonable. And we know that isn't true. Our men share with no problems. They don't attack women in the street or each other."

"So, Ilda found out you were going to steal Jord?" Keld asked.

Tears filled Cara's eyes. "No, when we realized another colony ship had been here, I knew I'd have to strand Ilda and Teryl on the surface. If word arrived back at Haven, they might destroy this world and everyone on it to prevent men from leaving this planet.

"Veta and Fahyim would cooperate and lie, but we didn't think Ilda and Teryl would. What we didn't realize is Ilda had secret orders. Seems Haven suspected we might mutiny and each crew had a woman aboard who was ordered to release a beacon at first contact.

"She sent the beacon?"

"She did."

The grim way she said it made Geir shiver.

"I'm not going to let the *Odyssey* report."

A scowl on his face, Keld glared at her. "What does that mean?"

"I know there are others aboard the *Odyssey* who will help me. We'll take the ship."

"Just like that?" Eyes narrowed, Geir held her away to see her face.

She shrugged. "I have no choice. I plan to try to talk them into helping, but if that doesn't work, I'll have to stop them by any means necessary."

"Any means?"

"Geir... I love you. I would do anything to be with you, but were talking about the murder of a planet."

"Are you sure they'd kill us? Maybe whoever told you lied to gain control of the planet for themselves."

She hugged him tight, resting her face against his. "I wish that were true, but I saw the plans myself. My mother is on the council. The council has plans in place to move weapon platforms to keep anyone they consider hostile on their planets, and if they believe the threat sufficient, they'll destroy the planet." Cara rubbed her cheeks. "It sounds crazy harsh, but you need to understand the foul conditions women endured for thousands of years. They're terrified of going back to that. On Earth, women were forced to do as men wished with no control over their bodies at all. It was only late in Earth's history that a small majority of women began to receive 'equal' treatment.

"To them, equal meant being able to say no if a man wanted sex or being able to live alone and choose your work, although most jobs remained out of reach. By the time the colony ships prepared to leave Earth, wars had broken out, the treatment of women being a major issue. The women in the more civilized countries of Earth want to rescue their fellows from enslavement."

A sad grimace on her face, Cara took Geir's hand and kissed it. "Now we know you can bring men up to respect women and they can live peacefully like you do.

My sister Bridget is a leader of the underground and on Haven right now planning the thefts. We knew finding a colony was a remote possibility, and we planned for this too, but I never thought... the chances of finding a colony planet were so slim as to be almost impossible.

"Yet here you are..." Keld said.

She left Geir to hug Keld. "And I'm glad I found you. You're a miracle. I love you, Keld."

"I love you too, Cara. Can we come to the *Odyssey* with you?"

"I don't know. It depends on what pilot is on the shuttlecraft and her crew. If it's one of the underground, there's a chance they'll have not sent the beacon on to the *Odyssey*. We could fake reports showing this planet was too dangerous to colonize and that the original settlers had died out.

"Haven might send a second ship to check, but at least we'd have a chance. God, so much depends on who comes. My sensors only showed a few populated areas; we might be able to disperse the population to fool a second ship. We have four years before *Odyssey* is scheduled to return to Haven.

"They can't send a message ahead?"

"No. Only *Odyssey* is hyperspace capable. We communicate long-range within the system only with the help of buoys."

"How many are aboard *Odyssey*?" Geir asked.

"Two thousand, three hundred, and twenty give or take a few hundred depending on what ships are aboard."

"And of those, how many are you sure are in the underground?"

She turned in Keld's arms to stare at him, her face grim. "Twelve."

"So, twelve of you will take the ship?"

"We might have to destroy it."

"With you aboard?"

"There are lifeboats."

He strode forward and yanked her from Keld's arms. So furious his hands shook, he had to pause before he could speak without yelling. "Look at me." He shook her lightly when she wouldn't meet his eyes. "Cara!"

She yanked away and placed her hands on her hips. "Geir, I'm doing the best I can!"

"There must be something better you can do than blow yourself up. And it won't work. Won't Haven send another ship to investigate?"

"What am I supposed to do? Let them blow a planet up because they're afraid of men?"

Keld stepped between them and pried his hands from Cara's arms. "Okay, we're all friends here."

"Keld." Geir glared.

Keld's eyes narrowed, and he tensed. Geir took a deep breath and spun away, pacing the small room. She hunched miserably, peering between him and Keld. She hated when they disagreed.

Keld said, "Go back to Haven and tell everyone what you've told me. I'll come with you. We're no threat to anyone. From what you've told me, your citizens won't attack us unprovoked. Can't they stop your government?"

"Maybe, but that's a hell of a chance to take. If we destroy the *Odyssey*, you'll have ten years or so to hide your people, and the underground will have ten more years to infiltrate, *Sojourn*, the ship being built right now. It'll be at least ten years before they have another hyperspace capable ship to send to check, even if they make it much smaller with fewer scout ships. "For sure, they'll spot the wreckage and the mines around this planet as easily as we did, but maybe more sympathetic women will arrive. Meanwhile, you can prepare to show the women of Haven you're no threat. If you're as kind to them as you've been to me, you can always try to sway the citizens of Haven then. Weapon platforms wouldn't be so bad if they'd let you live here unmolested."

Geir said nothing. She'd be horrified with how his town treated women and rightfully so. The people of Jord were violent barbarians who fought each other constantly.

"Cara, you can't do it. You're irreplaceable to me."

He was ready for her tears. She laughed and cried freely without shame. Her reactions felt spontaneous and honest. He wondered if all women were like this or if this was a personal trait.

Ready or not, her tears hurt him. He gritted his teeth and glared at her, she flinched. Keld pulled her close and rubbed her back, murmuring endearments too soft for Geir to make out.

"Keld, she can't do it."

"She won't. Cara loves us. She'd never leave us miserable like that. We'll go with her, or she won't go. We don't need to settle this right this second or even worry about it till she speaks with whoever arrives. Let's worry about right now. She needs food to eat and warmer clothes. She needs her ship."

Geir threw his hands up and spun away.

Soft and low she whispered his name as if she feared he'd reject her.

"I'm not angry with you; I'm worried."

"Me too," she said in a small voice.

"Keld's, right. Let's go to your ship tomorrow. I figure it'll take us eight days of hiking."

She shivered.

"We'll bring the furs and all the mega meat. Keld and I will keep you warm."

Her cheeks flushed, and her eyes lit, making him grin. Keld moaned softly and slid his hands under her shirt. Her gaze locked on him, she arched her back and turned her head so Keld could kiss her neck. Familiar with what she liked now, Keld kissed her neck while fondling her breasts.

Geir began removing his clothing. Keld touched her, but she wanted him. It was evident in the way she stared.

"Kiss me," she whispered in a breathy voice.

Geir obliged. Keld stepped back and dropped his pants then hers and took her from behind, making her cry out. Moaning Keld's name, she thrust back. Her hands braced on Geir's hips, she leaned forward and took him in her mouth as Keld surged behind her.

Geir threw his head back and groaned. The feel of her lips on his cock made him throb. Her soft excited cries made him clench his fists in her hair, trying to hold back his orgasm.

"Cara," Keld pulled away and turned her to face him, walking her backward to the bed. "Lay down, it'll be warmer."

"I'm hot now."

He chuckled and pushed her onto the furs. Geir knelt beside the bed. Keld drew the fur around her shoulders, rubbing his hands across her back and arms. With his back against the cabin wall, he lifted her and settled her on his lap. Face to face with his cock inside her, he held the fur around her shoulders.

"Let her suck you now," Keld said.

Cara moaned and reached for him.

"See, she likes the idea."

"You get me so wet," Cara said and kissed Keld hard.

"Come for me, Cara." Keld clutched the fur around her shoulders with one hand and played with her nipples with his other.

She turned and reached for Geir.

Geir stepped forward close enough she could suck him again. He was surprised when Keld began rubbing his balls. He was shocked when Keld began licking his cock too. Cara moaned loudly and began jerking her hips against Keld. The two of them took turns sucking him. His excitement grew as hers did.

"God, that's so hot." Head thrown back, she rocked hard on Keld and came with a long drawn out groan.

Her pleasure made him come. Geir pulled the fur away and spurted across her breasts. Keld cried out and came too. Geir fell to his knees and hugged them.

Collapsed across Keld's chest. Keld held her up with one arm and hugged Geir with the other. Geir pulled the fur over her back. Cara fell asleep with her head on Keld's shoulder.

"No sex on this trip, Keld. It's going to be tiring for her. I wish I could leave her here with you and go get what she needs, but the ship won't open for me."

"We should've gone sooner." Keld smoothed her hair and frowned at the blond strands that stuck to his fingers. "If she dies..." Keld stopped speaking and turned his head to hide the tears.

Geir took Cara from Keld and laid her on the fur, then covered her with the other fur and their cloaks. "We'll use the door as a sled and pull her across the plains. The mountains will be rough. We'll need to make her eat. If we stop to let her sleep a few hours in the afternoon and travel at night with the light from her comp, maybe we can shave a day off. Her comp will warn us if a large animal is close."

"Ten feet... And only she can fire the gun."

"We'll lay her between us on the door and take turns keeping watch. Keep your hand on hers and pull the trigger for her if she's asleep. Wrapped in my cloak with the furs and us she should be warm enough."

Keld stood, stepped carefully over her, and began dressing. "Let's make the deer skin into mittens and a hat. She can cut two more holes in the door so if we can carry her on it. Cut the deer hide into extra strips in case we break one."

Geir kissed Cara's forehead before dressing. "Pack all our food in your pack. I'll carry the leather. If we cut thin strips, maybe we can sew the two skins together. When she isn't in the sled, we can take turns wearing it like a poncho. She'll do better in our cloaks, the skins are too heavy for her to carry."

"What'll we do if we get there and others are still there?"

"Hopefully, Cara can shoot them and get us inside her ship. Once inside, assuming they haven't broken in and wrecked the place, it'll take her ten minutes to program guns for us."

"And if they have wrecked it or ruined her food?"

"We take her back to Ludger. What else can we do? There's fruit there and fish. There'll be leps and honents, maybe something will help her."

"They'll never let us keep her, and she'll hate it there."

"We'll tell them about the ship. A woman for all of them if they treat them nice. And tools. We'll tell them everything. What do we have to lose?"

"Everything."

"We'll lose it all if we do nothing too."

"I know. This scares me to death."

# -17-
# CARA

Cara huddled beneath the furs and shivered. The crude mittens on her hands made holding her pack awkward. Keld and Geir pulled her through three feet of snow. She should've made them go weeks ago, but she'd been selfish. The days in their rough cabin filled with love and learning had been the happiest of her life.

She missed the freedom of flight but could happily spend years with just them. She understood them now and only tripped occasionally on their language. They'd learned some of hers too. She'd have to teach them more. Enough to speak to whoever came to check the beacon in case she died.

The first two days of travel hadn't been too bad. The hike through the burnt woods to the plain had tired her, but they'd laughed and joked as they pulled her across the plain. She'd fallen asleep not waking till they reached the hills. The climb to the top tired her. The climb to the bottom after a night trying to sleep in the painful cold exhausted her. They'd pulled her across the plains again.

She'd collapsed halfway up the next mountain. Too weak and dizzy to stand, they'd carried her to the top. She didn't remember much of that. The effort to focus had been too much. Snow had fallen that night. The men had made a quick igloo and laid beside her, all three shivering. She'd been amazed to wake in the morning, sure they'd freeze to death in the night. The foot of fresh snow had insulated the igloo, and for the first time in two days, she'd been warm. They let her sleep a day, making her eat and drink every time she woke.

While she'd slept, the sun had melted the top layer of snow, which refroze into a sheet of ice easier to pull her across but harder for them to trudge through. Each step plunged their feet through the top layer and took effort to remove. They wouldn't let her try to walk, insisting she stay beneath the furs. Because the sled flowed easily across the frozen snow, she'd agreed.

Her comp kept them on track. Geir wore it on his wrist. She'd explained how it worked to both of them, but Keld never really grasped the map. Geir understood it and used it as easily as she.

While they pulled her, she told Geir all about her ship. The simplest things sometimes took hours to explain as he had no words for them or she lacked the words to make her meaning clear.

She'd woken this morning feeling sick. Nausea roiled her stomach, and she was sure she had a fever. A bitter wind threw snow into the air. Snow that felt like fire on the bare skin of her face. She'd dozed and woken needing to vomit.

She'd fought with Geir when he tried to carry her, finally getting her way. Carrying her would exhaust him to no purpose. Only reaching her ship would save her. Now they skidded and slipped, hurrying down a mountainside. The night air felt surprisingly warm. It angered her how weak she was. Too weak to throw off the smotheringly hot furs.

Bright light and darkness jumbled. Keld held her and sang a sweet song from his childhood. Then Geir yelled at her, making her cry. She forgot how to speak to him and realized she dreamed when he cried.

Darkness clouded her vision, and her sleep deepened.

# -18-

# GEIR

Dim yellow radiance from the  comp on his wrist illuminated the snow before Geir. Keld followed, pulling the sled they'd tied Cara to two days ago. Exhausted like never before in his life, Geir broke the trail with only the weak light from her comp to guide him.

Fatigue made him slow and clumsy. He fell every few feet, tripping over interlaced firtin branches or rocks hidden beneath the snow and too sluggish to react. Snow, disturbed from his passage, showered down on him. Every hundred yards or so they had to wipe snow off Cara. Dread filled him at each stop. One of these stops she wouldn't be breathing when he checked.

Filthy, lying in vomit and shit, he was scared taking the time to clean her would use up her allotted minutes. She'd stopped raving and sunk into unconsciousness hours ago. He and Keld hadn't slept in two days. Instead, they'd hiked through the night. Keld pulled her while he led the way. Geir pulled her during the day. The small red dot representing her ship on the comp grew closer with maddening slowness.

They were close now. Fire had swept this plain. She'd said she'd run through a mile-long swath of burned plain before reaching the trees.

The dot on the comp appeared to be right on them. He'd wanted to scout first and ensure no one waited, but she couldn't wait. He hoped to the gods he remembered the code to enter and how to use her equipment.

"No fires," Keld said softly.

"When we arrive, I'll find the door."

She'd described her ship so he knew where it would be, but he didn't know from what direction he would arrive. A faint glimmer caught his eye. He halted and pulled the scope from his vest.

An amazed gasp escaped him. Despite knowing what to expect, the sight of her ship awed him. Two hundred yards long and equally as high, a long metal fin with a jagged edge cut a deep furrow into the ground. Tilted on its side, the graceful man-made nature of its design was obvious. No one seeing this would believe for a moment it was a rock fallen from space.

"This way." Excited their journey was ended, a boost of adrenaline propelled him through the snow. He caught his shin painfully on something beneath the snow and grunted a warning to Keld.

Geir found the door easily. Her limb body thrown over his shoulder, he pressed her cold hand to the metal plate and sobbed when it turned green. Cold and fear made his finger shake as he punched in the ten-digit code she'd made him memorize.

The door hissed open, letting out a wave of fetid air. He handed her to Keld to scramble inside, having to pull himself up four feet. The awkward angle of the craft made footing treacherous. On his stomach, he leaned out and took her from Keld.

Without waiting for Keld to enter, he put her over his shoulder and headed to their med-bay.

"Close the door behind you," he called over his shoulder.

The inside of the ship felt much warmer than the outside. She'd tried to explain about the metal polymer of the ship's hull, but all he'd understood was it somehow insulated from the cold of space and heat of reentry, keeping the interior a pleasant seventy degrees.

The odd shapes of unknown equipment, which at any other time he'd have found fascinating, failed to distract him from his goal.

Her med-bay was as she described it. He left her on the floor beside the door and closed his eyes to better envision her mumbled instructions.

He needed to find the red table and hit the black switch on the lower left corner. If the table top lit, that meant the emergency power still worked. He could close the lid over her naked body and leave her there. A screen would show the sensor's diagnosis, and the drawers along the right side would dispense medicine. She'd told him how to set the machine to automatic, but he was afraid to try it. She'd worried the machine would reject his commands as he wasn't programmed for its use.

The bed was easy to find and to his relief lit up. His hands trembled as he stripped her clothing. By the time she was naked, Keld joined him. Keld used the remaining water he carried to clean her as best he could, and they lifted her to the table.

"Captain Cara NiClearin Martason."

The mechanical woman's voice made him jump.

"Condition critical. Immediate action needed. Close the hood and step back."

Geir was relieved the table had built in ties. The machine had repeated itself twice, growing louder each time as he and Keld fumbled with the unfamiliar material. The angle of the ship made it impossible to just lay her there. Tied by her hands, she dangled in a sure to be uncomfortable manner but didn't wake.

The glass top wouldn't budge.

"Stop, don't break it. Look for a lever." Geir pulled Keld away. "This machine is meant to be used by untrained people. It'll be obvious." Geir found the small red lever in moments.

The top hissed as it touched the table. The surface on which she lay leveled itself. A hard thunk followed, and a green screen sprang to life. White writing flowed across the screen.

Nothing happened for ten minutes. Minutes Geir spent clenching his hands and trying to remember her instructions on the uses of the various devices the machine might dispense.

A low tone sounded, and a yellow light blinked as a drawer on the side of the machine slid open. "Use the clear liquid to clean injection site. Dispense antibiotic in the right shoulder." The mechanical voice repeated the instructions till he picked up the thin metal tube. On the screen, an image of Cara appeared with a red circle on her right shoulder. He examined the metal tube carefully with the comp light.

As she described, it had a pointy end and a plunger on top. Beside the syringe lay a soft hank of material and bottle of clear liquid. He used it as the machine instructed to clean the area before injecting her, then replaced all the materials and closed the drawer.

He didn't understand a word of the next instructions.

"I think that's the inhaled stuff," Keld said as he peered over his shoulder.

Geir examined the strange device. It looked like the one she'd described. He gingerly placed the two rubber tips in her nostrils and pressed the plunger then replaced it in the drawer and closed it. The machine prescribed three more shots and four bags of liquid attached to a metal cuff that slid over her wrist, then told him to close the cover again.

A smoky haze filled the interior, and the table glowed with a yellow light. Writing he couldn't read filled the screen.

A tone sounded, and the fog disappeared. The light dimmed, and hood rose. "Condition stable," the mechanical voice said.

The drawer opened, and Geir spent ten more minutes injecting, rubbing white ointment over the red rash on her face, and green ointment over the irritated red of her inner thighs. He replaced the cuff on her wrist with new, bigger bags of fluid before the machine told him to put her on the green bed.

Inert, the green bed had a softer surface and the same glass hood. Daringly, he hit the black switch on the front left corner and grinned at Keld as tiny lights sprang on around the edges. The bed whirred as the legs adjusted to keep her level. He straightened her as best he could. Keld kissed her cheek and smoothed her hair back.

"Will she be okay?"

"I'm not sure. Stable means to hold still and critical means urgent, so maybe." Geir kissed her lips and stepped back. Without him doing anything the hood lowered across the bed. Beneath her, the bedding glowed a soft green. A thick liquid emerged from the green bedding. In moments, it covered her body.

His shoulders tightened as the liquid approached her face. Beside him, Keld tensed. Both relaxed as the bed whirred and her head rose from the thick goop. Green puffy protrusions held her head up and slightly tilted. Fog again filled the interior and a comp screen lit. White writing he recognized as her numbers, but couldn't read, raced across the screen, then settled into a display that changed by one symbol every second.

"A timer I think." Geir stretched and dropped his cloak on the floor, then kicked off his boots and stretched out. "Get some rest. I'm sure a tone will sound when it's finished, or she needs care."

He kept the light from the comp on his wrist on till Keld laid beside him. The soft glow from the red table threw shadows over the strange room. He fell asleep pondering the amazing changes in his life.

Keld still slept when he woke. The numbers on the comp screen still flickered, changing every second. He recognized the individual symbols and counted down with the machine, "Nine, eight, seven, six, five.... When he got to zero it began again, and the larger number seven beside it flicked to six. A long string of numbers remained. She'd be in the box quite a while longer.

He used the light from his comp to examine the room. The artistry of the metal work impressed him. Every surface fitted smoothly together. The sheer amount of metal in the room left him in awe.

In his lifetime, he'd never seen nor imagined there could be this much metal in the world. Metal tools and weapons were the town's prized possessions. As far as he knew, the only way to get more metal was to steal it from another town. Stories were told of meteorites containing metal. He'd never considered where the metal came from in the first place, but now that he thought about it, he'd assumed it was all left from the ancients.

At one time, his ancestors knew how to take it from the earth and form it. His people could still form it but crudely compared to this. But he didn't think anyone anywhere took it from the ground.

Everything about his people was crude compared to hers. And yet she loved him. He was certain of that. She'd raved for hours worried for his safety. She was willing to kill herself to see him safe. She was willing to kill anyone, and he knew how much death upset her. Even the death of an animal.

Cara had a gentle soul. *Brave and daring too*, he noted as he contemplated the courage it must have taken to leave the safety and comfort of her world and venture into the cold loneliness of space.

Pressure from his bladder sent him back to Keld. He shook his shoulder lightly. "Stay here with her. Call me if any tones sound or anything changes. I'm going to explore and see if I can find a bathroom."

Keld leaned his face to the glass, but thick fog shrouded Cara completely. "Be careful."

Geir slapped his shoulder and retraced his steps to the door. This time he peered about him, taking the time to examine the walls and floor. Small lights glittered along the edge of the corridor, giving off barely enough light to show his feet. He examined the frame and numbered box beside the sealed door he knew led to the command center but made no attempt to touch it.

After ensuring the outer door remained closed, he retraced his steps, passing the open door to the cafeteria and playing the light along the floor not wanting to fall through the open hatch that would lead to the lower level of the ship.

When she'd described her ship, she'd told them she'd left the doors to their private rooms open. Each would contain personal effects and adjoin a private bathroom. The bathrooms wouldn't work, but he figured using one to relieve himself was better than going on the floor. The tilt of the floor made entering her room impossible but Veta's room he managed to enter by pulling himself along the wall and bracing against the furniture that sprouted seamlessly from the floor.

The small attached room contained a square box and small round sink with two levers. No water appeared when he turned the handles. The shiny white material of the toilet glowed beneath the thin beam of his comp. Glass shards glittered on the floor, and he wished he'd worn his boots. He made a mental note to keep them on in the future while exploring. The warmth of the ship's floors made boots feel superfluous, but danger remained. He couldn't afford to lame his feet.

He stepped forward carefully and urinated in the toilet, wincing as his urine splashed to mar the clean room. His shit lay in a lump against the side of the bowl. Her toilet paper felt soft. Slightly moist, it cleaned well. He snatched extra toilet paper, the blankets, and pillow from the bed, and headed back to Keld.

"Use the door and pee outside. Don't close the door behind you. Only Cara can open it from outside." From inside, it was a simple matter of pressing a red or green button to open the door. She'd told him she could introduce him to her ship and allow him to enter from the outside if she could power the main comp. "While she's in the box, one of us better stay inside in case the door closes."

"Find any food?"

"Didn't look yet. I came back for my boots." As he spoke, he sat on the tilted deck and pulled his boots back on. "Keep yours on inside. There's broken glass on the floor."

"Be right back." Keld headed out the door.

Geir checked the numbers on the comp screen on her bed. He wasn't sure, but he guessed she'd be inside for three days. The thought worried him. Locked in the box without food and water or even air... "I hope this thing knows what it's doing," he murmured and laid his hand on the side. To his surprise, it felt hot. He ran his hand along the top of the hood.

"Patient requires immersion. Health will be compromised with early release. Do you require release?"

"No." He jerked his hand back.

"Unknown voice print. State ID."

Umm..."

"Unclear, repeat."

"Uh-oh," he muttered. "Geir," he said as clearly as he could.

"Voice analysis no match. Place palm on the lit screen." The numbers disappeared from the comp screen, and a glowing outline of a hand replaced it.

For a moment, he debated, then placed his palm against the screen. She'd warned them her ship had security measures and told them not to touch the keypads on any closed door, but this was a machine meant to help.

The screen turned red. "No ID. State full name for the record."

" Geir Helge Septemsz."

" Do you require assistance, Geir Helge Septemsz?"

"Not now."

The screen darkened.

He wiped his sweaty palms on his pants. A distant yell jerked his head toward the door.

He ran up the sloping corridor, using his hands on the walls to balance. Keld yelled again. Geir drew his sword. Right outside the door, Keld struggled with a man, holding his sword arm in both of his. Keld's leather leggings, and sword still sheathed in his belt dangled around his ankles. It was clear his assailant had come upon him while he was relieving himself. His attacker spotted Geir, and his eyes narrowed, his gaze traveling Geir's sword. He pushed Keld back and shouted.

"Get inside," Geir ordered and offered Keld his hand. Two men appeared, running around the side of the ship through the deep snow. Both held drawn swords.

Geir yanked Keld into the ship and slapped the red button. The door slid closed with a soft thunk. The sound of the men yelling cut off abruptly. Geir pressed his ear to the door and heard nothing.

"How many?"

"No idea." Keld stood and straightened his pants. "He surprised me. They must be camped on the lower edge of the ship, using it as a wind break. Think they can force the door?"

"No. But maybe they can break the keypad."

Beside the door, stacked in neat rows, hung emergency packs identical to the one Cara carried. He grabbed two and noted with relief eight remained.

"Should we go out and fight them?"

"No. Cara needs us." As he spoke, Geir turned and hurried back to the sickbay. "What if she needs more medicine or can't open the bed from the inside?"

"What if they send for more? Give me your sword, and I can take three men."

"No. It's too risky. And there could be more than three. When Cara wakes, she'll give us guns. We can point and shoot from the doorway faster than they can charge us."

"Cara is going to freak."

"Did you understand what they were yelling?"

"Yes."

"We can try talking first then, but don't let anyone inside except us. Whether she likes it or not, we do what's best for her. Go back to her. Rest if you like, but don't leave the room. I'll go look for water."

The small lights glittering along the edge of the corridor were enough to lead Keld back to Cara. The doorway of the sickbay emitted a weak green glow from the table.

Geir headed into their cafeteria. The foreign words felt odd in his thoughts. Chairs had slid across the floor, landing in a heap against the far wall. The tables remained in place, seeming to sprout directly from the floor in one seamless piece. He slid across the empty flooring and had to use his hands and knees to pull himself to the long counter against the left wall. Thick shards of broken dishes and glasses caught in the corner of the floor and filled the sink. He searched for the cabinet she'd told him contained supplies that didn't require preparation and found it exactly where she'd said he would. He examined the contents and shrugged, grabbing a random assortment and stuffing them in the bags he carried.

He was tempted to open and rifle the other cabinets but couldn't remember if they were on the list of doors to avoid touching or not.

He did examine the cooking equipment, saying the strange words, naming the odd metal appliances softly as he touched each with his fingertips. "Microwave, refrigerator, sterilizer—"

Keld called him. He had to scramble from the room on his hands and knees.

"The fog changed color," he said as Geir entered.

Geir hurried to the green bed and checked the timer. It still ticked steadily. The fog now had a rosy tint. Geir shrugged and backed away.

"Don't touch it. It asked for my ID when I did. Too many strangers might alarm it."

Keld chuckled. "It isn't alive."

"No, but it's smart and powerful. Best to respect it." He handed Keld one of the bags.

Inside each, cloth straps held a full, metal canteen against the side. A scope and charging station fit in interior pockets exactly like Cara's pack. Colorful wrappers covered the food bars. Geir grinned when he handed Keld the plastic-wrapped square packet containing a shiny metallic square.

"Mylar blanket."

Keld waved his square. "Gods, too bad she lost hers the first night."

Geir winced. "She's lucky she didn't lose her life. A family of beringei is nothing to mess with."

"Thank gods she took the pack when she buried her shipmates."

"Not gods, good planning. Standard protocol when you leave the ship."

"Imagine if she hadn't? Or what if she stayed inside? Or we hadn't found her?"

"She'd have come back and who knows, maybe these men would help her. Maybe they still will."

"I wish we could just take her away. Just us three somewhere safe and warm."

Geir snorted. "We all wish that, but you know she won't stop trying to save Jord. This makes me an awful person, but I couldn't give a damn... well, that isn't true. I would save the women on the planet if I could."

Keld laughed.

"Not because I want them, but because they deserve our protection." Geir opened the metal water bottle and sipped. "We could treat them better. We did treat them better in my youth. Ludger became cruel. I think the deaths in Winter House changed him. When I was a kid, we'd hear laughter and singing behind the sanctuary wall.

"By the time I was a teenager, the wall had double in size, enclosing a bigger space but higher and thicker and the laughter stopped. When the men returned victorious from the sack of your town things changed. Suddenly, we had double the women and needed more food. The men were around more, and fights broke out all the time. I get that's why he built River House, trying to keep the men happy, but making the women unhappier made it worse."

"Inkeri," Keld said in a tight voice.

"She haunts me." Geir opened a foil-wrapped packet and chewed the meal bar absently.

"Why did you bring her back?"

"Honestly, I didn't think I could win a fight against the other men. I think they thought the same. Her begging hurt. Until that moment, I thought the women were happy behind the wall. Bored maybe, but content. Inkeri was terrified. It never occurred to me they might resent having to switch men. Shit, it never occurred to me they might resent men period."

"In my town, the women kept their children till a boy wished to leave and join the men. We could see our mothers and sisters if we had them whenever we wished. Once a woman had a child, she got to choose her mate for her next. They were allowed anywhere inside the walls of the town and sometimes the men would take them outside the walls. They seemed happy for the most part."

Keld twisted the food bar in his hands. "Your town scared me. At first, I was glad to be with my mother, but when we reached Ludger, I never saw her again." Keld closed his eyes and breathed hard a moment. "I heard her crying though. She would come to the wall and speak to me till a guard dragged her away. I stopped going, afraid they'd hurt her for talking to me, and afraid they would kill me or put me out. I should've tried to save her."

"You were twelve..."

Keld laughed suddenly, a hard, bitter laugh. "I'd hoped to become a warrior strong enough to gain a place on the council and be able to talk them into adopting our towns methods. When I heard of Inkeri's injuries, I knew that was a pointless ambition. Men who'd hit a woman, and leave bruises on her body, wouldn't agree to be kind."

"What did you plan to do?"

"Kill them."

Geir's eyes widened.

Keld snorted. "Ludger was a clever man, sending his strongest and smartest away. If they returned with more women, he won; if they never returned, he won. Notice he kept his cronies close? The men happy with him, or uncaring about women, happy with their male lovers, he kept home."

"I realized, but it makes sense. Men who want women would fight harder to steal them."

"Ever notice how the unhappiest men died 'in battle?'"

Geir frowned. "Because they fought recklessly or were sent on harder missions."

"Sometimes, but they were sent to die. And sometimes the dying was helped along. I saw Rainer stab Glendal in the back. I'm pretty sure that's why we were sent away. If they had any real intention of following and confronting the escapees, they'd have sent more than us two."

"So you planned to do some backstabbing yourself?"

"Yes. Not to everyone, but if a few key people died, the way would be open for a change of command, and meanwhile, I told stories of my youth to those I thought might listen without complaint, hoping others might want a life where women lived among them and sang and laughed. Like your town, the men in mine fought to be allowed access to the women, but unlike yours, the women choose from among them.

"Our women flirted and giggled. Any eligible man could approach any eligible woman, but she could turn them down. They were proud to become pregnant, and the men doted on them."

"Like Cara's world."

"Similar, yes. No women were allowed to abstain, but they knew that and picked before the jarl picked for them."

"And the men didn't mind never getting a chance?"

"Of course they minded so they tried harder to please the woman of their choice. A sure method to displease one was to be violent. Woman are soft. Like Cara. She likes it when we speak kindly to each other."

Geir blushed.

Keld chuckled. "Aye, she likes it when we cooperate and touch. I knew it would get her hot to see me suck you and I like her wet and to feel her orgasm. I have to work harder to feel one than you do. But now I know how to make her wild. She loves to see you excited. Did you know she never has sex with me without you present?"

"No. I assumed you two made love while I was outside the shack like we did when you were outside."

"No. She pulls away. She'll cuddle or kiss, but waits for you."

Geir's heart swelled. He couldn't help the proud grin, then frowned.

"Don't worry about it. I'd be proud and happy too if she loved me best. I'm grateful she loves me at all."

"We both love you."

"I know." Keld smirked. "I also know you'll never make love to me willingly and that's okay."

A hotter blush burned across Geir's cheeks.

Keld surprised him by leaning forward to kiss his lips. "I prefer Cara too, but you're beautiful. Making love to you isn't a hardship, and it gets me so hot to see her excited. I like that she wants both of us at once."

"She does like it," Geir said thoughtfully. He hesitantly cupped Keld's head with his palm and drew him closer for a kiss. The kiss didn't excite him, but the sound Keld made did. Keld pressed closer and ran his hand over his arms then over the growing erection in his pants.

"How long till she wakes?" Keld murmured.

"A few days I think."

"Too long." Keld stood and removed his clothes. Already fully erect, his cock jutted eagerly. Once naked, Keld knelt again and kissed him, dropping his hand to his own cock and stroking. He moaned loudly when Geir's hand covered his. Again, the feel of Keld's cock didn't excite him, the sound he made did. Keld's excitement excited him.

He stood and began removing his clothes. Keld stared. The glow from the tables made his excited expression clear. As soon as Geir's cock was freed from his trousers, Keld took it into his mouth, sucking till he was fully erected.

Geir knelt beside him and stroked Keld's cock in firm, hard strokes. Keld moaned and matched the movement with a hand on Geir's cock.

Keld's free hand trailed his body cupping his ass and pressing him forward. Geir realized Keld liked his body, he wasn't doing him a favor but enjoying himself. The thought surprised him.

He'd always considered that men loved other men because of the lack of women, not from choice. But the eager way Keld caressed him proved that wasn't true. He ran his thumb over the head of

Keld's cock in a move copied from Cara that he enjoyed. Keld moaned, making him chuckle.

"You like it. You like me. This isn't for Cara, or because you want release, you want me."

"Yes."

"It gets you hot when I touch you."

"Gods yes." Keld groaned when Geir kissed his shoulder.

Geir lay back on the warm deck and let Keld kiss his body. On his side, he stroked Keld's cock as Keld fondled his. "I'm going to come," he warned.

"Me too."

Geir withdrew his hand as Keld came. Keld grasped him and himself and moaned at each spurt. Geir pulled him closer. The two men hugged as they regained their breath.

"Cara will be happy." Keld's breath caressed his skin as he spoke.

Geir chuckled and ran his hand over Keld's head. "I'm sorry I'm not as aggressive a lover as you want. I do love you."

"This is enough." Keld ran his hand along Geir's body again. This is more than I ever expected. I know men don't turn you on. Do whatever you're comfortable with."

Geir fell asleep with Keld's head on his shoulder.

# -19-
# CARA

Cara woke stiff and sore. When she opened her eyes, Keld and Geir leaned over her with anxious expressions.

"I feel much better." She reached to touch Geir's face. "You need a shave."

He smiled, lightening her heart.

Both men straightened and moved back to give her room to rise.

Cara laid her hand against the comp screen. "Med-comp, I'm stiff and sore. What follow-up care do I need?"

"Prescribe vitamins and rest, a pain reliever and mild exercise. Visit physician at the earliest opportunity."

"Med-comp, do I have permanent damage?"

"Negative."

She sat and swung her legs to the side of the bed. "Hand me the bottles from the drawer there, please." She pointed to the drawer that opened at the foot of the bed and scratched at the gel stuck in flaky patches to her skin and coating her hair. "This room smells foul. Can we throw the skins outside?"

"Yes, but there are men out there, and they might take them." Geir kissed her cheek. She turned to kiss his lips and press against him. The feel of his naked chest against hers aroused her.

"Keld, hop on the red table. I'll introduce you to the comp. Both of you could use a checkup." She released Geir to hug Keld.

"Are you well, Cara?" Keld asked.

"Yes. Tired and sore, but I'll be fine in a day or two." She kissed him again then pushed away to examine him. "Take off all your clothes."

He grinned.

She laughed. "Examine first."

"Whatever you say," he said cheerfully and dropped his pants not at all embarrassed to be fully erect before her. The sight tempted her, and she couldn't resist running her hand along his thick length.

"Mmm, do that again," he said huskily.

She laughed and pointed to the table. "After. The quicker we finish the examine..."

Laughing, he lay on the table, holding himself in place with bent knees and braced feet.

"Med-comp, Keld Vigintisz, full access." She placed her hand against the lit screen and punched in her ID number. The hood lowered.

"Report condition. "

"Male, approximately twenty-six standard years old. Missing two teeth. Two misaligned ribs. Enlarged spleen. Skin density abnormally high." The machine spoke for twenty minutes before concluding, "Tests needed. Genetic diversity too great for a complete diagnosis."

"Keld, I'm going to authorize the tests. You'll fall asleep. It could take a day or two, but you'll sleep the entire time. If the machine and I think it's safe, can I fix the ribs and teeth and whatever else it thinks needs fixing?"

"Yes."

"There is some risk. Complications are rare but do happen. The chances are greater because of the differences in your genetics."

"Do what you think best." He sat and reached for her. "Can we make love first though?"

I want to, but... there's so much to do..."

"I'll be fast," he said so seriously she laughed.

"Not too fast."

He chuckled and trailed his hand across her breasts. Geir began removing his clothes. She fondled Keld till Geir was naked, then turned to kiss him. Keld pressed against her back and hugged them both.

This was the part she always found awkward, deciding which to take first. She didn't want to upset either of them.

"Keld first," Geir murmured.

A soft breath of laughter escaped her. Keld slid his hand to her clit.

"Mmm, wet already."

She widened her stance to give him room, awkward on the tiled floor. "God, I'm a mess. You sure you wouldn't rather wait till I clean up some?" She rubbed the flaking gel on her skin.

"You taste funny, but I want to be inside you."

Keld's words made her moan. Geir knelt and drew her to the floor. "Hands only. We're all too dirty for mouths. It's been days since we washed."

Keld jumped off the table and knelt between her knees. "You're sure you're well enough for this?"

"Yes." She trailed her hands over her breasts and down to her clit and began to rub it.

"Let me," Geir said and pushed her hand aside. Staring into her eyes, he drew his hand along Keld's cock.

"Yes." The sight surprised her but filled her with heat.

Keld laughed and ran his hand over Geir.

"God, yes." She reached out and grasped both of them, stroking them as they stroked each other.

Keld slid his fingers inside her, making her buck and groan. " Geir you too; I want to feel you both.

Geir smiled and fingered her too. He released Keld's cock to rub her nipple. His thumb on her clit as he stroked her made her squirm and pant. Keld played with her other nipple now as he stroked her. Deep groans escaped her as she came. Keld pushed inside her and threw his head back, letting her thrust against him.

"That feels so good." Balanced on his hands above her, Keld began to thrust as her orgasm continued. She cried out, and he thrust harder till he pounded while Geir held her legs back and braced her body. She screamed when she came again. Keld grunted as he came. Before the muscles of her vagina stopped contacting Geir knelt between her legs.

"Oh..." long and low she moaned, then shrieked as she came again, squirting with her release, she continued to squirt with each thrust and didn't realize she screamed and moaned till he stilled. A hot blush flushed her cheeks.

Geir smiled and laid his hand against her face. "That was amazing. I love how much you like it."

"Me too," Keld said in a husky voice. "I'm going to fall asleep dreaming of the sounds you make when you're excited. Make them for me when I wake?"

"Yes." Her legs trembled, too weak to stand. "I need a minute."

Keld grinned and laid beside her. "We have time. Sleep if you want too."

She wanted to, but first, she wanted to start Keld's treatment. She waited till her heart stopped pounding, and legs felt less rubbery. Geir helped her stand. His warm chest against her back supported her as she motioned Keld to the table.

"I love you." She kissed Keld's lips and closed the lid. The machine hummed and fog filled the interior.

"Sleep, Cara," Geir said as fog obscured Keld, and drew her to the floor beside him.

"Did you find water?"

He handed her a water bottle. She took the pills and laid her head on Geir's shoulder. His presence comforted her in a way she'd never experienced before. If they never had sex again but spent their days talking and laying together, she'd be content. "Does it bother you when I make love to Keld?"

"No. I like seeing you excited. I love how hot I get you." He stroked her back with one hand. "Does it bother you when Keld and I touch?"

"No. I like knowing you like each other. You don't have to touch him to please me though."

"He likes it too. I wish I desired him more like he does me."

She giggled. "I wondered if you knew or noticed."

"We worked it out while you recovered. I don't mind if he touches me. He's happy enough if I hug him or touch him with my hands. I don't even mind light kisses. His excitement when I touch him excites me. Not as much as yours though. I love Keld and want him to be happy. A touch or two is worth his happiness."

"If I take you on my ship, there'll be other women, and all will want to make love to you."

"I'm content with you."

His instant response made her smile. "Good, but it's okay to have sex with them too. I won't mind as long as you return to me."

"Will you have sex with other men?"

Surprised, she considered for a moment. It hadn't occurred to her that many men would be available here. "Maybe. I can't imagine wanting to, but maybe. No one will replace you in my heart though."

"Cara, tell me if your affections begin to change. Give me a chance to please you before you choose another."

She searched his face. He looked serious, but not sad. Her smile got instant reciprocation. "I promise. You promise too."

"I promise."

"Sex can be confusing. It feels so good, and lust can strike over the oddest things; the way a man smiles or smells or the flex of a muscled arm. In ancient times, men and women fought over that a lot. They didn't seem to think you could love more than one person or there were different degrees or types of love. On Haven, we don't mistake lust for love. I won't be jealous if you have lust, but if you prefer another's company over mine, I'll be jealous."

"Me too." Geir kissed her and stroked his hand over her breast before resting it on her hip,

"If you feel jealous, tell me right away." She searched his eyes, happy to see he appeared serious but not discontent.

"You too."

"Our future will be hard, Geir. Cultural differences can be difficult to overcome. Honesty will help. I want us to live together and you and Keld to father my children. I want to share my life with you and be privy to your dreams and fears. If we decide to have children with others, I want to discuss it first so we're both happy about who and how many."

"That must be so amazing— having as many children as you wish." Geir rubbed a thumb over her fingers, then cupped her breast. "My world is dying. We're losing skills, and the population is less than when I was a child. I hadn't considered it till now, but if the trend continues, in a few generations we'll die out.

"My town is the biggest I've ever seen. We have forty-two women and two thousand men. Of the forty-two, three are young girls. Three... Three new girls born in my lifetime."

"My comp might be able to learn what's causing the low birth rate. The medics on *Odyssey* will be able to help for sure." She answered absently. His off-hand revelations on his life before her shocked her.

"If *Odyssey* doesn't destroy us."

Cara winced. The worry never left her. Plans tumbled through her head. The lesson learned from Ilda haunted her. If she'd been ruthless, and placed her in cold sleep or killed her as soon as the first sensor reading came in, they'd not be in this predicament. She might have been able to lie and confer with others aboard *Odyssey*, restock *Intrepid*, and return here. While she wanted to spare the crew of *Odyssey*, her compassion might get Jord destroyed. She needed to be ruthless.

She fell asleep on Geir's shoulder and had nightmares all night.

# -20-

# GEIR

The dim lights on the bridge brightened, and Cara made a soft triumphant sound.

"Intrepid, identify the person in command-chair two."

"Geir Helge Septemsz," a mechanical voice stated immediately.

"Allow level three access for Geir Helge Septemsz." Cara tapped her screen and entered her ID code.

"Order acknowledged, Geir Helge Septemsz has level three access."

"Lock chair two's screens in training mode."

"Screens locked," the Intrepid replied.

"Okay, Geir, the top screen to the left will show Keld's vitals and announcements from the medical bay. Don't close that one. The top right will be my screen, but you can ignore it for now. The bottom three you can use to study as you wish. The screens there are in training mode so no command you give on those screens can affect the ship. With level three clearance you can affect the ship if you're not in that chair, so use care giving comp commands."

"Is that wise? Giving me that access?"

"You'll need it if something happens to me. Only level two and one can change comp programming though so if you use care it should be fine."

"Nothing's going to happen to you."

She shrugged, "I could fall and hit my head or something. With level three clearance you can authorize weapons for Keld when he wakes."

"How badly is your ship damaged?"

"Pretty badly. It'll take me months to repair."

"You can repair it," he said amazed.

"Hopefully, but first I have to run diagnostics." She had to explain the word to him.

"Then we have to do something about the men outside." Cara glanced at the large screen before them that showed the exterior view of the ship in a continuous loop. Five men camped ten feet from the main door in a cleared pocket of snow. They'd used the snow to form a windbreak and only lit a fire to cook with. Every five minutes the cameras showed that section. The men didn't venture far, huddling together without a fire.

"Can't we just ignore them in here?"

"They can't get in, but they could interfere with my droids." Cara grinned ruefully. "Too hard to explain, just take my word for it, we'll eventually need to do something but that's weeks away. The interior can be fixed first."

"So, what do I do while you fix the ship?"

"Learn. Ask the comp whatever you want to know. To activate the ship's comp call it by name. The ship will answer you if you're wearing your comp or are inside. Use the headset there if I'm distracting you with my commands, or you can use the screens in one of the cabins, but without the interior adjusters the ship is going to remain tipped."

"Can you fix that?"

"It's on my list."

Geir nodded he understood and put the headphones on. Cara had already loaded his main screen with what she called a language primer. He glanced over his shoulder, but she was already hard at work, fingers flying over her screens, a frown of deep concentration on her face.

He smiled ruefully and turned back to his screen. She was extremely polite about it, but he knew the headphones were for her sake. If she could prepare a spot elsewhere for him to study she would. His questions distracted her from her work.

He rested his hand on the gun at his waist and glanced at the comp on his wrist to ensure both were fully charged. Light glimmered along the sword he'd laid beside the chair. Although the gun was unquestionably a better weapon, he couldn't bring himself to leave his sword behind.

He glanced at her uneasily. She believed the men of this planet were like he and Keld and didn't understand the danger the men outside this ship could be to her.

His town would sicken her. He would sicken her if she knew he'd abandoned the women there to their fate without a backward glance. Inkeri gnawed at him. Fear for his sister and mother gave him nightmares. All were in the complete power of a cold, cruel man.

He fingered his gun again thoughtfully. Already he was more powerful than anyone in his hometown could imagine. Her ship held many wonders. With her help, he could rescue the women of Ludger. Or … if he learned enough, he could go alone, and she need never know what kind of man he'd been.

He tapped the blinking green light on the screen and followed the directions the comp gave him. Aa he wrote with his stylus, then Bb. Eyes narrowed in concentration he set himself to learning her language.

* * *

Two days later, the melodic tone from his top left screen grabbed his attention. He was already standing as Cara jumped from her seat and ran down the hallway.

"Intrepid, report condition on patient Keld," she said as she ran.

"Condition stable. Testing confirms subject is human."

"Genetic diversity?"

"Matching genome."

Cara stood before the table on which Keld now lay and examined the screens before her. "Adaptive differences, see, Geir?" She pointed to a graph displayed on the screen. "I need to run more samples to be sure the differences aren't just a genetic fluke for Keld, but I'm betting they aren't. The cold doesn't bother you either, so you likely have thicker skin too. And I'm sure your intestinal differences are the same, they'd need to be to survive on the food here. Med-comp, are the intestinal microbes constructed or natural?"

"Ninety-eight point-five-six percent probability they were constructed."

"Can subject impregnate a Haven woman?"

"Chance of successful impregnation three-point-nine-six-four percent."

"Assuming conception, chance of successful birth?"

"Zero percent."

Geir inhaled sharply.

Cara flashed him a small smile. "Don't worry yet. Med-comp, what steps need to be taken to ensure a live birth from subject and Haven woman."

"Many options, beginning— The fetus would need to undergo in-vitro gastric infusions of aplinticid-AD to suppress the growth of microbes, nutrient injections, and—

"Stop. Second option."

"Before conception host could acclimate to microbe with infusions—"

"Stop. Most successful method."

"Removal of microbes from the male. Sperm production would increase by eighty-nine point three-two-four percent. Fetus would have an eighty-six point-seven-nine-eight percent chance of viable birth without medical attention. With medical attention, the number increases to—"

"Stop."

"What harm does procedure cause to male subject."

"Short term loss of appetite. Potential temporary loss of hair. Potential temporary pain in lower intestines. Long-term effects; the inability to process native food. Without a different food source, the subject would die."

"Med-comp," Geir said. "What is the probable effect of these stomach microbes on a woman?"

"Haven women would experience weakness, vomiting, and diarrhea, increasing in strength to life-threating proportions. Without medical intervention to balance Jord microbes with native ones, Haven women would die. A native woman would experience a decrease in viable eggs and increase in gene SRY on the Y chromosome—"

"Stop." Cara tapped the screen and scrolled a moment. "Med-comp, can you determine which food source affects the rise in SRY?"

"Negative. More samples needed. Hypothesis— all food containing cellulose would impact production as Jord microbes emit DTN as a byproduct, which directly contributes to the production of SRY."

"Med-comp, pause." Cara took his hand. "I need time to go over these results to be sure I'm not missing anything, but as I understand it when your ancestors landed here, they discovered they needed to make microbes to digest the food in ways the human body could absorb. The side effect was lower birthrates, a problem they probably didn't consider too bad as they had the technology to ensure a high successful birthrate. What they didn't realize is it also affected the chromosomes that determine the sex of a child. That probably became clear in a few years, but by then it was too late.

"To fix the problem, you have to kill the microbes. Kill the microbe, and you starve to death. I'd love to get my hands on their records to see what they intended to do. Any mathematician could predict that the women on this planet would die out. They must have been working on something to either get off this planet or fix their microbe."

"Does it matter what they were doing?"

"Not really. Just scientific interest. But you have a choice to make—"

"No choice. Take them out. Where you go, I go. We'll starve or live together." Geir placed his hand on her stomach. "Will you conceive now?" The thought of making her pregnant filled him with tenderness and a fierce protectiveness.

"Not for four more years. When we join Stellar Command, we agree to ten-year sterilization. Our training costs too much to waste. We need to remain focused, which means no children." She stood on tiptoe to kiss his lips. "We'll have children, Geir."

He deepened the kiss till they were both breathing harder. As much as he wanted to continue, he wanted Keld safe first. He pulled away and laid his hand on her cheek. "Go over the reports and talk to your comp. I'm sure Keld will think as I do. Remove the microbes if it's safe to do so. I'll go get us something to eat."

He returned with two meal bars and bottled juice. She sat on the tilted floor with her legs braced against the green bed and spoke with the comp. He handed her the food, which she accepted with a smile and a finger upheld indicating she needed a minute. He understood about one word in ten.

Twenty minutes later, she pushed herself to her feet and leaned over Keld to kiss his lips. "Med-comp, re-run all tests. If tests show same results, repair missing teeth and realign all breaks." She turned to him and grinned. "Will he mind if I use facial hair suppressant on him? I can have the effects wear off in time."

"Go ahead."

"Med-comp, apply facial hair suppressant, male, standard one. Modify nails too standard three. Apply pubic hair suppressant six months, male standard one."

Geir cleared his throat, making her laugh.

She peered over her shoulder and grinned. "Six months of no hair. If he hates it, he can let it grow back, but I like it..."

"Then I'm sure he will too." Geir contemplated the removal of his pubic hair and blushed, but only she would see him like that and if she preferred it... "Six months," he said, making her laugh again.

"Med-comp, apply body hair suppressant male standard one. Begin longevity process. Do not commence microbe removal yet. Estimated time?"

"Two days, twelve minutes, and eighteen seconds. Longevity process is proscribed. Class two verification required." A countdown appeared on the screen, ticking down every second.

"Damn it." She leaned forward to read the screen. "I don't have the authorization to override the locks. I bet Bridget does though."

Geir placed his hand on her arm and drew her away. "Don't go back for that."

"It's a big deal, Geir. I'll live to three hundred...two hundred years without you."

"You'll never be without me. I'll always be right here"— he ran his fingertips across her brow before resting his hand on her heart — "and here." He kissed her until she relaxed against him. "We have time. Healthy is enough for now."

Cara stood to stretch and tore open the food packet. "You're right. We have time to reprogram the comp to gain access. I need to study the microbes more, but removal shouldn't take long. I want the bay open if he experiences cramping or has complications though and I really want to get the ship's systems running so we can heat food and use the bathrooms." She frowned and sat on the floor to eat.

Geir sat beside her. "You look worried."

"I want to stabilize the ship, but I could hurt the men outside if I do and doing so will leave the belly of the ship exposed."

"Exposed how?"

"There's a gaping hole there that allows access to the lower deck. Equipment we can use if we can reach it, but equipment they could potential harm if they tamper with it."

"Then wait for Keld. He speaks their language."

She rose an eyebrow and paused with the meal bar halfway to her mouth. "And you don't?"

Her surprise made him laugh, and he couldn't help the spurt of pride he felt that she assumed he would know anything Keld did.

"Keld wasn't originally from Ludger. Let's worry about that when he wakes. Do you know how many are outside now?"

"Yes." She rose a hand to cover a yawn.

"Tell me later. Finish eating, then get some sleep."

Her eyes lit, and she lifted the meal bar to her lips again. The anticipation on her face got him hard. He hadn't meant to imply sex but was more than willing if she was. The kiss she gave him when she finished the meal bar left him in no doubt she was willing. He kicked off his boots and pants and waited impatiently for her to be naked.

"I can't wait to make love to you in a proper bed," she said as she knelt astride him. She made a deep sigh of contentment as he seated himself deep inside her. Hands resting on his chest, she began to jerk her hips.

He settled his hands on her hips and thrust with her. The small sounds she made excited him. "Cara," he gasped, making her moan and thrust harder. "That's so good, feeling you all tight and wet." She moaned again and thrust faster. "Come for me, Cara. Scream my name."

"Geir," she said in a thin breathy voice then, "Geir!" she yelled as he thrust hard. With a deep moan, she came and collapsed across his chest.

"Cara and Geir," she whispered in his ear, and he came too, each thrust a glorious release.

Snuggled on the floor in a pile of blankets and pillows they slept wrapped in each other's arms.

She made love to him again when she woke, kissing him a long time while fondling his cock as he rubbed her nipples. Astride him again she swayed as she ran her hands over his body. He drew her down for a kiss, and when she pulled away to arch her back and rock faster, tears filled her eyes.

"I love you, Cara."

She stilled and smiled, leaning down to kiss him again. "And I you, beloved."

They made love so long he was afraid it was hurting her knees and rolled them over. She pushed herself up on her elbows to watch as he slid inside her. The aroused sound she made tightened his balls. His cock glistened from her wetness in the low light.

"Soon," she said in a panting breath as her body tightened.

He kept his strokes slow and even until she convulsed and called his name, then let himself go.

Her body trembled against his, and she clutched him tight.

"Cara, it's okay to make love to Keld when I'm not there. It would kill me to always share you. I love this best, just us two."

"I don't treat him well, do I?" She sounded sad and sorry, not all what he intended.

"Believe me, he has no complaints."

"I'm a selfish lover with him."

She was quiet a minute, running her fingertips over his face and through his hair.

"I love Keld now. That first night I wouldn't have made love to him if you both hadn't expected me too. I did it to please you, and I enjoyed it, but somehow afterward it felt like betrayal to have sex with just him." She leaned on an elbow to see him better. "I would never betray you. You're right though, I need to stop treating Keld as lesser and give him equal attention. My feelings would be hurt if you only made love to me with another present as if I were a toy to get you excited, but she the main event."

Geir smoothed her hair and ran a finger over a dark-blond eyebrow. "You're the main event for both of us. It'll always be Cara and Geir."

# -21-
# CARA

It's just like taking a nap," Cara said a week later as she leaned down to kiss Geir's lips. "It won't feel like days to you."

"It doesn't hurt at all," Keld said.

"I'm fine. Let's get this over with."

Cara stepped back. Keld surprised her by kissing Geir before stepping back, but Geir surprised her more by returning the kiss. He winked at her and closed his eyes.

"Med-comp, run program Geir medical." She'd spent days going over the program to ensure there'd be no complications.

The hood closed over the red table. Fog billowed under the glass, obscuring Geir. She waited to confirm the testing had started before leading Keld to the bridge. He settled in seat two and began the language lessons, but his gaze strayed to the main screen every few minutes.

"Cara, more men are arriving. Let me talk to them from the doorway before so many are here it becomes more dangerous for them and us."

Cara glanced at the screen and frowned. She'd repositioned the probe to sweep a three-hundred-mile perimeter. A group of eight hundred or so men headed their way. Keld was right. Talking to the five outside now was better than waiting. By her estimate, the eight hundred would arrive in four days.

"Stay inside the doorway."

"I will, and stay out of sight unless I call you." Keld buckled on Geir's sword and opened the door.

The ship's sensors worked in a five-hundred-yard radius around the ship. Cara focused on the doorway and put the picture on the big screen.

"Comp, record this to private log Cara one-three."

As soon as the door opened, men sprang to their feet and dropped their hands to swords on their waists.

"Peace," Keld said. "Stay there, please."

Cara only caught a few words of the man's reply, enough to know he asked Keld who he was and where he was from.

Keld answered first in their language and then repeated it so Cara could understand. "I'm from Jord. This ship is from Haven, a planet far away. It crashed here, and the captain is attempting to repair it. For your safety, don't stay closer than fifty feet or you might be harmed when the ship moves."

Another spate of words followed of which she caught the word women and no.

"Yes, the captain buried crewwomen who died in the crash. The captain has no wish to hurt anyone here." The men yelled something, and Keld replied, then called her.

"Cara is the captain. Cara placed her hand on Keld's shoulder.

The men outside surged forward but stopped as the biggest man held up his hand and spoke rapidly.

"Just her," Keld said in reply. He turned to her. "I'll tell them what you told me, but go back to the bridge, or they won't hear a word I say."

She nodded, wanting to kiss him, but not sure that was wise in front of the others.

He ran a thumb over her bottom lip, then hastily withdrew it. "I love when you look at me that way. Go." He gently pushed her back.

"I'm going to call your name loudly tonight," she said in promise and giggled when he groaned.

Back on the bridge, she kept her eye on the monitor, but Keld had stopped translating, so she understood very little of what was said.

"Cara, can I bring Mark inside if he leaves his weapons?"

"Yes. Tell him to touch nothing though." No systems would respond to Mark, but she wanted to see if he listened.

Mark turned out to be the older, stocky man with the graying hair and beard. Deep lines radiated from the edges of his bright eyes. A scar lined the side of his face, another cut jaggedly down his arm.

"Cara," Mark said in a gruff voice and inclined his head. His wide-eyed gaze darted about the room, landing on the main screen, which showed his men outside the door.

"Can you show him pictures of your crew?" Keld asked.

"*Intrepid,*" Cara said and put the official picture of she and her crew standing before *Intrepid* before its launch. The women wore their uniforms and smiled brightly, knowing this shot would be the ones the histories used when future generations of Havenites researched the *Odyssey* and her voyages.

Tears filled Cara's eyes at Veta's wide grin.

Mark said something, sounding sad.

On a whim, Cara replaced *Intrepid's* picture with the one taken of *Odyssey's* crew before they boarded.

"Odyssey."

Behind the two-thousand-women, *Odyssey* hung in a star-speckled sky. Behind *Odyssey,* Haven rotated in all her green and blue glory. The men stared at the gathered women.

Keld looked awed as he ran his finger from face to face. The screen reacted to his touch, making each portrait life-size a moment. Bright smiling faces gazed out from the picture. Blond, brunet, redhead, even a few who preferred no hair. Everyone wore their uniforms with hair either pulled back or regulation chin length or shorter. All were clearly women.

Mark and Keld spoke a moment.

"Do you have more pictures?" Keld asked.

"This is my most treasured possession." Cara tapped a moment to access her stored backup and showed them Michaelson. "My relatives." A moments manipulation and Michaelson blurred as the background women became clear.

"He sired them all?" Wide-eyed, Keld turned to stare at her.

"Most, some are nieces like me, and lots more didn't come. Last I knew Michelson had three thousand and twelve daughters and seven sons."

"How old is he?"

"One hundred and forty-nine, but his sperm will still be viable twenty years after his death. Each ejaculation contains millions of sperm, and only one is needed for conception. Most of the women visited a clinic to conceive."

"How many women live on Haven?"

"As of the last census six-point-two billion."

Keld looked blank. Cara put the number on the screen in its long form.

"I know you told me, but I never really pictured it before. There are more women on *Odyssey* than people in my town."

"Did you tell him what might happen if Haven hears of them?"

"Sort of. I told him if the women are afraid they'll fight, and if he wants them to stay, he must treat them nice."

"Good enough, I guess. Nothing he could do anyway. Does he know *Odyssey* is returning?"

"Yes. Will it land?"

Cara changed the picture again to show Fleur before her ship with her fifty-women crew.

"A ship like this one will come. *Odyssey* can't land on a planet. That woman is my best friend like Geir is yours."

Keld grinned and made Fleur's picture bigger.

Cara laughed. "She'll love you. In fact, she'll love you so much I might be jealous. Don't forget you love me too."

A serious expression on his face Keld turned from the picture and hugged her. "I could never forget that. "Are you and she lovers?"

"No. I prefer men."

"But you love her?"

"Very much."

Keld nodded thoughtfully, then turned to Mark. The men talked quite a long while. Keld finally led him back to the door.

"Should we offer to let them sleep inside?" Cara peered at the temperature readings and frowned.

"I believe Mark, but Geir would kill me if I took a chance like that. You're more tempting than you know, Cara. Besides, I want you to scream my name, not whisper it afraid others will hear."

Cara giggled and kissed him. He laughed at her eager fumbling of his laces and moaned when she knelt to take him in her mouth. She stopped quickly and grimaced. "You taste medicinal not like yourself. It's clean, but tastes yucky."

"Let me see how you taste." He pulled her shirt off and licked her breast, then made a face.

"Kiss me," she murmured and pulled him close for a deep kiss. With her fingertips, she stroked his cock till he tightened her hand around it. Smiling, she withdrew her hand and removed her clothes then pushed him to the floor to kneel astride him. She was so wet for him, he slid inside easily despite his size. Hands braced on his chest, she began to swirl her hips. "I love you, Keld. Will you give me babies someday?"

His hips bucked hard. "Now if you could."

"God, you feel so good. I want to take my time but..." she began panting and thrusting on him "Keld," she moaned as she came and collapsed on his chest. She moaned again as her muscles contracted, squeezing his thickness.

For a minute he lay without moving, then thrust hard.

She screamed.

"No wonder Geir likes to go second." He thrust again, then flipped her over to push her legs back and pounded hard.

"Keld, Keld, Keld!" she lost track of what she yelled as she came again in a wet rush, her body convulsing around his. He threw his head back and yelled her name and thrust in short, sharp jolts as her hips jerked uncontrollably against his.

"And here I thought Geir was generously letting me go first all this time."

Cara blushed.

"The second orgasm is stronger, imagine how good the third is going to feel."

Cara groaned as he began rubbing her clit with his thumb, sliding two fingers inside her. "It's too much. "Oh... Keld..." again she lost track of her words as she moaned and panted, pressing against his fingers and writhing like a wild woman.

She screamed so shrilly when he entered her, he stopped with an alarmed expression on his face.

"Don't you dare stop!" She flexed against him and screamed again. She growled with frustration when he slowed. "Please..." a blush burned across her cheeks at her begging tone, but she wanted him to surge hard. To sensitized to enjoy slow, hard felt amazing. "From behind and hard."

Her hands shook as she pushed away and turned and thrust her ass at him. One part of herself was embarrassed, but the part that wanted him didn't care. On her hands and knees, she pushed back against him and began to keen as he surged hard against her.

Flesh slapping flesh echoed in the room. Her thighs were wet with her come and liquid dribble with each thrust until she came so hard it almost hurt. It did hurt when her face hit the floor when her arms collapsed. Her entire body felt limp. The warmth of Keld's semen jetting between her legs filled her soul; she felt every pulse and moaned with each.

"Are you okay?"

"Sore and too tired to roll over and hug you like I want to, but that was amazing."

He chuckled and gathered her close, laying her across his chest. "Four in a row might be one too many."

"Mmm."

He laughed again and kissed her brow.

Her heart still thudded, and her loins twitched, jerking against his pelvis.

"I love you, Cara. You have the most beautiful smile. I want to make love to you in the sunlight and see it sparkle in your hair." He ran his hand over her back in long, slow strokes. "And moonlight. The summers on Jord are short but warm. You'll like it."

She drifted to sleep as he spoke of the days he wished to spend with her.

When she woke, she was encased with blankets, and he sat beside her looking worried.

"Are you okay?" Blankets clutched to her chest she sat.

"Your face is bruised. I hurt you."

She lifted a hand to her cheek and winced, then snickered. "I hurt myself, and I want to do it again, but not today. I'm sore today."

"How bad did I hurt you?"

His grim tone and worried look alarmed her. She pulled him close for a kiss. "I like it. I'll feel you all day. By tonight I'll be fine and want you again, and all day I'll be thinking of your hard cock inside me."

His eyes darkened, and he kissed her hard, pressing her back into the blankets. Despite the mountains of work that waited she held him close till her bladder forced her away.

All day he grinned at her when he caught her eye. Mark returned with another of his men who he introduced as Gunter. Both men examined her face, then glared at Keld.

"Tell them I tripped in the dark."

Keld repeated it. A hint of a blush appeared on his cheeks. She couldn't resist kissing him. She'd meant it to be a fast kiss, but his soft sigh enticed her. Mark clearing his throat brought her back to herself, and she blushed to her toes as she realized she had her thumbs tucked into Keld's waistband and pressed against him.

Keld stepped in front of her, and the men spoke a minute while she regained her composure. She pressed her hands to her burning cheeks and took deep breaths. *What the hell was wrong with her?*

She practically molested him before strangers, and right now it was it all she could to not drag him down the corridor and have her way with him.

She rested her forehead against his back and breathed in his scent, wanting to hug him more every second.

He peered over his shoulder, his eyes concerned. "You okay?"

"Yes." Suddenly she realized she was worried she was losing him, that he'd rather go do man things with them than be with her. Keld was no longer just pleasure, she loved him too. Not the sudden overwhelming attraction she'd felt for Geir but just as real and deep. Sharing his attention hurt. It hurt more when she realized she wouldn't have him to herself much longer, and he might prefer it that way.

"Cara..." he lifted a hand to frame her face. Turned halfway between the strangers and her, he hesitated. "I can't leave them unsupervised in the ship." He turned back and said something she didn't understand to their visitors, then ushered them from the room. She followed and burst into tears when the door closed behind them, and he remained inside.

"What? Did they frighten you?"

Embarrassed by her lack of control, she ducked her head and hugged him tightly. "Make love to me."

He laughed uncertainly but cooperated when she tugged his pants down and grunted in surprise when she threw her legs around his waist, but he supported her weight with both hands on her ass. He pushed her against the wall for leverage as she fumbled trying to guide him. She cried out in a mix of pain and desire when he entered her.

"You're hurt." He stilled

"I need you. Come for me. Show me how much you want me."

He groaned after every word she said and jerked his hips.

"Don't let me go," she cried when he finished.

He sank to the floor, holding her and cuddled her as she cried. "Tell me what's wrong."

"Will you go with them?" she rubbed her eyes hard. "I mean; I know you will, but you'll come back, right?" The desperate, whiny voice made her cringe. She took a deep breath and wiped her eyes again. "You can go where you want, with whoever you want, but you'll come back eventually, right?"

Proud of her steady tone, she sagged in relief.

"I'll never leave you. Those women are beautiful and exciting, but not you. I prefer you. They might be fun to meet, but you're my soul."

She started crying again and clutched him hard. "I'm so stupid. I'm sorry. It just suddenly hit me we won't be alone much longer."

He stiffened. "You want him?"

"Who Mark?" she asked, shocked he thought that. "Not at all."

Keld held her so tight now she knew he was worrying over it too. After a while, she said tentatively. "Fleur has been my friend forever. I don't remember not knowing her. We've shared a lot, and both of us have other close friends. She's had a few lovers over the years; some, she's really liked, and I was never worried she'd cease to be my friend and prefer another. I think because of our shared history. Our friendship grew slowly, and I really know her.

"With you it's different. It hit like a lightning bolt. Within a day, you and Geir became the most important people in my life and without the shared history I'm afraid to lose you, and the pain of that will kill me."

"It isn't history, Cara, its trust. Fleur has earned your trust, so you're free to love her unconditionally. Time will prove you can trust me the same way."

His body relaxed against her. "I already trust you."

She sagged against him, enjoying his closeness. "What did you tell them," she finally said.

"That you wanted to have sex."

"You didn't," she shrieked and covered her face with her hands to smother the giggles.

"Of course, I didn't." He laughed and ruffled her hair, then pushed her away to rise and fix his pants. "I told them strangers frighten you and you needed a few minutes."

"Not a lie."

"I'm more barbaric than I thought. I wanted them away from you too. I used to think I was more enlightened than the men in Ludger but I wasn't enlightened just stupid."

She giggled and kissed him. "Have your meeting, but be careful. It'll kill me to lose you."

Keld smiled after her as she headed to the bridge.

# -22-

# GEIR

Geir opened his eyes. The first thing he noticed was Cara's smile, the second, that the room was now lit with a soft, yellow light. Keld offered him a hand to help him rise. He'd expected to feel different, but he felt normal.

The table now lay on a level floor. A barely discernable hum, more felt than heard, rose from the soles of his bare feet.

Keld wore a uniform like Cara's and had cut his hair short. A handgun was clipped to his belt, and a shiny new sword swung from his hip.

Cara laughed when he kissed her absently and reached for Keld's sword.

Keld snickered and handed him the sword. "Careful, it's razor sharp. I can take a mega's head in one blow." He winced and hugged Cara. "Sorry, Cara."

"I'm okay. I know the animals need to be killed to make you safe."

"What holds it to your belt?"

"A magnet. The red button on the hilt releases it. I made it myself."

Geir rose an eyebrow.

"Well, designed it or copied the design... whatever. The comp has a ton of weapon designs. I picked one I liked, then fabricated it in the machine shop with the comp's help."

It's called a katana. And check this out." Keld plucked a four-inch-long cylinder from his waist and flicked his wrist. The cylinder elongated, becoming a thin, six-foot-long, stick with a four-inch metal arrow-shaped blade on the end.

Keld hand it to him and pulled a flat one-inch-wide by six-inch-long matte-black metal rectangle from his belt and flicked his wrist. A knife jumped from the end of the box. "Switchblade. I made you some too."

Afraid to cut Cara who still hugged him, Geir declined to take the blade. "You two have been busy. Am I finished in medical?"

"Yes, microbe-free and healthy as a honent." Cara grinned. "Horses are prettier, but honent are impressive. Don't forget you can't digest the plant life here anymore. It'll give you a stomach ache. The meat is okay, you could live quite a while on it, but eventually, the lack of nutrients will make you weak, and your systems would shut down, resulting in death."

She glanced worriedly at Keld. "I hope I did the right thing with that. The hydroponics will be repaired soon, but if *Odyssey* confiscates my ship, you'll be in trouble."

"We aren't worrying about that, remember." Keld tucked her hair behind her ear and kissed her forehead.

She left his arms to hug Keld. Geir felt a spurt of jealousy and told himself he was being stupid.

"The ship is stable, and I have power to eighty-percent of the ship's systems now." Cara tugged him to his feet. "We're staying in my cabin. Keld has been redesigning it. You two can arrange it however you like."

The comp on her wrist sounded a tone. "Damn, I have to go, or my cultures will be ruined. Keld, take him to our room and show him how to shower." She kissed them both quick and ran back down the hallway.

"Don't freak, but we have guests aboard," Keld said in an apologetic tone.

"What?" Geir stopped dead.

"She's perfectly safe. They can't leave the ship without one of us authorizing it. Our bedroom door locks, and we're armed, they aren't."

"Who?"

"Five men from a town called Hjalmar. Jarl Hjalmer is on his way here. Eight hundred of his men are already here."

Geir's shoulders tensed.

"She could kill them all in less than a minute. Don't tell them that though. They're camping four hundred yards off the starboard bow. Not that she'd ever harm them. She'd more likely sit in here and starve to death. I'm learning how to though."

"How long was I out?"

"Five days. She did the cosmetic stuff to remove your scars and apparently you needed to grow a new stomach to repair damage from the mega attack."

"You did all this in five days?" Geir gestured vaguely around him.

"The men were already on their way and arrived three days ago. She straightened the ship, and Mark and his men have been cleaning it up. With the help of the droids of course." Keld pointed to circular metal object the size of a rotte crawling across the wall. "A droid. Don't touch them if you can help it. That one is checking hull integrity. Others are cleaning and repairing."

Keld glanced over his shoulder. "The bloodstains made her cry for hours," he whispered. "Don't bring up her crew. I have our guests packing up the belongings in the other cabins, and I'm going to repaint them. Seeing their things hurts her."

"Where did she run off too?"

"Hydroponics. She's considering stealing this ship, but it'll be hard as hell to hide from *Odyssey* because it can't leave this system. The comp would need reprogramming and doing so could wipe the hard drive."

"I have no idea what you're talking about."

Keld shrugged slightly. "It's dangerous. She's preparing the ship though and frankly working too hard. The maintenance droids need almost constant supervision. Hydroponics needs daily tending. She's working with medical to find a cure for the Jord microbe.

"Our guests help with that, bringing her samples to test. They've been very friendly and helpful. Cara is getting portable med-bays ready to go to Hjalmer and help their women if the jarl okays it."

"Help them how?"

"She can scan them and give them the vitamins and minerals they need to produce healthy offspring. If any need it, she can bring them back for more comprehensive treatment. The med-bay here can cure quite a few prenatal problems. Problems with fetuses, unborn babies." Keld clarified at Geir's blank look. "She could even artificially inseminate the women to bear girls.

"We're running the men here through sickbay one at a time and fixing them up. It's earning a lot of goodwill.

Geir stopped in the doorway of Cara's room and whistled softly.

"Like it?" Keld asked proudly.

Geir strode forward and placed his hand on the wall above the bed almost expecting it to pass through into the sunlight. He breathed deep, but the lily trees weren't real despite the lifelike movement of the fronds as if a gentle breeze ruffled the blossoms.

Instead of the off-white color of Veta's room, Cara's walls were a soft blue. Her furniture appeared to be polished burl wood, which only the oldest men had in their homes as it was rare and expensive. Plush mega fur covered the bed, which could fit all three of them stretched out.

"The fur is fake. The room is warm enough we don't need fur, but I like seeing her on it. The trunk at the foot of the bed contains light blankets, but the comp can raise or lower the temperature in here by voice command."

Burl wood covered the wall across from the bed. Keld pressed against a wooden panel on the wall. "This is your closet. I already made clothing for you like mine, but you can make whatever you like. Her closet is between ours. Store loose items in closets or drawers or attach them to the magnetic strips, so they don't shift when the ship maneuvers."

"Does the ship maneuver?"

"Not at the moment. There's a giant hole in it, but Cara insists on the shipboard protocols. We have two smaller flying vehicles though called copters. She took me for a ride in one. They only fit two people. Flying was both the most exciting and terrifying experience of my life. I've been practicing in the simulator and can show you how later."

"You're sure she's safe?"

"Intrepid, display Cara."

The image behind the bed changed to show Cara. Reddish light cast shadows across her face as she pressed her eyes against a black cylindrical object. In her hand, she clutched a thin, shiny knife.

Small squares of glass rested on the table before her.

Geir watched for a moment then turned to her bathroom.

"Intrepid, resume wall art," Keld said.

The sunny glade reappeared. A single culmba flew past and disappeared into the trees. A family of lep scuttled from the underbrush and scampered into the tall grass.

"No mega I hope."

"No, it's supposed to be peaceful and relaxing." Keld pushed past him and showed him the cleaning controls in the bathroom. "Grit your teeth and wait it out. It doesn't hurt, but it's unpleasant."

Geir stepped into the box and sealed the door, already not liking it. It was indeed unpleasant. The high-powered blasts of air and lights didn't bother him at all, but the shaking felt odd and just on the verge of painful. The flaking gel disappeared from his skin, even the dirt beneath his nails disappeared, he noted then did a double take remembering he had new nails now. Super nails.

Keld had left him clothing and a full-length mirror. For the first time in his life, he saw his complete undistorted reflection.

*Not bad*, he mused as he flexed his arm. The absence of pubic hair didn't look bad either. He thought it actually made his cock look bigger. And she liked it this way. The thought made him slightly hard. He ran his hand over his cock till it stood up straight and watched in the mirror as he stroked himself.

A wad of toilet paper clutched in his hand he continued to stroke himself till he came. "Still works," he murmured and grinned at his reflection, then leaned closer to examine his bright-white, perfect teeth. He no longer had a chipped incisor. His skin felt soft and stubble free. He considered asking the comp for a haircut like Keld's then decided to wait and ask her. He loved when she ran her hands through his hair or tugged him close for a kiss with her fingers fisted in it.

He dressed in the provided clothing and went to explore the ship. With lights on and leveled, it looked bigger and even more imposing. In the cafeteria, he ran into the visitors. All five rose when he entered.

"Crew, me Mark," the oldest man said and offered his hand.

Geir shook his hand. "Geir. You're learning her language?"

"Yes, small language. Cara, good. Keld teach much."

"Where is Keld?"

"Food Cara." Mark gestured to the table and returned to his seat. "Sit, eat."

The chairs had been replaced beside the tables, and new plates and glassware set out. A glass pitcher held a pale amber liquid. Two half-eaten trays of a thin, sauce-covered bread lay on the table.

"Beer and pizza," Mark said the words proudly and filled a glass to hand to him. His grin widened at the appreciative noise Geir made when he sipped it.

The pizza smelled good and tasted better. Whatever fruit covered the top was delicious.

"Good," Geir said in a massive understatement.

Mark laughed and rubbed his stomach. "Intrepid, show my men."

The wall behind the table became a picture of night as if dimly lit. The scene scrolled past men huddled around campfires, some sleeping, some eating jerky. The picture clouded a few times, and Mark made an obscene gesture. Geir bit back his laugh. Cara had told the comp to give privacy.

Mark pointed at the screen. "Unhappy." He grinned and stabbed his chest with a thumb. "Happy."

Geir smiled

"Intrepid, show *Odyssey's* crew," Mark leaned forward and stared intently at the picture the computer displayed. "All happy soon."

Geir hoped so. His thoughts flit to Inkeri again. She wasn't at all happy and had no hope to be. He needed to do something about that.

# -23-
# CARA

She fell into bed exhausted and slept without moving till her alarm woke her. Geir sat to watch her dress.

"Sorry, I can't stay. Hydroponics needs attention right now. I love you." She winced as she rushed from the room. Geir was unhappy with her. He was being a good sport, but she felt his discontent.

So many things remained to do that every moment not spent working worried her. When the ship came, if she couldn't convince the pilot and crew to lie, the next best thing would be to make them sympathetic to the men.

The men from Hjalmer were trying hard to learn her language. She had no time to learn more than the basics of theirs.

Droids had set up screens that gave lessons around the clock. More droids built shelters and helped the men hunt and prepare food.

Jarl Hjalmer had arrived yesterday, and she needed to find time to meet with him but medical needed attention after hydroponics and medical was a priority because it wouldn't do a spit of good to convince *Odyssey* to leave if they were going to die anyway.

She missed Fahyim and Teryl her science experts. She tried not to think of Veta.

"Damn Ilda to hell," she muttered as she had to prepare another slide because she prepared the first one incorrectly. She rubbed her face hard, rotated her neck, then took a deep breath before preparing the next slide.

"You need to eat," Keld said and slid a sandwich to her. "Eat!" he handed her a thermos of juice and stood with his hands on his hips till she drank it.

She hadn't noticed him enter.

"What can I do to help?"

"How're the classes coming?"

"Mine or theirs?"

Instantly remorseful of her neglect, she hugged him. "I'm sorry. There's just so much to do, and the clock is ticking away."

"I wasn't angry. My lessons progress at a rate the comp is happy with. Theirs... some are slow, some adequate, a few advance quickly."

"Put the quick ones together, so the slow ones don't hold them back. If you or Geir could check to see if any droids have priority red signals that would help. Probe-seven reports deposits of adamantine, but I didn't have time to finish the report to see if it was in amounts with bothering with...." she cleared her throat and tapped the stack of slides before her. Keld's confused expression told her she was wasting her breath. It would take longer to explain how to read the report than reading it herself.

"Can you make sure the jarl is comfortable and show him around or whatever till I finish this? Or ... just work things out without me? You'll have to do all the talking anyway."

"I'll work out what I can, but some questions only you can answer, and some decisions only you can make."

"Do your best." The cryostat microtome dinged, and she scrambled to her feet to remove the tray. Keld left her as she grumbled over the results and absently ate the sandwich.

# -24-

# GEIR

"Y our woman works too hard," Hjalmer said and nodded to Cara who slept face down on the dining room table.

Keld picked her up and left the room. She snuggled into his shoulder and murmured sleepily.

The gathered men stared enviously.

"She's worried her ship will return before she finds a cure for the microbe," Geir said.

"Will her ship force her to leave?"

"She isn't sure what her jarl will do."

"Are you not her jarl?"

"No. Stellar Command is her jarl. And like a jarl, to cross one brings drastic repercussions."

"So, she tries to anticipate what it wants to cozen it."

"Yes. And she prepares to defy it, but Stellar Command has many to command with strong weapons, and she wishes to remain in her jarl's good graces."

"A severe dilemma."

"One which you can help by presenting a desirable face. The women of Haven like men. If we show them we're not to be feared, Cara won't fight Stellar Command alone."

"Will they like us enough to stay?"

"They can't stay without fixing the Jord microbe."

Hjalmer pursed his lips clearly puzzled by the word.

"They can't survive on our food. Our food is what causes the low birth rate of girls. Within five generations there will be no more women born."

He had to explain for minutes before Hjalmer understood. It took two hours of talking with help from the comp to convince him. He stared at the graph in deep dismay.

"Can they take us with them?"

"Not all of us. Cara estimates there are eight million people on this planet. Their big colony ships can move two hundred thousand at a time. So technically, yes they could move us all, but where?"

Hjalmer stared at the map with his lips pursed.

"Cara can grow food to live on here, but it requires equipment that can't be hidden from *Odyssey*. She thinks the first colonists didn't notice the problems with the food till too late. The difference is small and hard to spot even with her science, and her science is leaps and bounds ahead of what our ancestors had.

"She's impressed they found a solution at all and one they probably thought was a great one. The problem is the damage is accumulative and genetic. Your children will have a harder time digesting the food than you and produce more DTN as an offshoot of that. She can help our women become pregnant and bear girl children, but the job is huge, and she is one."

"We need to become smarter to learn to use her equipment."

Geir nodded.

Hjalmer leaned back and traced his fingers absently over the tabletop. "Her machines are amazing, but without them she is weak."

"As are we without our weapons." Geir drew his nail along the tabletop, leaving a deep scratch behind. "She has made me like herself, and her planet has heavier gravity. Her muscles are denser, making her stronger than a woman here of that size could be."

Hjalmer waved his hand in a dismissive gesture. "Not what I meant. I meant we're strong— with her machines we'd be unstoppable."

"Never let her hear you say it." Geir peered over his shoulder and lowered his voice. "If she thought for a moment you were cruel to women or forced others to your will, she would run. But worse, if *Odyssey* heard, they would destroy us utterly."

"Ahh like a father protecting a beloved daughter."

"Exactly."

"And yet she loves you. Doesn't she know you were on a raid and what that means?"

"She has no idea." Geir stirred uneasily. "Never let her find out either, for all our sakes."

Hjalmer dropped his hand to his belt and touched the hilt of his new sword with a fingertip. "She arms us though."

"Because our world is dangerous. Many large animals threaten us. From men, she's only seen cooperation and been treated with kindness."

Geir told Hjalmer of Earth's history as he'd heard it from Cara. Keld joined them, and the pace of the story picked up as Keld didn't need to stop and explain every other word through mime and pictures.

Geir left them talking and headed to the gym. The first time he'd sparred with Cara he'd been amazed at how easily she'd beaten him; amazed and relieved she wasn't as defenseless as she looked. He practiced every day for two hours, and now it took her a few seconds to defeat him. Mostly because she paused to correct his stance or hand holds.

Virtual fighting was even more fun with the floor level, and he wished he had more time to do it. He reviewed his schedule for the day as he took another three-minute shower. Before heading to the bridge for more study, he entered his bedroom.

Cara lay naked on the furs, half on one side with a knee bent, sound asleep, clutching a pillow. She didn't wake when he ran a hand down her side. A spurt of jealousy tightened his shoulders as he wondered if she and Keld had made love. He left her to sleep.

✦ ✦ ✦

Two months later, he found himself standing over her in the same exact position, but this time his jealousy raged like an inferno. Time slipped through his fingers like water. He understood her systems best so worked with the droids while she slept and slept while she worked with bare hours of overlap.

In two weeks, they'd made love twice. As a youth, he'd naively thought that having sex would ease the need. Instead, it exacerbated it. He missed her more now than he'd thought possible and easing his own need left him aggravated.

Keld had passed him in the hallway ten minutes ago and gave him an apologetic grimace.

"Cara..." he removed his clothing and lay beside her, running his hand along her side as he repeated her name.

She murmured sleepily and curled against him. Her soft warmth against him felt so good he moaned. The mattress beneath him adjusted to his movement supporting and yet soft on the knees.

She was right, it was much better than the hard floor.

A soft sigh ruffled his hair as he caressed her. Not quite awake, she murmured his name.

"Cara, beloved."

Eyes cracked a bare slit she peered at him then smiled and reached for him. His questing fingers found her and stroked her till she opened her legs wide and his fingertips came away moist before he slid inside her.

"Mmm, you feel so good." He bent to take her nipple into his mouth as she let out a deep breathy sigh. Before his heart stopped thudding from his release or he brought her to orgasm, she fell asleep again.

"Don't be angry with me, but I have to go."

She didn't stir.

"My mother and sister are there, and I promised myself I would help Inkeri. You won't even know I'm gone."

He left her sleeping and stole a copter.

# -25-
# CARA

The comp dragged her from a sound sleep with an increasingly irritating tone. "Copter two has left the designated training area.
"Pilot?"
"Geir Helge Septemsz."
"Connect me to pilot."
"Pilot refusing all connections."
"Override controls and return to base." As she spoke, she jumped from the bed and grabbed her uniform.
"Unable to override. Safeties disengaged.
Cara's palms began to sweat.
"Connect me to Keld."
"Cara?" Keld sounded concerned, but not upset.
"Geir has been kidnapped. Or— Intrepid, scan for Geir Helge Septemsz."
"Last know location, copter two."
"Who was with him?"
"Geir Helge Septemsz entered the copter twenty minutes ago, alone."
"Backtrack position. Keld, how could they force him away?"

"I... I don't think anyone did. I'm reading the flight plan—"

"Map of last ten hours of locations on screen," the Intrepid interrupted.

"Cara, he's headed home," Keld said.

"Without telling us?" Her hands began to tremble, and her breath left her in a rush. "He left me?" she whispered. A sick, cold feeling overcame her. She scrambled to the bathroom and vomited.

Keld ran into the room. "No, he would never, I swear it. He must have gone back for his mother and sister and— " Keld cut off abruptly and spun away to his closet. "It's dangerous there. Too dangerous for him to go alone."

Cara grabbed his arm. "Will they hurt him?"

"Maybe. Gods, why didn't he tell me and take me with him?" He stared at Cara, and his face paled.

"No, Keld— they'll kill him?" she heard the high-pitched terror in her voice and couldn't control the tremble of her hands.

She turned and ran for the hatchway to the lower level.

Keld grabbed her arm and yanked her to a halt.

"You can't. All your work here will be ruined, and you need this food. Ludger is no place for you!"

She pulled her arm away and jumped to the next deck, landing hard and scrambling to her feet to run to the next. The copters were kept on the bottom level with the probes.

"Cara, wait. Please— we need supplies and weapons. You promised to never leave me!" he screamed.

She paused and turned. "He has a twenty-minute head start. If we go quick, I might be able to catch him."

"Wait five minutes. You better wait for me!"

She had the copter idling when Keld appeared, carrying two emergency packs and all his weapons. Hjalmer followed him, nodding his head as Keld yelled instructions as he ran across the open ground between the ship and the copter.

Cara pulled up at a sharp angle and immediately went to maximum speed. G-force pushed them both back into their seats. Her fingers flew over the keyboard.

"Cara, the ruling men of Ludger aren't nice. You can't go in the town. Are you listening to me?"

"What do you want me to say? I'm going. They can't have him."

"He left without us because he knew it was dangerous and didn't want you along."

"Like it or not I'm going."

Keld clamped his lips together and said nothing.

"Will we catch him?" he asked ten minutes later.

"No, he's landed."

# −26−

# GEIR

Geir came in slow and low after circling to land in the high grass of the plain. He walked into town unchallenged by guards. No one had seemed to see the copter. The young men hunting leps in the high snow gathered and followed him. He wasn't sure if it was his odd clothing, his bright sword, or the fact that he'd been sent to scout and returned months later.

By the time he reached the outskirts of town, a parade followed behind him. He beckoned to Ulf, one of the younger boys he knew.

"Go find Geoff and my friends on the hunting crew. Tell him I've come to speak to the jarl."

Ulf ran off, skidding on the hard-packed snow.

The two guards outside the double doors to the floor straightened and eyed him with a mixture of distrust and amazement.

"Tell the jarl his scout has returned with news."

"Did you find a town?"

"Did you find women?"

"Two-thousand of them." Geir couldn't help the grin that spread across his face.

One guard stepped back as if struck.

The other stepped forward. "You mean two thousand men, right?"

Geir fished in his pocket and handed the man a printout he'd made of the crew of *Odyssey*. "Two thousand and two hundred women. Let me speak with Ludger."

The guard stepped even closer and lowered his voice, his nervous glance going to the gathering crowd. "The jarl hasn't been himself. Best you tread careful like."

He stepped back and opened the door.

"Wait," Geoff called and pushed through the crowd. He hugged Geir, then held him at arm's length to examine him. "Found something didn't you, boy? You look a proper treat. Never seen such duds. And the sword... impressive." He slung his arm around Geir's shoulders and stepped forward. "Don't speak to him alone," he whispered.

"I'll come with you." He rose his voice and spoke loudly over his shoulder, "I'll listen and report. You all wait patiently." He followed Geir up the stairs into the jarl's rooms.

The door closed behind him with a resounding thud. Ludger stood with his back to him, peering out the window that overlooked the women's sanctuary. Rainer lounged on a honent hair sofa.

Excited yells could be heard through the walls from the men gathering below. Rainer placed the paper Geir had given the guard on the table beside him. As old as the house, the table was finely crafted in a manner lost to them.

"An impressive picture from an ancient text." Rainer gestured to the ragged books on a shelf above an empty fireplace. "Most pictures are much more faded."

"That is a copy of a picture taken three years ago." Geir stepped forward and handed Rainer his scope. "My tale is fantastical but true."

The deep thwap of a copter's rotors passed over the house. Outside men hollered. Geir turned to the door. She'd followed. Furious with himself and her, he strode toward the door.

"Wait. Did you lead enemies to us?" Ludger glared, leaning forward with his hands clenched.

"No, my woman followed."

Rainer straightened, and Ludger smiled.

"You've brought us a woman in a flying machine?" Ludger grasped his arm. "You've located an ancient village? Are they truly filled with women and machines?"

The guard stuck his head in the doorway. "Keld has returned with a woman. She demands to speak with Geir."

"Wait here," Ludger said to Geir. "Bring them to the summer room," he said to the guard. "Rainer, Geoff, keep him here." Ludger strode from the room. Geir hesitated then sat. If he wanted Ludger to listen, it was best to treat him with respect.

# -27-
# CARA

Keld stood before her with his hand on his sword. His tight shoulders told her how nervous he was. The guard returned and motioned for them to follow.

"Nice catch, Keld, she's beautiful," the guard said as she passed.

"Catch?" The guard's eagerness puzzled her. She'd expected some fear over the copter but no one had paid it much attention. Every man they passed had stared as if strangers were unheard of.

Keld flushed.

The guard cleared his throat. "The jarl wishes you to wait in the summer room."

She followed him up a steep flight of stairs to a porch with a low wooden roof. The porch overlooked a small garden studded with snow-covered fruit trees. Four, two-story, wooden homes bordered the garden. A much smaller wooden shack peeked from a copse of overgrown bushes. No smoke drifted from any of the chimneys. Paths had been beaten through the three-foot snow drifts.

Older men peered up at her. Animal skins hung over their backs, and they carried spears. Whips hung from thick leather belts beside long knives.

Their cold regard chilled her. She turned her back to examine the porch. Four chairs woven of thin tree limbs sat before a rough-hewn table. She admired the craftsmanship a moment. On Haven, handmade furniture of this sort commanded high prices. An older man entered the room. The guard bowed and stepped back. Thick black hair shaded to gray at the man's temples. A thick, gray beard covered his sallow, sunken cheeks. A tumor distended his neck, and she wondered if it made talking painful.

"Bring refreshments." Yellow teeth flashed as he spoke.

The guard left the room at a run.

"Keld, a woman for Summer House— very impressive."

"May I speak with Geir, please?" Cara asked as politely as she could.

"My name is Ludger, and I'm jarl here. Geir and I were just speaking. Please stay and refresh yourself. We're thrilled to meet you, and I look forward to speaking with you again."

Ludger took her hand and kissed it. A shiver traveled her at his voracious gaze so at odds with his pleasant tone. One hand continually rubbed against the rabbit-skin pouch dangling from his belt. The skin showed signs of wear as if he rubbed it habitually.

"Geir is just in the other room. Let me speak him to him first before you're reunited." He stepped back and examined her a minute. A bright smile on his face, he left the room.

"That was odd," Cara murmured.

But she supposed she'd react oddly too if confronted by an alien for the first time. The wall separating this room from the next appeared to be formed to come apart, likely to open the other room to breezes in the summertime. She pressed her ear to a crack.

"Yes, she's very beautiful," Geir said. She couldn't hear the jarl but assumed that's who he spoke with. "Why would I give her to you," Geir continued in a sneering tone. She missed the next few words "At least unlimited access to Summer House, but that's not what I want. I want Inkeri."

"She isn't mine to give you," Ludger said, his voice so clear she knew he must be right in front of her now. "Besides, you know she's barren. Or is this one barren too?"

Another man spoke, but she only caught the words, "Let him have her."

"I admit it appears to be more than a fair trade."

Cara's heart pounded. Geir was trading her.

"Can you use her tools and flying machine too?"

The guard returned and cleared his throat harshly as he set the tray he carried on the table.

Cara thought she might be sick again.

"What?" Keld jumped to his feet and grabbed her as she swayed.

"He's trading me. I heard him."

"No."

"For Inkeri. Who's Inkeri?"

"She's— You heard wrong. Sit with me, and we'll speak to him in a moment. Your hands are freezing." Keld hugged her tight.

Her anxiety surged. He shook. Keld's calmness was a fake.

"Can she have a blanket, Treig?" he asked the guard.

Instead of going for one, Treig stuck his head in the hallway. "Frant, bring a blanket."

"We should go," Keld whispered as he rubbed her back. "We could make it back to the copter now.

Ten men in the sanctuary and two on the back gate.
We could cut our way through the wall."

He stopped speaking as Treig approached.

"Geir said thousands of women live in your
village," Treig said.

Cara squeezed Keld's hand so hard he hissed.
She lightened her grip and licked her dry lips.

Treig leered at her. His posture was
threatening, though neither she nor Keld held a
weapon or had made a threat. The town hummed
with the feel of a storm about to break, as if
violence were a breath away.

Sudden loud yells of men outside the wall made
her jump. A man she assumed was Frant ran into
the room carrying a blanket. Keld snatched it from
him before he could touch her.

"Cara," Keld said pleadingly.

"I don't know what to do."

"Trust me."

She nodded.

"We're going," he said in her language

She nodded again. The sounds outside had
grown in volume. Deep, ugly growling. Her
thoughts confused her. One moment she wanted to
rush to Geir, the next horror filled her as she
remembered him trading her away. She was going
to get Keld killed and herself raped.

The way the men eyed her as if were a bone and
they starving dogs, sickened her. Hjalmer's men
had greeted her with smiles and the occasional
lustful look, but not this sneering lewdness.

She pulled her gun a second after Keld. The two
guards thumped to the floor.

Keld began firing on the guards in the garden.

"Come." The wooden rail creaked as he swung
himself over. A horn blew. He dropped and rolled
as he hit.

Cara climbed over and let herself dangle by her fingertips before letting go. Keld caught her, and they both tumbled into the snow.

The guards had scattered at Keld's first shot. A horn wailed again, piercingly loud. The snow hampered their flight till they reached the trampled path. An arrow arced past her face and hit Keld's shoulder. It didn't penetrate but was sure to be painful. She turned and fired at the man shooting at them.

"Don't stop," Keld said, sounding desperate. "If I go down, leave me and get to your ship!"

Ahead of them, thick, black smoke bloomed from glass bottles launched from the windows of the building.

"Don't breathe it. Hold your breath, Cara." All around them bottles fell. Keld yanked his shirt up to cover his face. She copied him and ran through the smoke with him.

Her eyes began to tear. Another arrow hit Keld, then two more in rapid succession, staggering him. If he'd been wearing a linen shirt, not his uniform shirt, he'd be dead. The thought made her sob, and she swallowed a mouthful of smoke, making her cough hard. He grabbed her hand and dragged her into the deep snow between the houses.

The burning glass bottles broke against the house walls sending up more thick black smoke.

Keld stumbled. The smoke wavered and swirled becoming a starry night sky. She stopped to admire it.

"Run, Cara!"

She turned from the sky as he fell in a graceful pirouette and landed in the snow with his arms outspread. *Yes, she wanted to sleep too.* She laid beside him and watched meteors shoot across the night sky till sleep took her.

# -28-

# GEIR

"Cara isn't for sale or trade. Neither do I owe you. She's a free person. They're all free people. And if we treat them well, everyone in Ludger will be happier. Why can't you understand this?" Frustrated, Geir slammed his hand onto the table before continuing to pace.

"Ludger, we saw her flying machine," Geoff said in a calm voice. "Look at the weapons she's given him. He speaks the truth. We have no hope of capturing them when they out-arm us by such a degree. It matters not if he's lying about where she comes from, whether new ship or ancient village, the facts are indisputable."

Lugar tossed the glass ball in his hand absently. "Our people want answers. Can't you hear them?" he lifted the ball to his face and sniffed the cork.

Geoff nodded, his gaze riveted to the ball. Geir sighed and tried again to get through. He swung the bag he carried to the tabletop.

"This is a portable med-scanner. Try it, and you'll see how advanced they are. I can bring you to her ship to show you."

"Think I'm that gullible, boy?" Ludger stalked toward him. His brown eyes glittered with furious anger. "You came back to make yourself jarl. One woman, that's all you brought. I brought this town to life! They're all mine!"

Foul panting breath misted his face as Ludger continued to yell inches away from him.

"I've had men killed for less treason than this. Your shiny new toys won't save you."

"I like his shiny new toys," Rainer said in a dreamy tone. He stood at the window overlooking the garden, peering through the scope. "I'm a god. Look! See how I can make men large on command?" He waved the scope at Ludger who stopped glaring and strode away to take the scope. The two man spoke too quiet to hear, but their laughs were clear.

Ludger handed the glass ball he carried to Rainer who left the room.

"She is only one. Attacking her will provoke her fellows," Geoff called after him. He grabbed Geir's arm tight as he tensed. "Can we not try sweet words first?"

Ludger spun from the window and threw the scope at Geoff. "I am a god. The women see it and fall at my feet. Soon the men will see it too."

Deep and melodic the horn sounded, shockingly loud right outside the room. Ludger turned back to the window and laughed. "Beautiful."

Geoff and Geir ran to the window. "You'll kill them all," Geoff said in horror and turned to run from the room.

Geir starred stunned. The guards threw flaming balls at the walls of the houses as Keld and Cara ran. Unbroken balls littered the snow around them, some still burning, sending up thick clouds of smoke. He leapt at the window as the first arrow arced through the air.

"Ancients glass," Ludger said mildly as Geir hit the glass and rebounded.

Thick, black smoke crept into the room from the stairway.

"No need to panic. They'll sleep and dream of being gods." Ludger inhaled, a blissful smile on his face.

Geir turned and ran for the balcony door. His last sight of Cara— Keld yanking her into the deeper snow.

He cursed himself for rushing in. He should've brought Hjalmer and all his men, surrounded this place and then demand to speak publicly to Ludger. But copters made travel so quick he'd thought he could come and speak and return before she even knew he left.

Yet she'd arrived moments after him.

More thick black smoke crept from beneath the balcony doors. Geoff covered his face with his arm. "Lily smoke. The burning oil is more potent than burning blossoms, smoke just touching your skin can absorb it."

Clenched hard in his hand Geir's gun mocked him. What use was a gun against smoke? He flicked the setting and cut through the wall into the next room.

A cloud of black smoke billowed into the room from the new opening, buffeting his face and making his eyes sting.

Ludger laughed a high-pitched giggle, and thumped to the floor.

Scintillating waves of light warped the room as Geir leaped forward and drew his blade, intending to kill the man on the floor before him.

Keld and Cara lay in the snow. He hesitated caught by longing to be with them. Geoff yanked his arm.

"The roof." Muffled by his shirt over his head, the words sounded indistinct, and it took a second for their meaning to penetrate. The laser from his gun wavered crazily, and he couldn't help but admire the brilliant beam of light as it sliced through the roof. Wooden beams crashed around him. Ludger was right, he was a god. He played the light over the ceiling and walls, enjoying the crash and shrieks of men as the building fell in around him.

# -29-
# CARA

Cold metal clasped her wrists. An even colder breeze covered her naked skin in goosebumps. With effort, she pried her eyes open. She lay on a lumpy bed bare of bedding. Open windows let in the cold winter air, making her shiver uncontrollably. A man holding a spear stood inches from her face.

He spoke to another man as if unaware she was awake.

"Two guards should be enough. The fires are out; you can let the other women return. When Ludger wakes, he'll organize the fights for this one."

"You better close the window and cover her."

Cara turned to see the speaker. Three men stood right inside the doorway. All three carried swords. The speaker laid his hand on the hilt of his. Cara shrieked as his hand melded to the metal and his body distorted. For minutes, the room wavered, morphing into terrifying shapes of men merged with walls and weapons before settling into a scene she understood.

"— water and time and she'll be fine." The spear carrier ran his hand over her breast.

She kicked up and out, sending him crashing into the wall. The wall grabbed him. Cara shrieked again. She shrieked louder when the blanket covered her. It slithered over her skin, and she waited for the strike of fangs with mounting terror. Hands held her down as she thrashed and screamed. The fangs struck on her ankles, and the snake contracted around her till she could barely move.

The room resolved into walls and men. The snake became a blanket that encased her.

"Help, something's really wrong with me," she gasped between deep panting breaths.

"Lily smoke. Relax and let it wear off." The man who'd stood by the door now leaned over her to smooth her hair back. "You'll get used to us very soon. This doesn't need to be scary or a battle; we can enjoy each other. Don't you want daughters of your own?" He smiled kindly at her.

His yellow teeth elongated into fangs. She squeezed her eyes shut and tried to stop her harsh panting breathing, but terror jittered along her nerves. Knowing a hallucinogen affected her didn't make the sights less scary. The scratchy blanket became a million ants crawling across her body, and she shrieked again as she tried to brush them off and couldn't move her hands.

Geir had done this to her. Given her away to be raped and tortured and where was Keld. Had they killed him? Crying deep racking sobs, she struggled with her bonds.

In her next moment of clarity more men surrounded her. Rope had joined the metal manacles. The rope crisscrossed her body holding her to the bed. Treig offered her water. When she wouldn't drink, they forced her, holding her nose till she had to gasp for air. Choking and sputtering, she drank it.

"You'll kill me. I can't eat your food or drink your water." The water had soaked her hair and the blanket. Both lay like icicles against her skin. "Please, I'm not from here. It's too cold for me. Why do this? I would've helped you."

The room began to shimmer in her vision. Eyes squeezed tightly closed, she tried to think of something pleasant, the touch of Keld's hand against her face, the art he hung above their bed, but the memory of Keld evoked Geir who had given her away, and the chains and rope tied about her forced her to think of them.

She couldn't help the scream as the ropes transformed to writhing snakes.

A woman sat beside her when she next opened her eyes. Pain radiated in waves from her head to her stomach. Muscles ached from straining, leaving her limbs feeling weak and wobbly.

"I need a bathroom," she warned as her stomach gurgled loudly.

The woman slipped a shallow pan beneath her and glanced at her fearfully. "Are you ill? The men say you're sick from the water."

"I'm not contagious, but I am ill. How long have I been here?"

"Three days."

"Keld?"

"They let him come as is the law." The woman ran her hand over Cara's breasts and abdomen. "You don't look pregnant." She cast a glance behind her toward the open door and leaned closer to whisper. "If you lie and they find out, you'll be beaten and your man will never be allowed another visit to any house." She glanced again at the door. "I would help if I could, but they'll hurt me if I'm caught. I must report when you bleed."

The stranger was obviously sincere and afraid, but her words made no sense. "Is Keld well?"

"They keep him chained, but he walks on his own. He orders that you be fed from your pack." The woman glanced at Cara's bag leaning against the far wall.

Cara couldn't stop the voiding of her bowls and blushed in humiliation.

The woman patted her arm and cleaned her with a professional air as if she often took care of such chores and they held no meaning for her. When she finished, she offered Cara her metal canteen.

Cara drank gratefully. Dry and scratchy, as if she'd screamed for hours, the cool water soothed her sore throat. She realized she was in a different room. A fire burned in a fireplace, taking the chill from the room. A softer quilt covered her, and thin sheets covered the mattress. Still fettered by her hands, her feet were free. The chains clinked as she pushed herself up to sit against the wooden headboard.

The woman shook the bottle. "Your water will be gone soon."

"You can refill it with yours. The bottle will clean the water and make it safe for me to drink. Can you release me?"

"No. I'm sorry. Only the guard of the day carries the keys."

Cara realized the woman was chained as she crossed the room for her pack. Thin chains on her ankles kept her stride short and rattled with a musical tink at each step.

"Where are we?"

"Winter House."

"Where is that?"

"Hell," the woman whispered as she handed Cara a meal bar from her pack. "I really think it's one of the Hells."

Sad despair filled her voice. She straightened and moved away as a man entered the room. Shaggy blond hair matched his blond beard both equally unkempt. "Has she drunk water, Inkeri?"

"Yes, and voided her bowels again. I've cleaned her and given her food." Inkeri stared at the floor and spoke softly.

"Have your wits about you?" the man said directly to Cara.

Despite the three feet of snow outside, he wore only a leather vest loosely tied with rawhide, revealing his chest hair. Stained leather trousers with undone laces, allowing pubic hair to peek out, sagged around his thin hips and new boots laced tightly to the knees.

Cara averted her gaze.

"Inkeri, Ludger will be visiting today. Your three months is up in few more days. Shall I ask him if you may remain in Winter House or would you prefer to return to Autumn House."

"Whatever the jarl wishes, Rainer." Inkeri's fingers clenched so tightly together her knuckles whitened.

Rainer threw his head back and laughed as if she'd said something funny. "The men miss you. Perhaps you prefer a return to River House?"

Inkeri said nothing.

"Here or there, it matters not." He smiled, spun on his heel, and sauntered out.

Inkeri collapsed to her knees and covered her face with her hands, her entire body shaking.

Cara eyed her uneasily. Her fear was evident. Inkeri was older than she'd thought she'd be. She'd pictured a young beauty, but lines marred Inkeri's face and gray threaded through her blond hair. Her face would be pretty though if it weren't scrunched with fear and her body was pleasing, large breasted and gracefully curved.

Geir loved her, and she could see why. She'd been kind and shown bravery. Inkeri deserved better than Geir though. She deserved Keld, A man who would fight for her not give her away as if she meant nothing as if he had the right.

Suddenly furious, she yanked on the chain holding her. She turned and placed her feet against the headboard and pulled. The frame creaked. Streamers of color swirled before her eyes with each furious yank.

"Stop," Inkeri shouted in a whisper as she scrambled to her feet. "Please." She grasped Cara's arm and turned her toward the door. "Wait. Escape is harder than breaking free of chains. They'll chase you. You'll need boots and clothes."

She jumped away as the sound of booted feet and men talking approached.

Cara settled herself against the headboard and pulled the blanket to her chin.

Ludger swaggered into the room. Two men carried in a portable med-scanner and set it on the floor.

"Can you use this?"

This further proof of Geir's treachery shook her.

"Anyone can use it. It's a medical device. Press the green button on the top and pass the black wand slowly along the patient. It has limited capacity to dispense medicine though. It's meant to triage patients or apply emergency care till the patient can reach a medic or med-bay."

Ludger snapped his fingers, making Inkeri jump. "Strip and lay on the floor."

"It works through clothing," Cara said.

"Did I ask you? Are you in charge here?"

His tone, though mild, chilled her.

Inkeri had already dropped her thin shift and lay on the floor. Without being told one of the guards hit the button and ran the wand over Inkeri. The machine beeped.

"The beep means it needs you to pause," Cara said.

"Blood tests needed. Patient exhibits signs of illness."

The men jumped back as the med-comp spoke.

Ludger stepped forward and glared at the machine. "What did it say?"

"The machine would like to take samples. Slide your arm through the cuff into the device that looks like a glove. It won't hurt. Warmth and a liquid sensation will coat your hands. Stay still till the sensations dissipate."

Inkeri licked her lips and sat to slid her hand inside the glove. Her tense shoulders relaxed fractionally, and she nodded slightly at Cara.

"Immediate treatment advised. Bacterial infection present. Quarantine level two advised."

"What's it saying?"

"Inkeri is sick and needs medicine. Can you bring the machine closer so I can read the screen?"

Ludger hesitated then motioned a guard forward.

"Keep your arm in the glove, Inkeri."

"Can the machine fix her barrenness?"

"Maybe." Cara patted the bed beside her.

Inkeri sat gingerly. The guard stood before her, holding the portable med scanner. Cara was afraid to say Inkeri had an infectious disease. Their conduct made her think they might kill her as a sure cure.

Her frown tightened on viewing the screen. Spirochaetes and highly motile ones. No known species but closely resembling Treponema Pallidum with two extra flagella and an extra inner membrane. Two small tumors laid against Inkeri's sacrum. Another attached to her coccyx and yet another against the L-three vertebra.

"Have you had rashes or any small fleshy growths?"

The men exchanged uneasy glances.

"Not since summer. I had a horrible heat rash this year. Most of the women suffer from heat rash during high summer. The walls keep the heat in and air out, and our wells don't produce enough water for soaking."

"Med-comp, can you remove the bacterium from her blood?"

"Yes."

"How many patients could you treat with this without recharging."

"Two hundred and twelve."

"If the bacterium is removed, will the tumors remain or is surgery necessary?"

"Microscopic surgery is called for, but not urgent. Tumors are beginning and noninvasive."

"How infectious is she?"

"Thirty-four to fifty-six chance to spread bacterium with blood or mucus membranes."

"What secondary conditions does she have?"

"Malnourished. Weakened muscles. Thirteen misaligned breaks, four chipped teeth, two missing teeth. Four misaligned bones. Non-life-threatening."

"Did the bacterium cause that?'

"Negative. Probability ninety-seven point two-three-five percent human interaction caused. Probability sports related injury three point—"

"Stop."

"Med-comp, do you possess solvent or any other means to weaken the metal on my wrists." Cara ran her hands under the scanner.

"Negative on solvents. Localized extreme vibration will make the metal brittle."

"Brittle enough I could break it with my hands?"

"Yes."

"Is the process loud or visible?"

"Sound spectrum of three-point-two hertz inaudible by human ears without assistance. Visible light spectrum NIR three-hundred THz."

Cara tapped her fingernails against the bed a moment, then turned to Ludger. "I can cure her barrenness, but the cure will require she remain celibate for one year. No sexual contact at all till she's fully healed. The procedure is painless but will take a good portion of power from my machine so it's pointless to do it if she can't remain celibate.

Cara bit the inside of her cheek as she waited for Ludger to decide. He looked angry like a child denied a longed-for treat. The two guards appeared amazed and hopeful.

His glance skipped to them. "Do it," he snarled. Inkeri trembled.

"Med-comp, administer blood cleaning and vitamins. Shine level three light on lower right abdomen. Commence weakening of metal around my wrists with vibration." She placed her hands on either side of Inkeri's abdomen and let the light shine for two minutes then turned it red, then green. As directed by the machine, she passed the wand slowly over Inkeri three times as it scanned for and destroyed bacterium in her blood.

"Inkeri the machine is going to give you a shot. It will feel like a pinch on your arm."

"Treatment complete," the machine said.

"You might feel tired, and it would be best if you remained here laying still and undisturbed a few hours before you resume your normal activities.

Remember, no sexual contact of any kind, not even self-pleasuring, to give the surgery time to heal."

"She's cured now?" the guard said with such hope in his voice Cara felt unwilling sympathy.

"In a year, yes," she lied again.

"Lay back, Inkeri." The man gently arranged Inkeri on the pillows and covered her with the blanket.

"Shall I check your men?" Cara asked.

"No, check the women first. What will repower your machine?"

"I need my ship to do that."

Without another word, Ludger stalked from the room. The two guards followed, talking excitedly about entering the fights. Both turned back to smile at Cara.

"I lied," Cara whispered when they were alone in the room.

Inkeri nodded.

"You had a sexually transmitted disease, and it's cured now. How many of the men here have you had sex with?"

"I lost count, but hundreds."

"And do they have sex with the other women too?"

"Yes, and each other."

So, likely all the sexually active people here are infected."

"Can you cure them all?"

"No. My machine will run out of power and supplies. I'm sorry about the lie. I can likely cure the barrenness, just not here; you'd have to come to my ship."

"I'm grateful for the lie. When you escape, will you take me with you?"

"If I can, but I promise to come back and get you if I can't."

Inkeri closed her eyes and sighed deeply.

"Really. I didn't prepare for a gas weapon. Next time their smoke won't work. My ship can level this town, and my friends are coming. I swear we won't leave you here at their mercy.

"What mercy," Inkeri said bitterly.

"In their defense, the disease they likely have causes crazy behavior. Have the men had rashes and mood swings? Things like happy one minute and angry the next?"

"Yes. They laugh for no reason, tears of laughter that change to furious scowls. They've taken to smoking lily flower. Fewer men come, but the ones that do are more violent, and inside the walls, they break the laws with abandon now. When I first arrived here, it wasn't nearly this bad, now..."

"What laws?"

"By law, the winner of the fight gets the woman for one cycle. If she becomes pregnant, he may visit her daily to ensure she's well carried for till the birth of a child. If she has a girl child, he stays her mate till her next conception. If she has a boy, he can choose to enter the fights again to try for a different woman."

"And the women have no say?"

"None. In my old village, we had a say. We could choose from the allotted men. We were happy there. The men were kind, and we could do what we wished as long as we stayed within the walls of town. Sometimes, the men took us out of town too if we asked to visit the river or see the orchards." She shook her foot, making the chain rattle.

"They never tied or beat us or fell on us like animals...."

"Outside the walls here they follow the law?"

Inkeri shrugged. In the distance, men hollered. She turned toward the window but didn't rise.

"The guards seemed kind," Cara said thoughtfully.

"The exterior guards haven't entered the sanctuary yet and shouldn't be in here now. They'll be eligible for the fights. Once a man enters the sanctuary, he's no longer eligible to be a guard till he's old and gray or injured in such a way he can't impregnate a woman. Boys under twelve can enter but don't. Men with breeding rights come and go as they wish. They used to stay with their woman the entire month courting and making love."

"And now?'

"The new ones still do, the older ones..." Tears filled Inkeri's eyes. "They pass us around. I think some can't perform anymore and don't wish the other men to know."

"Why do they fight to enter then?"

"It's considered manly, and they love to fight. Fewer of the older ones do fight though. The new ones are so enthralled they don't notice what's going on around them. The women are trying to keep the new ones away. We're afraid they'll see and join in instead of stopping it."

"Have they tried to stop it?" The room wavered and reformed as she spoke.

"Yes, boys are so stupid. They try to act honorably and report to the jarl. So many have died I can't believe the rest don't grow suspicions."

"Died how? The jarl kills them?"

Inkeri's words terrified her. The injustice and cruelty she lived with were worse than Earth's ancient history.

"Not honorably in fights. They slip down stairs, or a snake gets in their bed, or they brawled amongst themselves, or a woman killed them," she finished bitterly.

"You?"

"I would if I could, so I guess the beating was deserved."

"Tell me about the fights."

"The men gather, and the entire village comes to watch. We used to watch too." Pink crept across Inkeri's cheeks. "They fight naked on the Floor. Once you step onto the sand, it's considered a great shame to back down without fighting no matter who the jarl sends into the ring. He used to set fair fights, the young against the young, and older more experienced men fought each other. Now, he lets his cronies fight the weakest men and men he considers dangerous to him fight the strongest. No man can defeat ten strong warriors without rest."

"Do they fight with weapons?"

"Bare hands. Weapons aren't allowed."

"What if one kills another?"

"It happens more and more lately, but a man can tap out and killing one after that is still murder, so it needs to be done fast."

Cara grasped her manacled wrist and squeezed. The metal crumbled to dust. Inkeri sat and stared in awe. When both manacles were dust, Cara peeked out the window.

Inkeri peered over her shoulder. "They fight now for you."

"The town will be there?"

"Yes."

"Did you see where my copter landed?"

"Your flying machine?"

"Yes."

"Can you reach it?"

"Maybe."

"If you can reach it, and get inside, no one could force the doors. From there, you could contact my ship. A screen like the one on the medical scanner will light up. Repeat after me. "Autopilot emergency override, training flight failure new recruit. Teacher injured."

She repeated it five times till Inkeri said it clearly enough to please a comp.

"To enter, there will be a square box to the left of the left-hand door. Place your hand flat on the box; a square panel will emerge covered with small squares." In the dust of the window, Cara drew the panel and pointed to the buttons in sequence. "Hit them in that order. They'll beep, and the door will open, then hit the red button beside the door to close it. Say the words I taught you and the copter will return to the ship. Once there, tell Hjalmer we need help here. He's kind and will help you whether or not he comes here."

"And if he won't come?"

"Then, when my shipmates arrive, tell them where I am, and they'll rescue me."

"And if the men here kill you?"

"Then my shipmates will destroy this planet." For the first time, she wondered if Haven were right and men an evil that should be wiped out.

# -30-

# GEIR

Ludger and Rainer had stood over Geir smirking when he first woke and left without saying a word or answering his pleas, leaving him and Geoff naked in the cold room. Rainer had returned the next day alone. Cara was sick and getting sicker. He smiled and nodded pleasantly when Geir told him she couldn't eat their food or water.

He stood over him now, his cold, gray eyes flitted to Geoff, and he smiled. "I still owe you for Sven. Don't think we've forgotten. A year alone down here to think about it and you'll take his place willingly."

"And when Cara's crew comes?" Geir asked.

"That old fairy tale?" Rainer crouched in front of Geir. "You'll tell us soon enough where you found the ancient's artifacts."

"I told the truth."

"I hope you did. With lily fire, we can take them all. With that many, I won't have to stop when they start to scream. Ludger will realize how dangerous your woman is soon and let me finish her." Rainer giggled like a girl when Geir swore. "I'll be deep inside her with my knife and cock; I can hardly wait." He stood, but turned back by the door. "We got the idea of lily bombs from you, by the way, so thanks for that."

"Me?"

"Sure, we had to keep Inkeri quiet, and we couldn't kill her. Your suggestion of a flower to calm her worked like a charm. A single flower in her room kept her nice and quiet and the water it sat in still smelled. It worked better if you drank it. Lily flower infused in oil works amazing to relax them."

"You're drugging them?" Geoff said, sounding sick

Geir felt sick. He'd meant to help Inkeri, worried over the pain of her wounds, and instead weakened her to allow the abuse to go on unchecked.

"Some of them. They're more fun undrugged though. Burned Lily flower oil is incredibly potent. The longer it seeps, the stronger it is."

"You could have burned down the sanctuary," Geoff spat.

"Just the buildings." Loud cheers above him grabbed his attention. "Well, I don't want to miss these fights. She looks to be a lively one, and I love to break them in." He laughed when the chains brought Geir up short.

"Oh, by the way, she thinks you traded her for Inkeri. The lily flower makes her rave. Seems you broke her heart and all she wants is Keld now. We'll let her watch his execution."

The door closed with a soft snick. Tears of furious anger filled Geir's eyes as he yanked futilely on the chains holding him. Above him, the sound of men laughing and calling wagers drifted through the thick floorboards. He yanked again, harder.

"Stop, you'll hurt yourself for nothing." Geoff stood, making the chains around his right foot rattle.

"He's crazy."

"More so by the day," Geoff agreed.

"He'll kill them all."

"What possessed you to return without back-up?"

"I thought I could reason with Ludger. I didn't realize he was crazy. Anyone could see I told the truth. Only a crazy man would turn his back on the chance to acquire weapons like mine and make friends with a planet populated by women. I'm an idiot. Gods, she must be frantic. Inkeri, Lily... I needed to fix that before she saw."

Geoff snorted.

Geir pulled on the chain again. His finger caught in the center link; pulling it free left a long gouge in the metal he could feel. Of course— his nails. He'd forgotten they were stronger now. He began scratching at the metal. Small curls and flakes drifted.

Above them, the crowd cheered a victor.

"Try the wood it's attached to instead."

Short chains brought Geir up short as he tried to turn. Thick, metal, chains held his hands behind his back with bare inches of slack to allow movement. The chains connected to a metal ring in a wooden post less than a foot from the ground, forcing him into a sitting position in the middle of the narrow aisle.

Hunched awkwardly, and half squatting, he managed to bring his hands to the wooden beam to which his manacles attached. The wood peeled from his fingernails in long strips. In minutes, he was free. He freed Geoff next, ignoring the rough wood that stabbed his fingertips and made them bleed.

"Can you squeeze through the air grate?" Geoff asked doubtfully as he inspected the metal latch on the metal door.

Thick rock walls encased them. Casks and wooden crates filled the storeroom. Made by the ancients, a smooth rock floor connected seamlessly to the rock walls. Metal, mesh grates covered two-foot long slits in the walls meant to promote air flow between storage rooms. The two men restacked the crates to reach the grate. The wooden frame surrounding it was so old Geir pulled the grate out with one hard tug.

"I be smaller than you, boy. Let me try first. No great loss if I'm left dangling," Geoff said.

The men above them cheered another winner. Each cheer made Geir cringe. She must be terrified, living a nightmare come true. No way would she stay willingly. To keep her they would have to chain her as they did him. *And she thought herself abandoned or maybe Rainer lied*, he thought hopefully.

Geoff squirmed his way through the narrow opening. "Wait there," he called back softly through the opening.

Geir snorted, *as if he had a choice.* His shoulders wouldn't fit through that opening. Icy shivers traveled from his cold feet up his spine as he pressed against the cold metal door, trying to hear. The thick metal blocked all but the faintest sounds of a scuffle. Above him, the crowd quieted.

"Fight me if you're man enough. I am a free person, not a prize to be given at a man's whim. Or are you cowards, afraid to fight me in a fair fight?"

"No, Cara!" he screamed, knowing it was futile. She'd never hear him above the loud yells from the crowd. Men arguing drown out her voice as she continued to yell.

# -31-
# CARA

The men unwillingly parted for her to let her reach the edge of the sandy floor. Her elbows and kicks pushed them aside. They seemed unwilling to touch her.

"I have a right." She dropped the blanket and stepped onto the sand naked. "Will you drug me like cowards and use force? You'll never have me willingly without respect." The faces wavered becoming fanged animals before resuming their real shapes. She almost laughed. It was as if she saw their souls.

A tall, dark-haired man, who stood before Ludger, handed his sword to the man beside him and stepped forward. "This is no place for a woman."

One leg slightly back, the other forward and braced, she waited till he was in striking ranged. In one move, she stepped forward and pivoted as she grabbed at his throat. Blood droplets sprayed. The body tumbled to the ground at her feet. She flung the bits of bone and skin she clutched at Ludger. It fell far short, scattering over the corpse twitching on the ground.

For a moment, the corpse wavered in her eyes, becoming a crouching mega before resuming its human shape.

"Bring me Keld!" Her shriek got no response, and it took a moment for her heart to resume beating normally. Anger such as she'd never experienced heated her till she didn't feel the cold. She would kill them all, rip these man-animals to shreds with her claws and teeth. The room wavered again, spinning in dizzying whirls, and she cursed herself for not using the med-scanner on herself.

"Pathetic. Not a man here is worthy of me." She turned her back on Ludger and faced the naked men on the edge of the ring. "Your women are untrained, so you feel free to abuse them. I am not. You should be ashamed of the way you treat people in your care. But you're cowards too afraid of a sick old man to stand up for what you know is right. You can strip me and tie me, but I'll break free again and again, and when I do, I'll kill you. You'll need to bring friends to hold me down to rut like animals. I will never submit! Bring me Keld or have you cowards killed him?"

She waited for the yelling to escalate, then said softly, "Or you can fight me in a fair fight, and if you win, I'll submit. My children will be fathered by real men."

The last taunt did it. A man stepped forward. He approached her cautiously, his gaze on her hands. She kicked as he sprang forward.

He screamed shrilly as her foot connected with his balls. Moaning, he fell to the floor. She stomped down as hard as she could with her heel. He gagged and choked and slapped his hand on the ground.

"He submits," Ludger bellowed.

The next man charged in. Big and beefy, he threw his arms around her chest and squeezed. She let him, and pushed with his momentum, taking them both to the ground. One hand behind his head, she used the elbow of her other arm as a fulcrum and twisted his neck hard as they fell.

It took her longer to struggle from beneath his suddenly dead weight than it did to kill him.

The next man hit her face twice before she scored him with her nails, leaving deep gouges.

He tapped out.

She turned to the men on the stairs. "Will you wait till the boys tire me? If you're coming, come now!" Blood trickled across her naked breasts. She shivered and stamped her feet. "What about you?" She pointed to Rainer. "I see you in with the women all the time. You don't look old enough to be a guard."

"Rainer does as I command," Ludger said as the men began muttering.

"Ah, so the law doesn't apply to you or your friends. You're free to fuck who you wish."

"We oversee the safety of the women."

"Hah, terrify them to silence, you mean." She spun to face the crowd. "How many of you have seen tied and battered women and closed your eyes to it? How many women have begged you in whispers for help? How many men have visited the women and died soon thereafter?"

"You will stop your lies at once!" Ludger bellowed.

Cara laughed and spun to face him. "Make me! Come onto the sands, and make me. I can be an animal too. Or are you afraid to show your impotence? I've been here three days and already know—"

Rainer rushed forward holding a knife. She ducked from Rainer's swing.

"A knife in a fair fight?" she said
contemptuously. "See how they treat their women?"

With her forearm, she blocked the next blow
and scratched across his face.

"Your witches nail count as knives, this is fair."
Rainer stabbed at her again.

"Will you fuck my corpse then? Or do you only
like boys?"

He charged her. She grabbed his knife hand
with both of hers, spun and twisted. The arm in her
grasp broke with a sharp crack. She kicked his right
knee hard as he staggered back to clutch his arm.
Another man grabbed her, surprising her. With
both arms around her, he pinned her arms to her
sides before she noticed he'd entered the ring.

Without having to plan, years of practice placed
her foot behind his, twisted her hips, and rolled her
body. The air left his lungs in a whoosh when his
back hit the sand, but he kept his grip on her. His
body cushioned the fall. She used her head to bash
his face while kicking his legs with her heels.

From the corner of her eye, she saw Rainer
approach and was ready, connecting solidly with
her heel in his solar plexus, knocking him back
wheezing for breath. The hand she pressed to the
man's side flexed and came away with a gob of
meat.

He screamed and rolled her face down into the
sand. Hot blood spurted between her fingers again
from the wound she gauged in his thigh. He
released her arm and rose his hand to hit her. The
blow dazed her, but she scored another gash across
his wrist.

Coated in blood and sand, she rolled away and
kicked him in the chest as he grabbed for her.

"Stop," Ludger bellowed.

She ignored him and used her feet to break the man's neck. Gritty sand clutched in her hand, she stood.

Rainer backed to the edge of the ring.

"Coward." She turned her back. "You're all cowards, letting them cheat and break laws as they like. I'll die here, but I won't die a coward. I'll take as many of you with me as I can or give me Keld, and I'll go."

"She's right," one of the younger men waiting to fight said. "Calder, Bruno, Swen, all dead after visiting the women. And right before us they cheat. I won't let them use knives on her. Bring Keld to her. What use is killing her? Let them speak to calm her."

He strode into the ring.

"Kill him," Ludger bellowed.

"Stop!"

Cara turned at the shout.

Wearing an unbuttoned linen shirt and to large leather pants, Geir stood on the stairs on the opposite side of the room with an older man.

"Will you strike down an unarmed warrior? Kill him, and we know you for lawbreakers," the man with Geir yelled.

"Ludger has broken the law by not letting a scout speak before the council and locking him away," Geir shouted.

The deep thwap of a copter passing overhead made the crowd yell and push. Armed men pushed forward through the unarmed naked ones.

"I am Jarl. He speaks treason, kill him!" Ludger bellowed.

Cara turned from Geir to face Ludger. "Inkeri has left to my ship. Nothing you do here will save you now." Cara tossed her head to shift the blood-soaked hair from her face. A fierce smile pulled at the drying blood on her cheeks. "Kill every unarmed person here. Kill the women, and my crewmates will destroy this planet utterly."

# -32-

# GEIR

Blood coated Cara. Geir couldn't tell how much of it were hers. The bruised, puffy, face she turned to him made him wince. The cold expression when she saw him made his heart constrict. Rainer hadn't lied.

While she yelled for them to bring her Keld, Rainer smirked at him. The men would riot. He felt it like static on his skin. He wore a dead man's clothes and carried a stolen sword. Every second of the fight to reach her burned his soul. The desperate way she shouted for Keld, her pain and fury, the slurring tone she screamed in all alarmed him. Her actions were irrational and while the men here wouldn't kill her on purpose accidents happened. And then there was Rainer who would kill her for the joy of it. His palms sweat on the cheap tin sword, no match at all for the steel swords and shields of Ludger's guards.

She faced them with her bare hands.

"Cara," he screamed as Rainer threw the knife.

She staggered back and laughed, waving the now bloody knife she'd pulled from her shoulder.

Knife clutched in her bloody hand, she ran forward. Men yelled and pushed.

The man beside her grabbed her.

Geir lost sight of them in the sudden surge of bodies. Her soprano scream of pain cut through the others.

Beside him, Geoff cupped his hands around his mouth and bellowed, "The women need our protection right now. Stop fighting like animals. We'll have a trial. No one is above the law. Those of you who are armed surround the inner fence. GO!"

Geir leaped to the floor and tried to push his way through the throng to Cara's side. Every man in there was attempting to do the same. *Most to help her*, he thought in relief as a man pushed forward, stopping the fall of a sword aimed at her shoulder with his body.

The congestion in the room began to break as men ran to surround the fence.

"Eirick, Stian, organize a patrol. Einar, get fifteen men, seven from the retired barracks, and seven from the cadets, and we'll hold a fair trial and listen to our scouts. Drop your weapons and submit to the will of the town or be banished!" Geoff yelled.

"Treason!" Ludger bellowed.

"Not treason, law, and it applies to all. Are you afraid to face your accusers?"

Ludger and his cronies began shuffling backward. The unarmed men in front let them retreat. Loud yells of armed men, who couldn't squeeze into the building, got the unarmed men backing away to make room.

Geir reached Cara's side and grabbed her. She yanked her arm from his grasp and knelt in the blood-stained sand to press her hands against a wound spurting blood on a man's shoulder. "The med-scanner can help," she said to a man crouching beside her.

"Cara—"

"Save it. I'll never believe a word you say again."

She ignored the shirt he removed and offered her.

Two groups of men faced each other.

"Step armed into the sanctuary and you'll be treated as criminals," Geoff called as Ludger's men eased to the small door that led to the sanctuary. "Lay down your arms and submit to the law."

Cara snatched the shirt dangling from his hand and tore it into strips to tie around the shoulder of the man at her feet.

Muttering between themselves, the men with Ludger began to advance. Blades struck blade with a screech of metal. Cara jumped to her feet.

Geir pulled her back.

"No, stay behind—"

She hit him hard, but the shock of it hurt more. Blood seeped between his fingers from the wound in her shoulder where he grabbed her. The next swing he ducked. Hand-to-hand, he couldn't beat her, but if she attacked sword-carrying men she could be killed.

"Cara, please. At least take my sword."

As if he didn't exist, she turned from him and ran forward, kicking out at Rainer who fought with another man. Her kick connected. Rainer snarled and lunged at her. Geir intercepted the blow with his cheap sword.

Beside him, she screamed for Keld as she kicked another man and grabbed his descending arm, twisting and yanking to make him drop the blade.

Rainer slashed at him again, taking a hunk of metal from his sword. Cara's opponent fell, and he lost sight of her as men surged forward shouting and fighting.

Rainer gasped as someone jostled his broken arm. He tried to step back, but the wall behind him stopped him.

"We should have done this months ago, when Inkeri told us what a foul creature you are," Geir shouted.

Rainer laughed. "She was a nice piece of ass, but I preferred your sister. You knew you were a coward and you still are. They all knew and pretend not to, hoping for crumbs from a god's table." His gaze flitted to the man beside Geir. "Screams of passion right, Manu?" He laughed again. "You believed me, sure you did. You saw me visit Tres and turned the other way for a poke at Triginta."

Geir feinted toward Rainer's broken arm and scored a hit on the sound one. "Keep talking. We all want to know who broke the laws."

"That's a lie! I earned my chance with Triginta," Manu shouted as he parried his opponent, his furious gaze shot to Rainer and his opponent stabbed him in the shoulder.

Rainer chortled as Manu grunted and stepped to the side to block another swing. "Sure you did. Those fights weren't rigged to give you the best shot. We knew you were like us— a real man."

A woman's piercing scream halted the fight for a second as everyone paused to look.

Cara tumbled to the floor and lay unmoving.

The men beside Geir growled and surged forward. Geir blocked Rainer's feeble swing and again faked a cut at his weak arm. This time he stabbed low, catching Rainer in the gut.

Rainer's sword fell from his hand as he grabbed at the spreading red stain and crumpled to his knees.

"More and better than you ever had, boy," he muttered. The light fled his eyes. Geir turned to Manu's opponent, but he'd already finished him off.

A few men threw down their swords, but most fought wildly.

Ludger lay on the floor, his hand pressed against the severed stump of his arm, and appeared to be talking to himself.

Geir whirled to face another opponent as Ulf ran into the room, lugging the med-scanner.

Ulf dropped to his hands and knees and crawled through the fighting men to reach Cara's side. Once there, he shook her arm, trying to rouse her.

"Place her hand in the glove," Geir shouted. Hot and cold waves traveled him. Her death was his fault, and she would die thinking he'd betrayed her.

Manu swung to parry a blow. "Go to her! I can hold these two."

Geir ducked as a man with a spear stabbed past him at his opponent. His opponent screamed and sagged, dropping the sword to grab the spear impaling him. Around him, men shifted to make way for him to pass. More spear-carrying men entered, led by Tovald, as Geir knelt beside Cara.

"Hit the black button here and run the wand thing over her," he said as he took the med-scanner from Ulf.

"Apply cleansing foam to wound," the machine said.

"Then follow the directions on what it says to do. You won't understand the language, but the device it wants you to use will beep. See how this instrument is beeping. It means use that one on the matching spot in the diagram." As he spoke, Geir held the nozzle over Cara's wound. The machine beeped again, and he replaced the nozzle.

"Apply cleansing foam," the machine said again. This time the picture was of her shoulder. He grabbed the nozzle and applied the foam.

"Patient is stable for transport."

"Med-comp, can you repair the damage here?"

"Negative. Full repairs require a med-bay. Partial repair is possible. Place blue pad over wound."

Geri took the thick pad from the machine. Purple plastic rings encircled a darker blue box attached to the pad. He placed the pad against the slash in her side.

For a moment, it did nothing. Steam rose from her skin and the handle heated, but he kept it pressed against her till the machine beeped. He replaced it and removed it again to apply to her shoulder wound. At the machines urging, he flipped her over and used it on the small exit wound the sword had made in her side.

"Patient stable for transport," the machine said.

Geir scanned the graphs, but most of the words were beyond his skill level. Nausea burned his throat, and the cold had settled into his soul. Whether she lived or died, she was lost to him. She would never forgive his betrayal. Inkeri she would understand; his keeping the truth from her she wouldn't.

"Will she live?" Geoff asked.

"I think so." Geir glanced around, realizing the fighting had ended. "Bring me the worst wounded first.

# -33-
# CARA

Firelight danced on the stone wall of the room she was in when she opened her eyes.

Wavering shadows formed monstrous images before settling into flickering light. Keld sat beside her, holding her hand.

"Oh—" The sight of his battered face hurt. She'd done this by rushing away and dragging him with her. Constantly her choices injured her friends. "I'm so sorry."

"Shh— don't cry." He gingerly lay beside her and pulled her close. "I'm okay. Just a bit sore is all."

"Where are we?"

"Honestly, I'm not sure, but I think Winter House."

"How come you don't know?"

"I've never been inside one of the houses before, but few buildings are ancient constructed like this."

Cold to her bones, she pulled him as tight as she could against her.

"We're okay. Geir's outside."

She stiffened.

"Cara, he came back for his family."

"I heard him trade me. It doesn't matter anyway." Struck by a sudden thought, she pushed away to see his face. "Do you have family here?"

"My mother is in Autumn House. Or she was when I left. I feel terrible I didn't come back sooner. I thought it'd be better to learn everything I could first and come with a bigger group."

Cara snorted. "Are we prisoners?" her arm and side twinged when she leaned forward to hug him again.

"I don't think so. I just got here. Geir is outside talking to the guards like he's in charge.

"Check the door." She began shivering when he stepped away.

"Locked." A scowl etched his brow.

Wrapped in the blanket, she scurried to the window. The house faced a tall wooden wall.

"If this is Winter House, can we get to the copter Geir stole?"

"Maybe." Keld peered over her shoulder.

Both spun when the door opened.

"Geoff." Keld stepped between her and the man who entered.

The same man who'd promised laws and trials. "Is Cara well?"

Furiously angry again, she pushed past Keld to glare at the man. "No. Let me go to my ship." The man's face distorted, becoming bug-eyed and chiton covered. She clamped her lips against the scream and forced herself to stand unflinchingly.

"Geir has taken the copter for supplies. He'll return within two hours. You can go then. Can I get you anything meanwhile?"

"Our clothes and weapons."

Geoff resumed being a man. Cara wiped her sweating brow with a trembling hand.

Geoff placed an emergency pack beside the door. "I'll see what I can do."

As soon as the door closed, Cara tried to raise the window, but it wouldn't budge. Padded by the quilt, she tried to break it with her elbow.

"Ancient's glass. Nearly indestructible, you'll hurt yourself," Keld said as he pulled her away.

"We need to get away."

"Geir will be here in an hour."

Did he speak to you?"

"No."

"Than either Geir is willing to trade both of us, or Geoff is lying."

"Why would either do that?"

"Does it matter? Would the Geir who said he loved us leave without checking on us and before you say no consider he did it once already so either he doesn't love us and left us to our fate or Geoff is keeping him from us."

"But why would he do that?"

"Geir or Geoff?"

"Geir." Keld threw his hands in the air "Geoff. Either."

"Geir is smart, that's why. He believes me about my crewmates. Now that I know what the men here are really like, he can't let me go back."

"That's crazy. You would never condemn us to death for a few people actions."

"You believe that because you trust me and wouldn't do it either. He isn't willing to risk his family or the woman he loves on me. If he returns and claims I'm dead, my crew will believe him. I gave him access, shared my room, Hjalmer's men will all swear I trusted him. He need do nothing except make the new arrivals like him. To him, leaving me here probably isn't that bad, it's what he did before I came— stole women and brought them back."

Keld looked sick. "It isn't that simple, and I'm as guilty of that as he. Neither of us liked the necessity, but if we want children, then we need women and the only way to get them is steal them."

Cara waved her hand. "We can worry about that later. Geoff might believe Geir will be back. Hell, he might even come back, maybe with a story to tell us to convince us to stay here. The minute I try to go back, he'll stop me. Or Geoff is lying and Geir is locked up or dead, and any minute now we'll be swimming in lily juice. How far away are the closest lily trees?"

"About thirty minutes." Keld sounded even sicker. "Why put us together though."

"To keep me calm. If I believed them, we would lay here and wait quiet—"

She stopped speaking as the door opened. Geoff entered and placed a bundle beside the door.

"Why lock us in?" Cara asked.

"Only until Geir returns. Just to keep you safe. The woods and fields around us are dangerous—"

Cara slashed the air with an impatient hand, interrupting him. "You have a plague in this town. Inkeri was infected with a bacterium. A germ, a teeny, tiny, bug that can travel person-to-person through body liquids, saliva, blood, semen. This bug causes rashes and fleshy growths that you can see. It also causes lesions inside the body. These lesions can cause weakness, blindness, or effect the brain to give delusions or produce odd cravings. You'll notice some will enjoy tactile sensations like rubbing something soft against their skin. Some will scratch till they bleed and keep scratching. You can have no symptoms and still infect others. It also produces tumors that can affect other organs and cause pain."

"How many have this?"

"I'm guessing every sexually active person in this village because of the way Rainer broke the laws. Every person he had sex with, and every

person they had sex with, and so on. Your children
will be especially vulnerable as they were likely
born with it. Most will be clumsy and grow clumsier
as they age. Any child born within the last fifteen
years or so is at risk and a potential carrier."

"Can you cure it?"

"Med-scanners can kill the bug and fix some
damage, but brain damage and neural damage can
be hard to impossible to fix and can't be done with a
portable machine."

"You're positive we have this?"

"I'm positive Inkeri did. The med-scanner cured
her, and her internal injuries can be fixed."

"The council is going to love this news," Geoff
murmured as he closed the door.

"Was that true?" Keld asked as soon as the door
closed.

"Yes. It's worse than I said. The children will all
be sterile."

"Can a med-bay fix them?"

"I don't' know." Cara grabbed the bundled
clothes and shook them out. "My shirt, your pants,
no boots." She handed him the switchblade and
tapped the scope against her palm. "Enough
clothing to appear helpful, but without boots and
my pants, the cold will be rough."

Keld knelt beside the pack and turned to her
with a hard smile on his lips. "They forgot this." He
waggled the small Mylar packet.

Cara dressed in the clothes provided. Her bare
toes wiggled on the stone floor peeping from the
leather pants.

"You can't go in the snow like that."

"I can— I just shouldn't."

"You'll get frostbite before we're a mile away."
He flicked the knife in his hand. "How can I fight a
mega with this little thing?"

"It won't get easier when they chain us. Is there a canteen in the bag?"

"Yes."

"Then we run for it. Inkeri will have asked Hjalmer to send help, but Geir will tell them not to come. If we run into Hjalmer's men, we can come back in force for Geir, but we won't. We'll have to travel there on foot."

"We'll never make it. It's fifty days of travel on foot in the fall. Through deep snow, it's more like seventy days. We have enough food here for ten days."

"You can stay here. They might not kill you until they're sure I'm dead. I can't stay. They'll poison me and rape me every day till I die." Anger and fear had dissipated, leaving a cold emptiness. She wondered if it was from lily flower or Geir's betrayal.

Keld's lips tightened, and he began cutting strips from the bedding. "I'll call the guard, and we'll kill him and grab his boots. The river will be frozen out the back to the left. Anywhere we run, we'll leave tracks, but the wind scours that plain. They'll be two guards on the gate. We'll have to kill them too, or they'll sound an alarm."

"The room I was in upstairs had an open window, but it faced the front."

"All the upstairs windows will open. That was a later addition. Those windows close with wooden shutters. You carry the pack and the quilt." He finished knotting the material around her feet and stood. "Don't stop running till you're in the trees no matter what happens to me. Then put the boots on."

He kissed her hard. "Ready?"

"Yes."

Keld pounded on the door. "Cara's sick!" he crouched as the door opened. She stood to the left of the door ready to use her nails as weapons.

Cara kicked as the man entered, sending him into the door. Keld slashed and blood splattered.

Cara caught the body and lowered it to the floor. Keld began taking off the boots. She undid the belt and tightened it around her waist then tugged off the man's leather vest.

"Leave the rest." Keld peered into the hallway before darting for the stairs.

Cara followed. The stone stairs morphed into a fathomless black-hole causing her to trip and tumble before righting herself. Keld glanced back, and she waved him forward as she pushed herself up. He eased a door open and rushed forward to slit the throat of a man grunting atop a woman. The woman opened her eyes and said nothing.

"Sorry," Cara whispered. The woman's face wavered and became Bridget then Ilda. Cara bit back the scream and breathed hard with her eyes closed.

"Cara," Keld hissed. He stamped the man's boots onto his feet, scooped up the man's clothing and sword and eased the shutters open. The woman in the bed hadn't made a sound. Her dead expression made Cara shivered, the woman looked like she felt, cold and lifeless. The cold wind that whipped through the window made her shiver harder.

Keld caught her, falling backward into the snow. She wished she had her gun.

"This is Autumn House," Keld whispered as he tugged her through the snow.

He glanced back at the house with a troubled expression. She took the clothing from him and stuffed it into the blanket. At the gate, she dropped the blanket and drew her stolen sword. The clash of steel on steel sounded shockingly loud to her. They tugged off the injured men's boots. Both guards lay in the snow, clutching wounds. She knew they should kill them to prevent them from calling for help, but she couldn't make herself.

Keld examined the swords, picked two, then grabbed her hand and began running. Shivers wracked her as they ran. The blankets on her feet became wet and laden with snow. Each step became a cold, stabbing pain. The sun sank under the horizon, leaving a streak of golden rose to show where it had been. White flakes drifted down in lazy arcs, more drifted up tossed by the gusting wind.

A horn blew behind them.

Cara glanced back, but night and distance made the town indistinct. Tiny lights flickered. She couldn't tell if they were torches or candles in windows. *It didn't matter either way,* she thought as she turned to face forward.

The muffled thwap of a copter's rotors came from behind them. She tugged Keld down into a snow drift and began burrowing in.

"He was there the entire time and he's helping them," Keld said in a strangled voice.

Cara said nothing. She'd already lost all her allusions about Geir. "Stay still when he passes over. He might not know how to use all the equipment yet."

The copter cut to their left directly toward the northern pass. Cara pulled him up and began running again toward the trees.

"Cara, you're freezing. I can hear your teeth chatter from here."

Keld stopped running and glanced back at the town. "Only two can fit in a copter. What if we hijack it?"

"Geir will be driving."

"We'll have to kill him," Keld said grimly.

"I don't think I could. He'll have all his weapons too."

"You'll die, Cara. This cold will kill you."

"I can't."

"Will you die for him? Will you let me die for him?"

Cara sobbed and clutched Keld. "No."

"When the copter returns, lay in the snow. I'll pretend to drag you. He'll land. Let them pick you up. I'll kill whoever has free hands first. Geir will likely pick you up, just don't let him draw his gun till I get there."

Her tears froze to her cheeks. "I'm so sorry I rushed away and didn't listen to you. I'm so sorry I've ruined your life."

"Ahh, Cara, If I died right this second I had a better life with you than I dreamed possible." Soft and low, Keld's voice shook with emotion. "I wouldn't give you up to save this world or any other. Geir is a fool."

"If we can fix my ship before *Odyssey* returns, we're going to run, Keld."

"Wherever you go, I go."

"I love you."

"We aren't dying." Keld kissed her cold lips, his warm and sweet.

She shook out the blanket and wrapped it around them. If we get caught, and they take us back, tell them we made love and the med-scanner can see if I'm pregnant."

"They won't believe you."

"I just need access for a minute."

"No! We can break out and try again."

It surprised her that he figured her intent so quickly. "I can't take this. I really can't." Shivering so hard she couldn't stand, she collapsed against him. "All of this is too much. I killed people with my bare hands." Acid roiled in her gut, and she vomited.

Crouched in the snow, he smoothed her hair back and kissed her temple. "We'll get through this. Be tough a little while longer. Pretend he isn't our Geir, but a stranger."

"Our Geir," she said, and her voice broke. Deep sniffling sobs shook her shoulders. "I believed him despite what I know of men's history. I believed him because I loved him and wanted to believe he loved me too."

"Maybe your wrong and he had a good reason for locking us in."

She cried harder.

"If I left without telling you, to come here for my mother, would you think I was trading you?"

"If I heard you say so I would."

"But he wouldn't; I know it. You must have misheard, like maybe he said, 'I wouldn't trade Cara for a million nights in Summer House.'"

"He said, 'unlimited access to Summer House isn't enough, I want Inkeri.' Then Ludger said, 'that appears to be a fair trade.' I don't know any other way to take that."

The copter returned. Keld kissed her cold lips again and put his hand against her cheek then recoiled, staring at his bloody palm. "You're bleeding."

"It doesn't matter."

"Stop it!" He shook her shoulders.

The wound didn't hurt. A warmer patch on her frozen skin, it felt good. If they made it to her ship, med-bay would fix her right up. If not, she hoped it killed her.

The copter circled them before settling to the snow.

Keld stood as Geir approached. He'd come alone. She wished she were feigning weakness, but she really couldn't stand.

Dressed once again in his blue uniform with his weapons on his belt, he approached them with his hands out and empty.

"Keld, I'm sorry," she mumbled as she fell face first in the snow.

# -34-

# GEIR

"Back away." Keld snarled as he crouched over Cara and rose his sword in clear threat.

"What the hells are you doing? Help her!"

"The med-bay can help her. Let me take her there."

"Fine."

"Put her in the passenger seat."

"Keld, I don't know what she told you, or what she thinks, but you know I would never hurt her. You know it!"

"I want to believe you, I really do, but her logic is sound, and if you really wanted to help her, you'd put her in the copter and let me take her to the ship."

"I'll bring her and come back for you."

Keld's glance flicked to his gun. "Put her in the copter."

"Going to stab me in the back, Keld?"

"Going to let Cara die in the snow?" Keld countered.

Geir's shoulders tightened as he turned his back on Keld to scoop Cara from the snow. He wanted to believe Keld would never hurt him, but doubt niggled. Keld stepped back to let him lift Cara and took the pilot seat as Geir buckled Cara in. "I have no way back to the ship. Come back for me, Keld. I love her– and you."

Keld said nothing. Geir stepped back and closed the door. The copter sped away into the night. He kicked the pile of discarded clothing, wincing at the bloodstains, then began jogging back to Ludger.

The two people he loved had just abandoned him, and worse, thought he had betrayed them. With no way to contact them, he had no way to set things straight. He paused to pray to the gods that Keld's love was stronger than Cara's fear.

Geoff greeted him at the gate. "They killed two and injured two more in their escape."

"The deaths are on me, not her. She was frightened and injured, and again I thought I'd be back before she woke and missed me," Geir said in alarm.

Geoff laid a hand on his shoulder and spoke grimly. "We shouldn't have locked her in, and once we did, we should've been cautious opening the door. We saw what she was capable of. Will she return?"

"Maybe for the women here, but she won't make the same mistake twice. Next time, she'll have reinforcements."

"I thought she loved you?"

"I thought so too. Guess we were both wrong." He'd meant to sound blithe but instead sounded pathetic.

Geoff slapped his shoulder. The other men gave them a wide berth, letting them enter the sanctuary without comment.

Geoff said, "Consider this from her perspective, you sneak away, and she rushes to you. She finds herself tied naked to a bed and I'm sure Ludger and Rainer were unpleasant at the least. She fights, thinking she's alone with what to her eyes is savages. Savages you lied about. When she wakes, she's locked in and likely thinking she's to be kept as a prize."

"Oh, I see her point, but I thought she loved me enough to trust me."

"Like you trusted her?"

Geir stilled and rubbed his eyes, then squeezed the bridge of his nose. "Did the new med-scanners work?"

"Yes. But we have a bigger problem."

"What?"

"Plague. Bacter somethings in our blood."

Geir sighed hard and headed to the makeshift med-bay as Geoff told him what Cara had said.

The men injured in the fighting lay on pallets along the sandy floor in the jarl's house.

"Have the women come in. I'll examine them all." Geir began checking the men, most of whom were recovering already. The remaining elders gathered inside the doorway.

Geir beckoned to Ulf who loitered outside the door. "Gather another thirty men or so, of all ages, who can tell the others what happens here."

Ulf ran off with the high energy of youth. Geir remembered being seventeen; it felt like ages ago.

The first women hesitantly entered the room from the smaller door that led to the sanctuary. Geir scanned them all eagerly, looking for his mother, but none matched the memory in his mind. He spied Triginta holding the hand of a girl who resembled her but with dark hair. Both girls stared at the floor and flinched from the guards who escorted them. No longer bright and inquisitive Triginta appeared dull and lifeless.

An older woman placed her hands on their shoulders, then kissed their cheeks. Her blue eyes fasten on Geir.

"Septem? Mother?" *Not recognizing your own mother was surely a crime*, Geir thought as he examined her. With effort, he could see the resemblance to his memories, but her once-blond hair was white now and cut close to her head. Lines and wrinkles of a much older woman framed her eyes. No longer plump and soft, she was skinny to the point of starvation.

She nodded wearily. The fear in her face hurt. The men spoke in quiet voices amongst themselves, eying the woman uneasily.

"Please, everyone sit. I'll tell you all what I tried to tell Ludger." He spoke for hours. It took four more hours to show everyone the pictures of bacteria in their blood and explain what it meant.

Geoff rose and faced the men. "Cara said the illness caused the men here to act crazy, but we share the blame for turning our backs on our women. Because they were kept locked up, it was easier to abuse them. From now on, men enter sanctuary by their invitation only. Three men will be assigned as guards for each house and stay inside; the rest stay outside. The women should be free to come and go as they like.

Geir rose as Geoff sat. "We don't have enough medicine to cure everyone, so we'll start with the women and the men with the least exposure. The children are beyond the ability of the portable med-scanners to fix. When Cara returns, we can ask her for help. But when she returns, we'll have to prove we're worth helping."

Geoff stood again. "Some of you won't believe and will convince yourselves he's lying. Maybe you can convince others, and you'll form a group and leave, but you'll infect any woman or man you have sex with, and eventually, you'll become as crazy as Ludger. So think carefully before exposing your lovers to a deadly disease. Any women who have a preference for a mate tell Geir so he can be sure to cure them too."

"We'll let them choose their own mates now?" a man shouted, sounding affronted.

"Yes."

"That's not fair, they'll never choose some of us."

"Then work harder at making yourself pleasing to them. The med-scanner can tell us who the father is. They're free to choose and change their minds as often as they wish. Those who've been selfish lovers in the past are unlikely to be picked, but who's fault is that," Geoff yelled over the rising grumbles.

Geir waved his hands for silence. "With help from Haven we could have more women than we could imagine. Two hundred thousand can fit on a colony ship. We can't force them to come here, they must want to come, but would you come to a place like this? riddled with disease and violence where women cower from men? Never mind the crappy weather and dangerous animals. We're dirty savages compared to them."

"So, what are we doing this for?" someone yelled to loud mumbles of assent.

"Because they're our only hope for life for our children. Without help, humans will be extinct on this planet in two hundred years and possibly much sooner if our plague spreads. Someone brought it here, so that means it's spreading elsewhere too. I want to be worthy of being a partner and traveling the stars in search of a more hospitable planet to settle. I want to learn to use their machines and be able to build a real future not fight over useless scraps, " Geir said into the respectful silence.

"How do we do that?" Trovald called.

"We learn and study. It took Cara eighteen years of school to learn to be a captain of a scout ship. We have a year, but we don't need to be captains just competent, willing crew."

"I'm too old to learn a new language," a gray-haired man in the front shouted.

Geir smirked. "Then you better be a spectacular lover, so one wants to keep you as a pet."

The men snickered and yelled jokes.

"Pass the word," Geoff said. "We live under a new law now. Any are free to leave with their belongings. If Cara returns and agrees, I'll send those who wish to learn at her ship with as many supplies as we can spare."

"Does that include the women?" Erica, Lily's mother asked.

"Yes."

The men erupted into loud protests.

"We'll do our best to make sure they're safe wherever they choose to go, but they're free people and can go where they wish. If you're worried, speak to them and explain the worry. Most have never been beyond the walls and have no real idea of the danger. Teach them. Make them more able to face the danger here. And before you say women can't fight, remember the battle we just saw. If Cara had a weapon she knew how to use she would've held her own against an armed man."

"She's much stronger than our women," a man yelled.

"So, let's make our women strong. Our women are bigger than she with broader shoulders and hips if we teach them, they can be powerful fighters too."

Geir began the examinations of the women while answering questions and listening to Geoff talk. For the three day's they'd been locked in the basement he'd told Geoff everything he'd learned about Haven and what Cara was doing about it.

"Med-comp, generate new user ID for Septem— Med-comp, pause. Do you have a second name or a name you prefer?"

"Helge. I was happy with your father. He was kind and did his best to ensure I was happy. When Trig said she'd met you, I thought maybe you would visit, but you never did. Then Inkeri said you turned your back on her pleas for help. I was so ashamed my son never tried to help even though I didn't wish your death. Thank you for coming back for us, but next time plan better."

Geir laughed and hugged her. She began to cry. It took willpower to hold his tears back. She finally pulled away and wiped her face on her sleeve.

"Med-comp, resume. Generate new user ID for Septem Helge." The comp beeped and had him rescan her three times before it was satisfied. Multiple tumors lined her pelvis, some painful and inflamed.

"Med-comp, keep a triage list of the new users."

He scanned his sisters next and cried over Triginta's cracked ribs. She made no response to him other than answering yes or no. The comp removed the bacterium and cycled her blood to clean the lily tree residue from it. A bottle emerged from the bottom tray.

"She needs to take one pill sunrise, noon, and sunset, for three days for the lily tree addiction"

"She won't crave it anymore?" Septem asked as she accepted the bottle.

"I'm not certain, but I think that's what the machine meant."

Geir took his sister's hand. She stared at him blankly. "Come to me if you're in pain or need anything."

She nodded lifelessly.

Septem drew her away. "She needs time to recover."

By the twelfth woman addicted to lily flower, Geoff stood with his hands on his hips glaring at the men.

"If anyone is caught giving lily tree to any woman, for any reason, they'll be left tied beneath a tree to consider the folly of their actions. That's truly despicable, drugging them to—"

Manu stood. "Some begged us for it. I've given a woman a flower, but it was meant to ease pain."

"Well, no more! Let them recover. If some still want it, and the med pack can't help, we'll figure something out to help them, but we don't addict them to manipulate them."

✦ ✦ ✦

Manu approached Geir as the men began leaving. The women had left as soon as the last was treated for the bacterial infection.

"Your sister was my lover, and I knew she was addicted, but the flower made her happy." He glanced at Geir uneasily. "I remember Trig before when she was just a girl always laughing and so bright. I fought hard to be her first but lost. When my chance finally came— she wasn't as I remembered and I'd have done anything to hear her laugh again. My hand to the gods, I never hurt her on purpose."

"Was she your lover willingly?"

A flush covered Manu's cheeks. "None of them are. They submit but..." Manu sat and rested his cheek against his drawn-up knees. "My father told me stories about his lovers. I thought them lies when I got my chance. There was no laughter or flirting, no sweet sighs or caressing." He shrugged. "Maybe I just got unlucky or they hated me personally."

"How would you feel if you were forced to submit to any man who wished?" Geir stared at his feet. "I'm ashamed it never occurred to me till Cara. Honestly, I never thought about their lives at all, just how they affected me. We've all been selfish.

Those of you who saw them though have more to answer for."

Manu nodded.

Geir rose to continue the medical treatment. Ulf used a machine too but sometimes had questions that only Geir could answer.

By dawn, Geir was exhausted and laid on the sandy floor to sleep. Ulf woke him an hour later.

"The copter returns."

"Tell Geoff I'll come back as soon as I can," Geir called as he ran from the room. She'd come back for him. Relief made his hands shake. Men approached the copter but kept back from the whirling blades that spun on the sides.

*Not Cara, Keld*, he thought in dismay. Keld popped the door open but remained seated and glared at him. One handed rested on the gun at his hip.

"Is she—" A lump formed in Geir's throat, blocking his words.

"Under the hood recovering. You almost killed her. She'll be under two more days. Lily flower poisoning caused seizures. I thought she died." Keld ran a hand through his hair and sighed hard. "She's going to freak when she wakes and remembers."

"But she'll recover?"

"Physically. She doesn't have the microbes in her system to break down lily flower if ingested. The med-bay is working on inoculating her so it can't happen again but the poison damaged her."

"Episodes?"

"As if she just ingested it. Stress triggers it. The poison etched those nerve centers lily tree affects. When the nerves are activated, she hallucinates; to many nerves affected and she has a seizure. And the hallucinations terrify her..."

"But the comp is searching for a cure?"

"Yes. Did you trade her?"

"Gods no. Rainer lied."

"She heard you."

"Impossible. It must be lily flower.

"She heard you before they gave her any. You said unlimited access to Summer House isn't enough, I want Inkeri. Then Ludger said that appears to be a fair trade. Or are you saying she lied to me?"

"No, I said something like that, but I also said I wouldn't trade her for anything, that nothing he had was worth it and she was a free person. Then I told him about her crew."

"Why did you come here without telling us?"

"I thought I'd be back in a few hours and didn't want her to know about this place. How did she know I was gone? She was sound asleep when I left."

"The comp told her. She thought you'd been stolen. Neither of us could believe you left without saying anything."

A guilty flushed burned across Geir's cheeks. "Will you take me to her?"

"I'm not sure. She thinks you'll kill her and I'm not sure she isn't right. I want to believe you, but you know exactly how to manipulate me."

Geir paled. "Why would she think that?"

"Why didn't you speak to us and lock us in?"

"I thought she'd be unconscious longer and the wounded needed medical supplies. I told Geoff to lock her up with you and went for the supplies, but the copter has an emergency pack, which I didn't know till I asked the ship comp how many packs there were and where they were stored. Keld, you know she would've wanted me to help the injured."

"Everything you say makes sense, and everything she says makes sense." Keld stared at him a minute, then waved to the copter. "I don't believe you would kill her though, not for any reason."

Geir climbed in gratefully.

Keld lifted off, leaving the village behind them. "Just in case you're considering killing her though, it won't work. Inkeri and Hjalmer will tell her crew everything."

"Once she talks to me, she'll realize she misheard." Keld's mistrust was a knife in his gut.

"Maybe." Keld glanced at him. "You think she'll be okay with killing to escape over a misunderstanding?"

"Two men died, and I realize their deaths are on me."

"Do you remember when I killed that mega in front of her?"

Geir winced.

"Now add terror and self-doubt and magnify that by a thousand. How did she get injured?"

"Fighting."

"I'm not retarded, of course fighting, who did it and why? Did they force her?"

"I don't know if they forced her. She didn't say?"

"She was too terrified to say, all she wanted was away from there, but she was convinced they'd poison her and rape her till she died of it. I saw they beat her and believed her."

"She entered the ring and fought for herself. She killed at least three men there with her bare hands."

Furious blue eyes turned to him. If he hadn't been driving, Geir was sure Keld would've hit him.

"You let her fight in the ring?"

"No! I was busy escaping and had nothing to do with it."

The rest of the ride to Cara's ship passed in silence. It surprised him he thought of it as coming home. Keld's coldness hurt, and he realized he took him for granted too.

"I'm sorry," Geir said as the copter settled to the snow beside the ship.

Keld nodded but remained quiet. The ship was as he remembered. Droids scuttled around busily going about their programmed tasks. Men sat beside fires and peered at comp screens. A few new log shelters had gone up, and the smell of roasting meat drifted on the wind, making his stomach rumble.

Inside, the ship was quiet. Soft voices came from the cafeteria, but the med-bay was still. Inkeri left the room when they entered, giving Geir a wide berth, but nodding to Keld.

Geir checked the readouts above the red bed. The cuts were healed. A long readout it would take hours to go through listed the possible treatments and side-effects for the lily flower poison damage.

"I'll go over this, and we can decide what's best together."

Keld nodded woodenly.

Geir hugged him. "I'm so sorry. We *are* together. I should never have left without speaking to you."

To his immense relief, Keld hugged him back. Geir cradled Keld's skull and kissed his lips. Keld's breath caught on a sob.

"I love you too, not just her," Geir said. "We're a family, speaking of which, I met your mom. Go back and see her if you like. The comp is triaging people who need the facilities here to recover. You can begin bringing them back and visit your mother. Bring her back with you. Cara will be asleep at least another day."

"Inkeri is staying across the hall in Teryl's old room."

"See if my mom and sisters will come here. Leave my brothers with Geoff unless my mom wants them here and they agree to leave their fathers. They'll be too much for us to look after."

Keld snorted, making Geir chuckle. Geir's three brothers were all under twelve and barely civilized.

Geir laid his cheek against Keld's. "I'll apologize till she forgives me. We'll help her forgive herself. We better add the lily microbe to our studies too. The new crew will need that in case they're exposed."

"Don't break our heart," Keld murmured and kissed him again before leaving.

✦ ✦ ✦

Papers scattered as Geir jerked awake. He'd fallen asleep over a stack of printouts on the damage the poison had caused and the comp's suggestions for fixing it. He glanced at the comp on his wrist, rose and stretched, leaving the papers piled on the small table to the right of the door in the cafeteria. Garlic and onion flavored the air, making his stomach rumble. He grabbed a sandwich and juice and went to check Cara.

Inkeri glanced up from the screen before her.

"No change." She nodded to the green bed. "Septem is undergoing treatment to remove her tumors. Your sisters are in Ilda's old room. Keld's mother is in the room across the hall."

"Thank you. How are you adjusting?"

She pulled the screen closer and gave him a cold glance. "Fine."

"I'm sorry I didn't help you. I should've done more."

"You all should have." Inkeri pursed her lips before straightening her expression. "What the men of Ludger allowed to happen was an atrocity, but we're to blame too for being so meek. We should've never let you close us inside the sanctuary. Not all

292

of you are bad men. We all need to learn to see beyond ourselves though."

Inkeri rose and placed a hand on his arm. "The choices Cara makes, the lies or truths she's willing to tell can start a war. Our fears and desires, their fears and desires, all must be addressed and understood if we're to coexist.

"I'm trying to get better at it."

She smiled suddenly. "I know." She patted his arm. "Get some sleep. I'll call you if the comp beeps."

He kissed her cheek and plodded to his bedroom. The sonic shower felt like heaven. He emerged spotless, feeling clean for the first time in days.

Keld woke him when he entered.

"I'm awake," Geir said as Keld eased onto the bed after visiting the bathroom. He turned to face him and ran his hand over Keld's shoulder. Dim lighting made Keld's eyes a barely discernable glimmer.

It surprised Geir how much he missed Keld's touch. Usually, Keld came to him, offering light touches until Geir moved away. Now, he didn't know if Keld held back because he wasn't interested, or he thought Geir would rebuff him. It took courage to roll closer and kiss his lips, uncertain of his welcome.

Keld kissed him back but kept his hands to himself. They were at a turning point, Geir realized. Keld was no longer willing to be the aggressor, but he was willing to remain friends with Cara their shared lover. *Did he want Keld as a lover? If Cara left them would he still want Keld?*

"Make love to me, Keld," he murmured, flushing wildly and glad the room was dark as he reached down to fondle him. "I want you," he said, meaning it.

Keld gasped and pulled him closer, close enough their hard cocks rubbed together. Geir reached down and rubbed them both, making Keld moan. His fingers trailed through Keld's hair to his shoulders. With his thumb, he flicked his nipple. The tiny gasp encouraged him, and he pushed him over to suck his nipple. The cock in his hand throbbed.

"Feel good?"

"Yes."

"Tell me to stop if I'm doing it wrong." He began kissing his way down Keld's body. Keld's muscles felt tight, tense with anticipation, he hoped, and not dread. The loud moan Keld made when he licked him reassured him. His cock tasted like skin and a hint of musk. Geir took his time licking him, before easing him into his mouth while Keld groaned.

He sucked him like he liked it, hard on the head of his cock with his hand making small jerking motions.

Keld rolled until he could take Geir's cock into his mouth and mirrored the motion.

"Suck me like you like it," Geir said.

Keld gasped and began licking his balls before taking them in his mouth.

Geir copied him. Keld's growing excitement excited him. Thicker than he, but not as long, Geir could take Keld further in his mouth then Keld could him, but faithfully copied the licking at the base of his cock. Geir's hips began to jerk as Keld ran his lips up and down his shaft fast, sliding his tongue over the head of his cock, then repeating the motion.

In moments, Geir's hips pumped in time with Keld's.

"I'm going to come," he warned.

Keld kept sucking. He didn't want to come in his face, but couldn't hold back. Jerking and moaning he came as Keld sucked and licked him. Keld reached down and grabbed himself, pulling away as he came in thick jets. He knocked the tissues to the floor as he grabbed a wad to wipe himself off.

Geir crawled back up the bed and collapsed beside him, laying his head on his chest. "I love you."

Keld's voice cracked as he said, "I love you too." With a smile in his voice, he asked. "Was it as bad as you thought it'd be?"

Geir growled and squeezed him around the waist. "You know I liked it."

"I know you liked my tongue on you but wasn't sure you enjoyed your mouth on me."

"The sounds you make get me hot. I really like exciting you." He ran his hand over Keld's chest. "This is nice, being close like this."

"I have this fantasy—"

"Oh boy...."

Keld chuckled and kissed his cheek. "Me, you, Cara, and her friend Fleur, all together. Think she'll go for it?"

"Maybe, but don't suggest it the second we meet her; if we met her that is."

"Cara wants to run away with me. I'll help you, but you really have your work cut out to fix this."

"We should wake her before deciding treatment."

"That bad?"

"Can we talk tomorrow? It's going to be a long talk, and I'm exhausted."

"Yes." Keld kissed his forehead.

Geir fell asleep to Keld's steady heartbeat.

"Med-bay emergency." The mechanical voice pulled him from sleep. Keld wasn't there. He scrambled into his pants and ran to the med-bay.

"Sorry to wake you, but the monitors went crazy," Inkeri said

"You did the right thing." Geir placed his hand on top of the green bed. "Med-comp, report."

"Patient requires immediate scan. Place on red bed."

"Med-comp revive patient on red bed. We have to move Cara first," Geir said to Inkeri as he scanned the readout on the green bed. "Crap, a tumor beside the heart and inside the lung ruptured during removal. He'll likely need to return to the green bed after a complete scan. Can you get Hjalmer to take over in the med-bay? Cara is angry with me. I want to speak to her when she wakes."

Inkeri ran from the room.

The hood lifted from the red bed. Geir left his patient to check Cara. Wide, terrified eyes met his. She screamed and lunged backward, tumbling from the bed and smacking her head on the floor.

Shocked by the level of fear she displayed, he whispered her name.

# -35-
# CARA

Cara," Geir whispered in a heartbroken voice.

She peered around the med-bay. "KELD! Help! Where is he? Did you kill him?" She scrambled to her feet and edged to the doorway.

"Cara, no— I love you. You misunderstood what I said. I would never leave or hurt you. Keld is fine."

Inkeri and Hjalmer paused in the doorway.

"Thank the gods, get the green bed—"

*He'd convinced them to help him,* Cara thought in horror and slapped the emergency switch beside the door. "Intrepid, lock out all users except myself. Initiate full quarantine." Her eyes darted around the room for a weapon.

"Cara, you're not well. Look at me, It's me— Geir. Cara and Geir remember?"

"Back up. Tell your friends to leave. I don't want to kill them, but I will."

"My family is aboard now." Sweat sprang up on Geir's forehead as he turned toward the door. Inkeri and Hjalmer stood outside, staring through the window.

"The man in the green bed needs an emergency scan. Can I help him?"

"You had me under the hood?"

"Yes, you were injured, remember?"

"For how long?"

"Two days."

"You planned to keep me there?"

"No, the comp—

She struck, hoping the element of surprise would let her overpower him quickly. The room spun in dizzying colors, knocking her kick of course. He leapt back.

"Cara, please— just listen.

"Intrepid, where is Keld?"

"I'm at the door, Cara, let me in. Trust me this time and let me in," Keld pleaded.

She glanced at the door where Keld now stood alone.

"He's convinced you, told you I'm crazy?"

"Trust me." Keld pressed his fingers against the glass.

Her eyes met his, and her shoulders sagged. She could trust him. "Intrepid, end quarantine, open the door."

"Cara—" Geir reached out to her.

"NO! don't let him." She tried to make herself sound calmer but was terrified Geir had somehow convinced Keld to help him.

"Let's go to our room and talk." Keld smoothed her hair back and tried to lead her from the room.

"We can't just let him run around the ship. The women of Haven are right, men in packs are dangerous. Your bigger, stronger, and more ruthless than me. I need to be ruthless too." She reached for Keld's gun. As much as it would hurt to kill Geir, she couldn't afford any more mistakes.

Keld pushed her back and rose his arm, pointing the gun at Geir. "Sorry, Geir." Brilliant light surrounded Geir, and he crashed to the floor.

"I had to, he was going to kill me." Cara sobbed as Keld picked her up.

"Let's go talk. We're okay." Keld tried to sooth her but wild trembles shook her, and she thought she might vomit. Keld had shot his best friend for her, and she hadn't even checked to see if he were dead.

She didn't want to know. She wanted to pretend none of this had happened, that Geir still loved her and would return any minute with his deep voice and kind smile. The room wavered and her muscles seized. When her eyes opened again, she lay on their bed with Keld staring at her worriedly and acid churning her gut.

She ran to the bathroom and splashed cold water on her face till the nausea passed.

"What's wrong with me," she moaned as the water became silver bugs that scuttled over the sink. She slapped at them till they became water again. "Did he poison me again?"

Keld wrapped his arms around her and kissed her neck. His steady heartbeat reassured her. A blush covered her cheeks as she realized she'd run naked through the ship.

"I'm sick, Keld."

Keld grabbed her robe and placed it around her shoulders. "The lily flower poisoned you when you ingested it. The med-bay was trying to find a cure for the damage it did and a replica of the microbes the natives have that protect against that."

"Is there a cure?"

"Not a good one so far, but I don't know all the details either. We can both read the reports, but first—" he squeezed her hands and led her to the bed. "Geir had no intention of leaving us or trading us. He wasn't free there, but a captive himself."

"So he says."

"Do you trust me?"

"Yes."

"I checked his story, and I swear it's true."

"Then why lock us in?"

"As Geoff said, for our protection. You were dangerous, but they didn't want you to run into the cold either. Geir was busy with the med-scanners on the injured men and didn't realize you woke."

"So, I killed those men for nothing?"

Keld's embrace left her cold.

"No. They should've let you go. It isn't wrong to escape captivity."

"But you said I wasn't a captive."

"We didn't know that."

"I'm a murderer." She began to laugh semi-hysterically and rubbed her face hard. "I've murdered so many I've lost count. Ilda is right; I'm incompetent." The room wavered, becoming a star-filled void before resuming to be a room. Her laughter fled replaced by peaceful acceptance. She felt as if she could sleep a million years.

Keld kissed her cheek and smoothed her hair with his fingers, tucking the long, blond, strands behind her ears. "You aren't a murdered. It isn't wrong to protect yourself."

The skins on the bed slithered and hunched, and suddenly she was angry.

"This can't be fixed. The dead are piling up around me and for what? So I can have my lover? I don't deserve you. God, and I was going to beg you to run away with me, make you leave everything you've ever known and loved."

Shame and remorse made her want to curl into a ball and disappear. Keld's touch on her shoulder made her moan.

"Let me help you."

"How?" she closed her eyes against his misery. "I am who I am and can't change the past. But you deserve better." She swung her feet to the floor and perched at the edge of the bed. "You want the Cara I thought I was not the murderous selfish Cara I am. I want to comfort you, but don't know how."

She turned to kiss him. He murmured her name and deepened the kiss. She let him kiss her, feeling nothing except sorry for him. He was aroused, his erection pressing against her leg. To ease him she slipped her hand into his pants to caress him.

"Get undressed. I need the bathroom."

She took a shower, then used a lubricant before returning to him. She did her best to make him happy, holding him close afterward as his heart pounded. She grabbed his hand as he reached to caress her. "I'm tired."

"Cara— I love you," he said sadly and left the room.

She took another shower then, dressed in her robe, she lay on the bed and stared at the wall, considering her choices. Geir and Keld wanted a good woman, but it would be cruel to ask them to be celibate while they waited for the crew of *Odyssey* to arrive and what if the crew spurned the men here. Maybe it was only her who was so desperate for a man's attention.

She'd killed Ilda when she might have saved her. And not to save herself or others, but out of anger. If she'd taken the copter instead of sending Inkeri, all the men she'd killed would be alive, but she'd wanted Keld.

And to be honest, she wanted to hurt the men who hurt her. She had a barbaric streak, and it ran deep. She was too selfish to be in charge of anything, and they were too ignorant to run her machines.

Keld returning brought her from her musings. He'd brought food and Geir.

Silence hung thick and awkward. She wanted to run to Geir and beg him for reassurances of his love, but her need was sick, not at all a healthy

Havenite response to a man. She'd know this about herself, that she would become too attached and abstained from men. And here on a mission, where she should've been business-like and professional, she let her lust guide her, putting everything at risk with no thought for anything except that she wanted Geir.

"Did you read the medical reports?" Geir finally asked.

"Not yet." She clenched her hands behind her back and kept herself from him.

"We were talking about moving all the people together; it would be easier to help them—"

"Whatever you think best."

"Will hydroponics support this many?"

"I'll need to research it." She tried to put enthusiasm into her voice to stop their worried glances. "I'll get on that tomorrow." The food attempted to crawl off her plate, and she fought back the gag, but couldn't stop herself from slapping at the bugs that crawled to her. Sadness overwhelmed her, and she had to force the tears back. "I'm sorry, I'm still tired." Every hallucination heralded a change of mood, and she wondered if it were connected.

"Cara, I'm so sorry I left without speaking to you."

"Keld explained. It's me who should apologize." She faked a yawn and scurried to the bathroom, wishing there was a tub to soak in where she could remain undisturbed.

When she emerged, Geir sat on the edge of the bed in just his pants. Keld lay on his side naked with his hand under his head. Still in her robe, she lay behind Keld on the edge of the bed and feigned sleep.

# -36-

# GEIR

Cara slipped from the room five minutes after Geir lay beside them. Her body language couldn't have said any clearer don't touch me, so he rested his hand on Keld's hip after he hugged them.

"She wasn't tired," he murmured.

"No, she's exhausted and needs rest," Keld disagreed. He pulled him closer and kissed his cheek before rolling onto his back. "What she isn't up to is a confrontation."

"Will she forgive me?"

"She wants to. Can you imagine how hard this all is for her? Worried about us and two entire planets."

Geir sighed hard and rubbed Keld's back. "And now she feels alone and is worried we aren't worth saving, that her decisions will hurt the women of Haven."

Keld rolled on his side again to face him. His minty breath caressed Geir's cheek. Too dark to see his expression, Geir had to rely on his tone.

"When we made love, it was flat, passionless. Not at all like her. I might as well have used my hand, but she wanted so desperately to please me.

She said I deserved better than her; she's really doubting herself now."

"Should I go to her?" Geir asked.

"I don't know. I'm afraid to push her over the edge. She was going to kill herself if they captured her again."

"Oh gods." Geir brushed the tears that formed on the corner of his eyes away with his thumbs, hoping Keld didn't notice.

"I don't think she'll do that, but she might run away. Once this ship is capable of moving, one of us better stay aboard at all times." Keld held him for a minute. "Think really hard about what to say to her. I really want our Cara back."

"I think I killed our Cara." To Geir's horror, he began to cry. Keld didn't turn away in disgust, but held him tight, offering comforting words. He cried himself to sleep in Keld's arms.

Cara avoided him for the next week. In her defense, the work had tripled. They were planning to move *Intrepid* outside the walls of Hjalmer. Geoff was moving all of Ludger there too. Food and shelter had to be arranged for almost four thousand people. Work crews had to be rotated to ensure the livestock they'd left behind in Ludger remained cared for till they could gather and move it.

The med-bay was busy nonstop. Cara had droids building another, work only she could oversee. Hydroponics absorbed a good chunk of her time as did the research on the microbes. Working on the comp screen triggered hallucinations and sometimes seizures.

He'd had enough avoidance though and searched her out.

"— every day."

She stopped speaking and peered up at him through unruly blond hair. It touched her shoulders now and curled wildly if she fell asleep with wet hair. Reminded, he frowned, he didn't like her working outside in the snow.

She blanched and rose from the table. Inkeri turned to him with an irritated expression.

"Geir, Cara has asked me to oversee the condition of the women, including their education. I assume I can count on your support if Hjalmer or Geoff try to curtail their use of the comps?"

"Yes, of course, but they won't."

Inkeri sniffed. "Not blatantly, but we've been asked to perform many menial chores, and while we're willing to do our share of the work here, I've begun to suspect the men are purposefully producing chores to keep us in camp."

"This is still a wide open plain and dangerous," Geir said placatingly.

"I agree, but all the women should get equal time in school as the men. I'll make sure they do."

"Great, the more help we have, the better."

Inkeri flashed him a small, satisfied smile and hurried from the room. He smiled after her. The blue uniform and competent air suited her. She'd cut her hair in a short, layered style that flattered her thin face and made her look years younger.

"Cara, what do you miss most about your home?"

Surprised, she smiled fleetingly. "Bathtubs," she paused a moment. "Bridget, but I never saw her often; we were afraid to appear close. Books, green grass, and sunshine...."

"What about you?"

"You."

She cleared her throat and began organizing the papers before her.

Geir snagged the medical file and opened it. "Have you decided on a treatment?"

"Surgery, but I want to be sure the food can support you, and the women are organized first."

Geir said nothing, although his stomach roiled at her choice. She knew how dangerous brain surgery was and thought it might kill her— or maybe hoped it might. His muscles tightened, but this wasn't a problem he could fix with his fists.

"Do you have time—"

"Sorry, no free time at all today. Talk to Inkeri, and she can fit whatever you need into my schedule."

Cara kissed his cheek and hurried from the room, leaving her meal and files behind.

A thoughtful frown on his face, he went to requisition a droid.

# -37-
# CARA

Cara stopped dead when she entered her bedroom. The mural over her bed displayed her favorite spot beside the Gordon Sea. The long, sloping, green meadow led to white sand and turquoise water, but it was the tub that made her breath catch. Big enough for four to lounge in, it appeared to be a continuation of the ocean.

"Like it?" Geir asked softly.

"It's beautiful, but where will we sleep?"

He pointed to the ceiling. "The platform lowers and connects, but I was thinking we could expand and take over the room next door. There are three of us after all."

She couldn't help the tears that filled her eyes. "I want you to have everything you want, but the ship isn't mine to do what I wish with. How would I explain the ship changes? In my room, I can do what I like, but this ship belongs to Stellar Command, which means there are forms and permissions to fill out to request changes to the interior. If I steal it, I'll be a criminal and go to jail a long time if I'm caught."

"Okay, it was just a thought; it's nothing to stress over."

"You don't have to live aboard. The droids can build you a shelter or –"

"Cara, nothing's changed for me except how sorry I am that I left without saying anything. Remember how we felt when we made love last? I still feel that. It's Cara and Geir forever."

Bitterness filled her at the naïve girl she'd been a week ago. "I'm not her. I never was her. You intoxicate me, and I think made me a little crazy. One night with you and I forgot every warning I ever heard."

His hands on her hips sent heat through her entire body. She stumbled back from him till her butt hit the closed door.

"Are you afraid of me?"

"Not you. But you wreck my decision-making abilities. I'm not a good person, Geir. I've murdered people and have seriously contemplated how to murder the entire crew of *Odyssey*. And not to save this world, but so I can keep you for myself."

"That's not true, Cara. You were willing to blow up the ship with you on it."

"For you. I tell myself it's to save this world, and it isn't like I want them dead, but if you, Keld, and I, could go away, I wouldn't look back. What kind of person thinks like that?"

He pulled her against his chest where she could feel the rapid beat of his heart. "A scared one. One who loves and wants to protect what they love." Geir's voice rumbled in his chest. "These uncertainties and what ifs hanging over our heads are excruciating. I worry all the time you'll decide something for my own good that I'll hate. Don't do what I did. Trust me more than I trusted you."

With all her soul, she wanted to accept the comfort he offered, but she wasn't worthy of it.

As if reading her mind, he said, "Those two men killed while you escaped are on me not you. My actions put you there."

"If I hadn't doubted you..." she began to cry. Trusting and doubting were so mixed up in her mind she didn't know how to unravel it.

"You heard true but not entire." He took a deep shuddering breath and whispered. "It hurt so bad that you didn't trust me. Didn't you feel my soul when we made love? What we share isn't just sex. When you call my name— and whisper our names –" Deep and low, he whispered, "Cara and Geir."

And she was kissing him so passionately she felt the kiss through her entire body. They fell to the floor in a tangle of arms and legs, and she realized he was crying as he made love to her, then they were both crying, gasping and straining as they reached the peak. His face melted to a snarling visage of fangs. Black sparkles bloomed into white lights as the convulsion seized her.

# —38—

# GEIR

It took him a moment to realize it wasn't just a powerful orgasm but a seizure that gripped her. He waited it out with a pounding pulse.

"Uhh," she moaned and cringed from him, placing both hands over her face. "I know it isn't real, but it's so scary. I don't just see it; I feel it too. Why can't I see kittens or flowers or something?"

"What do you see?"

"Fangs and claws. Bugs and snakes; things to hurt me."

"Keld and I won't let them hurt you."

"I wish he were here, that we could cuddle together safe and warm."

The soft apologetic tone dismayed him.

"Me too. Intrepid, where's Keld?"

"Teaching in schoolhouse three. Connect?"

"Yes."

"Can you come home?" Geir asked as soon as Keld answered.

"Is everything okay?"

"Yes, we just miss you."

"I'm on my way," Keld said.

"Stop for food."

"Hah, you didn't miss me, you want pizza delivery."

Geir heard the pleased laugh in his voice though. So did Cara; she smiled and relaxed against him.

"Tell Inkeri we're taking a day off before Cara's surgery and to reschedule whatever needs rescheduling."

"Will do."

"I shouldn't take the time right now," Cara said.

"You're suffering, and there's no need." He frowned thoughtfully. "Suffering won't bring them back or help anyone."

"I'm afraid." She took a deep shuddering breath and spoke with her face hidden in his neck. "The surgery might affect my personality or leave me blind or even deaf. It could kill me outright, but that chance is low."

"Then try the medicine instead. I like that option better anyway."

"If I want to pilot, I need a cure, not a Band-Aid. It would be beyond foolish to trust a pilot who has seizures. Stellar Command will discharge me, and rightfully so. They likely will anyway, but I want to be able to pilot for the underground— and us."

"If the medicine works though..."

"How could we trust it? This ship moves fast and requires instant decisions while refueling and setting course. The stress then is real likely to cause a seizure, and I could kill everyone aboard before my crew could get control."

Geir nodded thoughtfully, He'd tried the simulator and crashed the ship every time. Moving at the speeds necessary to intake fuel, one moment of inattention or wrong course input could send you into the planet instead of space with no hope of slowing before impact. The autopilot could refuel a ship to about fifty-six percent capacity though.

"At half fuel, we could still reach the nearest planet in about fifteen days."

"Fuel is life in space, especially if we have to run from pursuers. The ability to reach orbit and swing out quickly refueled and heading where we mean to will be the difference between escape and destruction."

"I hadn't realized you planned it to this degree."

"I'm searching with the probes for a habitable planet." She kissed his cheek. Warm and soft, the light kiss reassured him more than their lovemaking had that she still desired him. The hands she trailed over his body as if memorizing him, scared him.

"I'm looking for mineral rich asteroids to replenish the droids, and meanwhile I'm planning escape trajectories for every planetary body with an atmosphere. And I'm mapping everything. We won't be able to use the probes without major programming changes and retrofitting, or *Odyssey* could follow the signal back to us."

Geir yawned and laughed at her insulted look. "Sorry, it sounds exhausting."

"Will your family come with us if we run?"

A bolt of unease wiped his relaxation away. "I hadn't thought that far ahead."

Keld entered, carrying a pizza balanced across two pitchers of beer. "Nice, I like the changes but let's add pillows to the floor," he said as he set the food beside Geir and grabbed plates and glasses from the table in the corner. "Nice thick padding and a fur rug right here would be good," he continued as he sat beside Geir with his back to the closet wall. "And the pool needs a ledge."

Geir ate his pizza, smiling as Cara and Keld talked about embellishments for the room.

"Keld, if we decide to run, will your mom come?" Geir asked.

"No, not without Hjalmer. I don't think he would go and leave his men behind."

"She chose him already?" Cara said, sounding surprised.

"My mother isn't stupid. He's a powerful man who can keep her safe."

"Not a love match then."

"No, but they both seem happy."

"Trig and Vigi won't leave their room still. My mother says I shouldn't visit yet, to let them a have a safe space. I hate the thought of leaving them to fend for themselves, but if we run the danger to them..."

"Our supplies won't last long with extra aboard. Don't forget extra people means more oxygen, so more hydroponics need to be set aside for that. We're going to get awful sick of legumes. We'll have to build more storage tanks for water too."

"How's the comp programming going?" Keld asked.

"Slow, like everything else. The code has failsafe's for just this scenario built in. I have to check every single line. If I printed it out, the paper would fill the bottom deck from floor to ceiling."

"Can we help?"

"Can you read comp code?"

Geir sighed. "We're too scattered, trying to do too much. Stop research on the microbes. Keld can research the changes needed to the ship and the maximum number of people it can carry indefinitely. Then he can begin construction, but not installation, to carry those people. We don't touch the integrity of the ship till Cara speaks to whoever arrives."

"I'll get on that," Keld said and began to rise.

Geir grabbed his ankle. "Day after tomorrow. Tonight and tomorrow is a day off for us, and we're all staying right here— and you have too many clothes on."

Keld laughed a light, happy sound Geir hadn't heard in a while. Cara smiled sweetly at him pleased with his laugh too.

"If *Odyssey's* crew wants to stay, they can research the microbes. "You're going to hate this, Cara, but if they plan on going back with a negative report, we use lily flower to subdue them. Not in their food, just a few blossoms placed around that should give us time to escape."

"What about those we leave behind?" Cara asked.

"When *Odyssey* leaves, we return and help them disperse. We can leave our families here and run. It's unlikely *Odyssey* will kill them without returning to Haven for instruction. We likely can't save everyone, but maybe we could hide enough that Haven doesn't bother to kill them just locks them on this planet with weapons platforms. Meanwhile, we'll look for a cure for the microbe and search for a new home and maybe even build our own *Odyssey*.

"If we could reach Haven or New Haven and speak to the women there and ask them for help... Or get in touch with the underground, we could save the people here. It's pointless to destroy *Odyssey* and proves their point that we're violent. Whatever happens isn't your fault. We'll make these decisions together and share the consequences— good and bad."

Cara relaxed with a deep sigh. "You're going to make a better captain than me. That's a great plan.

Her warm weight felt perfect against him. Geir reached over her naked back to pull Keld closer. This was his family. He and Keld with Cara between them. He'd never imagined he could change so much in such a short time. Cara had opened his eyes, and now he really saw the people and places around him. Keld had become an irreplaceable part of his life, a true partner. The three of them belonged together, and he would do anything to keep them.

"We're going to have an amazing life together," Keld said and rested his hand on Geir's bare hip. He kissed his lips, then Cara's.

Geir hugged them tight, willing to share any future that included them both.

## THE END

Books by Carol Edward
Star-Crossed Lovers
Rock the Boat
Coming Soon: Star-Bound Lovers